After the Orange

Ruin and Recovery

Also from B Cubed Press

Alternative Truths

More Alternative Truths:

Tales From the Resistance

Witch's Kitchen

When Trump Changed: The Feminist

Science Fiction Justice League Quashes

the Orange Outrage Pussy Grabber

by Marleen S. Barr

Coming Soon

Alternative Theologies: Parables for a

Modern World

Alternative Truths III: Endgame

Firedancer,

by S.A. Bolich

Digging Up My Bones,

by Gwyndyn Alexander

After the Orange

Ruin and Recovery

Edited by
Manny Frishberg

Cover Design
Sara Codair

Published by

B-Cubed Press
Kiona, WA

Introduction

It's been said that, at the turn of the 20th century, lots of people saw the automobile coming over the event horizon. Visionaries could imagine the country being connected, one day, by a vast interstate highway. But, it took a science fiction writer to foresee the traffic jam.

Science fiction writers are in the business of looking at the world through smoke-colored glasses and wondering, "What comes next?" Sometimes, that means imagining far flung futures of galactic civilization and planetary cooperation (though, for the sake of an exciting story, something must go badly wrong). Sometimes, to imagine things gone badly wrong, it is only necessary to read the headlines.

Submitted for your consideration, as Rod Serling used to introduce "The Twilight Zone," twenty-seven authors present a couple of baker's dozens of vision of what the world might face, if things go on as they are.... For the purpose of this collection, writers were asked to look at least a couple of decades ahead, to the world in 2032 or beyond. The idea was that, even if Donald Trump were to be re-elected in 2020, his second term would have ended eight years before. These, then, are stories of what comes after.

Most of these stories stay close to that timeline, looking a short distance into the future. Others are of people decades, and in a few cases, perhaps centuries after, coping with the world we are leaving them today. Some project the effects of climate change or another ecological collapse, still others imagine social disintegration or one of tighter regimentation and dog-eat-dog competition. Some are darkly funny, and some are just dark.

Science fiction has a reputation for predicting the future. And, like side-show psychics, we're right, maybe one time out of ten. Presenting these glimpses into a cracked crystal ball, I can only hope that we've scored much lower than that this time.

Manny Frishberg, editor
Somewhere near Seattle, Washington
March, 2018

Dedication

To my offspring, Jacob Liddil, David and Nicholas Hassell, and all the children of Earth. It's your world, we just live in it.

Acknowledgements

No book is ever the product of a single person, and that is obviously so for a collection of stories by a number of people. Many more people than have stories included in this anthology have been instrumental in its coming to life.

Thanks, first and foremost to Bob Brown, who started B Cubed Press with little more than the faith in an idea, and whose faith in me led directly to the volume in your hands right now.

Thanks, as well, to Robert N Stephenson, owner, editor, and publisher for Altair-Australia.com, who originated the idea that inspired the creation of "After the Orange." When he decided to cancel his planned anthology, "The Future of the American Trumpet," in 2017, he gave B Cubed his blessings to carry the project forward.

Of course, this collection would have been impossible without the more than 100 writers who contributed submissions to "After the Orange," those included in these pages and all those that are not. The unusually high percentage of excellent stories made the task of staying within the budget particularly difficult, for which I am grateful.

As hard as that task was, it was made much easier by the participation of my two assistant editors, Elizabeth Ann Scarborough and Janka Hobbs, who read dozens of the stories before me, and whose independent evaluations were invaluable. I owe you both.

Finally, I would like to thank Phyllis Irene Radford; she has always stepped up when a professional is called for.

Foreword

Elizabeth Ann Scarborough

At Worldcon in Spokane (Sasquan) I met an anthropologist who opens mass graves, seeking the identity of victims of genocide and the cause of their deaths. It is important work, unpleasant, uncomfortable and smelly.

We talked about the slain and why they might have been chosen to die--was one side able to gain such ascendancy as to butcher the opposing side and why. I said that I had always considered myself a moderate and the anthropologist replied, "Oh, moderates are the first to be killed." That was a rude shock to me, that essentially being Switzerland and being able to see the viewpoint of both parties in a conflict put you in danger from both of them. (Or if there are more than two sides involved, from all of them).

In this collection, a group of writers tries to imagine the future by the time the alt-right and the current administration are no longer in charge, say 20 years or more into the future.

Of course, science fiction writers have always tried to envision the future, but at this time, a lot of us don't like the picture we have to extrapolate from. Hard-won protections are being stripped away, putting the planet at risk as the US pulls its head in (while its leader shoots his mouth off) like a big old isolationist tortoise. Cruelty against immigrants (even those who have lived here since babyhood) is condoned, the Statue of Liberty's invitation is rescinded, and people are returned to their own countries to be murdered even though through heroic effort they finally made it to what used to be a safe place.

There is a scary schism between Americans of left and right persuasions and each side is tone-deaf to the other. The administration seems to be trying brain-washing techniques once employed by Communist China to make us believe lies by repeating them incessantly and ever more loudly.

Those of us who have studied history and paid attention to international disasters that have gone before can identify patterns that manifest before violent juntas that more frequently than not result in genocides such as the ones the anthropologist investigates. We see the rise of oligarchy (where the rich get richer by squeezing those with less into actual poverty) the feudal warlord mentality, dictator-like strategies, and maybe saddest and most irreversible of all, the sell-out of our precious natural resources from "sea to shining" (from oil slicks) "sea."

Whole species may disappear from the earth, as in "Maybe the Monarchs" by Brenda Cooper.

Spiritual erosion is an even more pernicious effect of capitalism so short-sighted and out-of-control that prosperity is the only measure of morality to such an extent that economic piracy may follow the less prosperous beyond the grave, as in Kevin David Anderson's "Dawn of the Debt."

In the following stories, the authors postulate the lasting damage to civilizations, to human beings as a whole, to individuals, animals and eco-systems should the current policies continue unchecked.

You might want to file this in the "horror" section of your library, though we fervently hope it will still belong in the "fiction" section.

Welcome to our nightmares.

The Business of Government

William Burns

Don't take it personal
This. . .?
It's just business

Shattered bottles
oil rainbow in the pothole
wet tire prints
so many worn shoes track the mud
and the grit
the eczema
the dermatitis

Don't you understand
this is the golden age brought by Lord Orange
Everyone wanted to run government like a business

The poor are dancing birds of fire
we the living
outnumber the dead
Techno-plast residue
a fine black filth sticks to the bottom
of every living thing
here

Tattered rags hide the passages
Cardboard walls
Soft leather for hinges
There's less noise that way
Dirty
Stained snow
Bleeds under the door
The rasping
Grit of cinders and sand

William Burns

On concrete
The bone clatter tink
Of frozen clothing
The only wind chime
Rats and roaches
The only wildlife

Tuberculosis and
Cholera blossom afresh
Plagues undreamed
In the future
Of the past

Hell
We'll have the population
Down to a manageable number
In no time
And under budget to boot

Bad Memories, 2032

K.G. Anderson

"They can't get rid of me. Trying, they keep trying, but, nope, won't work."

"Of course not, sir."

"Can't trust them. Not one of them. They can try all they want, make all the phone calls and write all the letters. But I'm too smart for them. We're too smart for them. Ivanka's on top of it, she keeps them in line. Fired the whole team of them a few weeks ago. Right down to the chef and that fat bitch who kept telling me what to wear. Don't see them around here anymore, do you?"

"No, Mr. President. They're gone now. Can I get you anything, sir?"

"Another Diet Coke. New team in place, doing a fine job. Had Wilbur Ross over here for lunch the other day. Know him? Head of the Fed? Great guy. Really knows finance; made billions on Wall Street. Chef made steak just the way we do it at the hotel. Great cut of meat, great seasoning. Ross loved it. Said it was the best."

"Mr. President, sir, your doctor is here."

"Doctor? Another check-up? Sure, sure. Busy scheduling. Keeping busy. Keeping fit."

"How are you sleeping, Mr. President?"

"Bad night last night, Doc. Couldn't sleep at all. Phone wasn't working. Couldn't log on the Twitter thing. I blame that dinner. Big state banquet. The biggest. Some terrible prime minister. Some awful guy from Teriyakistan. I let Ivanka handle him. Ivanka did great."

"Just a few questions. Do you know who the president is?"

"Do I know who's the president? Hilarious. You're some joker, Doc!"

"Do you know what year it is?"

"Do I know what year it is? Hah! Very funny! It's, ah,

2020! And we've got an election to win. Bannon's busy, you can bet on that. Man knows his job."

"Dad?"

"Hi, honey. Come on in. Doctor's just leaving. You look great, sweetie."

"Trina is going to help you get dressed, Dad."

"Who's Trina?"

"Your new assistant."

"New one? Good, good. Had to fire that other girl. Terrible. Terrible clothes. Fat. Needed to lose a lot of weight."

"Danielle's gone now, Dad. You have Trina. We all like Trina. She's going to help you get dressed."

"Gotta get dressed? Is this for another one of those state dinners? I've been in meetings all day, you know, honey. The Cabinet this morning. Can't what's-his-name handle this?"

"Dad, we have to go to this. You'll enjoy it. They're dedicating the Trump Presidential Library. It's just a few blocks away, in mid-town."

"Oh, honey, I don't want to go to a library. Bo-ring. Maybe we can drive over to Jersey, play a couple rounds."

"Here, Dad. Trina has your new blue suit. It looks great on you."

"Good tailor, only the best. Now where did you say we're going?"

"The Library, Dad. Today is the dedication for the Trump Presidential Library. Remember how much you liked the plans we showed you?"

"The plans for the Tower? Der Scutt, great architect. Great building."

"Yes. Well, the Library is right next door to the Tower, Dad. You'll like it. Tiffany is coming to the ceremony. And Barron. And Eric. And Donald Junior. And all the grandchildren."

"Is Melania coming?"

"No, Dad. Melania went back to...well, she lives in Paris. Don't you remember? It was right after you...well...the election."

"The election? That reminds me, we need to meet with Bannon. Haven't seen him in ages!"

"That's because he's —ah, don't worry, I'll take care of it, Dad. I'll, ah, call Steve as soon as we get back from the Library."

"How do I look?"

"Fantastic, Dad. The car is here for us. Trina and I will help you get downstairs. Watch your step. Careful there."

"Where did you say we were going?"

"The Library."

"Sure. If you want to go the library, we'll go to the library. Say, sweetie, do you think they'll have my books? *The Art of the Deal? Time to Get Tough? Great Again?* That one I wrote with Bannon about building the wall?"

"Absolutely, Dad. I'm sure they'll have every one of them."

K.G. Anderson

Candidate Games

Laura Staley

The camera zoomed in for a tight one-shot of Jerry, of the D tribe. He was holding a deep-fried lard-ball-on-a-stick, dipped in chocolate and sprinkled with iridescent tiger beetles.

"Start the clock on the Midwest Fair Food Challenge!"

Jerry lifted the stick to his mouth. He froze. His eyes were riveted on the bugs. Their legs waved vigorously.

Host Brinkly Bostock grinned into the lens. "That's right, those are live beetles."

Later, in the Debriefing Room backstage, he looked knowingly into the camera. "That hesitation cost the D team! The R team's Thom ate his lard ball in five seconds. And smiled while he did it." The inset picture showed a handsome man gulping a writhing mass of green and brown down, his grin never wavering.

Bostock turned to Thom, sitting on a weight training bench, one hand cradling a 20-pound barbell, the other relaxed.

"Tell us the truth. Wasn't that disgusting?" Bostock asked.

"It was. But I've got the self-control to do what's necessary for the American people," Thom looked deep into the camera. "Think of those bugs as terrorists, and my jaws as American military might. I won't hesitate to use it, and I can stomach the results!" His face froze.

"What an idiot," Leslie said, hitting Pause. She looked quickly at her boss. Bostock liked to be the one making judgements. Subordinates' opinions were not required, and ex-lover's opinions were even less welcome. She again regretted those first few weeks when she was infatuated with her job and her new boss.

"He's an idiot who stays on message," Bostock said. "And sticks to words of two syllables. That won the last

9

election."

"Forty-three million viewers," Leslie changed the subject. "Better than the last Game of Thrones IV episode." Given that this was the presidential election, they got their viewing numbers instantly.

"Good, but not good enough," Bostock said. "We need something really...visceral."

We're electing the President of the United States, Leslie thought. How much more visceral do you need?

~oOo~

"Welcome to the Spin Contest. The candidates were awake for 40 hours," Bostock whispered into the camera lens. "We've finally let them get a few minutes sleep. Now, we're going to wake them up, and ask them a very important question."

Bright lights flare as he shakes awake a sleeping candidate. "You've been caught with a dead girl AND a live boy. What do you say?"

Thom of R team blinks. "Photoshopped! By foreign service agents, trying to influence the election!"

"Fake news! Fake news!" Ted from the R team yells. "Who are you going to believe? Me or your lying eyes?"

"In your dreams." Lila, D team, stretched prettily and went back to sleep.

"What? Is someone hurt? I know CPR. It's 100 chest compressions per minute," Jerry said, and fell out of bed.

~oOo~

"If he gets eaten," Leslie said carefully, "we will never survive the law suits."

Or the rage of his supporters, she thought. She had already had to close her social media accounts, after Winny of the R team had been voted out. She'd saved the more vivid death threats. They would make an interesting detail in the movie she meant to make about this "modern campaign for the modern world." The show's slogan floated through her thoughts: the first season of "Direct Democracy" and the post-Electoral College presidential campaign.

Bostock laughed. "The lawyers spent months crafting those releases. Air tight!"

The audience had decided: Jerry had lost the D team spin contest. He had the whiff of a policy wonk about him. That was fatal in the spin game. The loss meant that he had to take the Tiger Team challenge for the D team, or he'd be voted off the island.

The Tiger Team was a simple idea. A president had to select a team of tigers—high performers ready to tackle the problems of getting a new government up and running immediately. It was Bostock's genius to replace metaphorical tigers with real ones.

Each challenger had to move the tigers from a spacious cage into a much smaller, darker, room. The politician was armed with a chair and a whip. The tigers each had twenty claws and a bad attitude. Ted of the R team had solved the problem by electrocuting all four of his tigers, through some quick work with a studio spotlight. It had taken him longer to drag the corpses into the target room than it did to solve the attitude problem.

He told Bostock later: "No one said they had to be alive. I guarantee you, when I'm president my next tigers will do what they're told." Some of his fans had instantly nicknamed him "Tigerkiller Ted." "Ted the Creep" was more popular. Ted the Creep won an immunity totem: a flag lapel pin.

Jerry from the D team was trying threats and treats. So far two tigers had made the trip to the conference room, but the other two were distinctly unhappy. One of the tigers had just shouldered him aside and he'd hit his head on the steel bars.

Audio recorded a resonant clang. Leslie winced.

"We need to amp that up for the broadcast," Bostock said.

"Already sounds like a concussion to me," Leslie said.

Jerry nearly fell. Leslie could practically see the stars circling his head. He wrapped a hand around the bars to support himself, snapped the whip wildly to discourage the suddenly intent tigers. It hit the surface of a tub of water and splashed the tigers at close range. Both tigers stopped, blinked, and backed up. Jerry started to fall, but some last instinct of fading consciousness made him snap the whip again. It sliced across the top of the water and drenched the tigers' faces.

They backed away and trotted off toward the smaller cage. Jerry hit the ground just as the last tiger left the arena. It was enough. Jerry won the lapel flag pin of immunity and Lila of team D was voted off the island. There would be no first female president this year either.

That particular episode, with the carefully leaked hints, had topped forty-seven million pairs of eyes.

"Funny thing," the tiger trainer told Bostock in the debriefing room. "Tigers love water. But they hate getting water in their eyes. Just hate it."

Bostock laughed. "It's better to be lucky than good any day, right, Jerry?"

Jerry nodded silently. He hadn't said much since he'd woken up in the infirmary.

The Vision Thing episode was almost a bust. The D and R teams had been combined into Team A for America. Tonight they had been summoned for a teambuilding campfire, and been served "special" punch. Ron, former head of the Darwinian Investor Fund and lately of the D team, was staring at the flames at the Team Council campfire, giggling.

"Bribery works," he sang.

Ted the Creep had fallen asleep, drooling onto his button-down collar. Thom was doing endless overhead presses with a medium-sized rock. "Fifty Ayn Rand," he counted. "Fifty-one Ayn Rand."

That little dash of LSD in the team punch seemed to have set off some deep-seated fears in Jerry. He shouted that there were demons dancing in the flames and retreated, only to be driven back to the campfire by the gleaming eyes of prowling tigers, invisible to all but him.

Leslie stared at the screen. "How did the psychologist team even allow this?" she wondered aloud.

"Funny thing," Bostock said. "Most of them were originally from the upper Midwest."

Leslie inhaled sharply. You were only from Minnesota, Wisconsin, and Michigan these days. The last President had sold the states—complete with those who had been unable to relocate—to Russia. "We got the GREATEST DEAL in the history of EARTH!" he'd crowed when announcing it. No one knew how much the US had made off the deal, or where the money had gone; it was as secret as the former president's tax returns.

The Internet was full of stories of children shipped abroad for labor, for "re-parenting," or for spare parts, but no one actually knew. The Great Wall the president had promised to build had been built, just not where people expected it to be.

"And the party brass allowed people from the Loser States to work on this show?" Leslie couldn't believe it. There had been a lot of ill-feeling over that particular deal.

"Like they had a choice," Bostock laughed.

Leslie nodded. The two parties ranked below serial killers in the public confidence polls these days. They'd been lucky to get seats at the planning table.

"One hundred Ayn Rand—aagh!" Thom dropped his rock. It landed on the head of the sleeping Ted, putting him decisively out of the running.

The Vision Thing episode was the highest rated broadcast in the history of the world. It broke the Internet for days.

~oOo~

"My friend Ted was an honorable man and wanted what was right for America," Thom told Bostock in the Debriefing Room. He wiped an invisible tear from the corner of his eye. "He had decided to support me in the final voting. I'm so sorry he passed before he was able to announce it. My thoughts and prayers..."

"He's lying!" Leslie pointed out as they watched the clip.

"Of course, he's lying," Bostock said. "So? We expect politicians to lie to us. We don't even hold it against them anymore. What are the ratings?"

"Two hundred million viewers," Leslie said. Once that figure would have filled her with pride.

"I am such a winner!" Bostock crowed.

He caught Leslie's look. "Listen, do you know how many people voted in the last election? Do you?!"

"One hundred million people," Leslie said. Everyone knew the number. When this new format was being set up, that had been the most often quoted fact.

"Last night we got 200 million sets of eyes! And this whole thing—it's only going to take a month. No more election fatigue! We are going to hit our eighty percent voter turnout rate—maybe even ninety percent! And the bonus will be fabulous!"

His eyes strayed to his personal dream board, where he posted the pictures that got his adrenaline going. "Maybe I'll buy the island and the submarine."

Leslie sighed. "Not to change the subject, but the CT scan on Jerry came back. He's got brain damage. The Tiger Team hit was worse than it looked."

At his Vision debriefing, Jerry would only say, "We eat their faces before they eat ours." This had concerned the psychologists enough that they had requested tests.

"Are you sure?" Bostock didn't sound concerned.

"Yeah. They compared it to his intake scans, and there's definitely damage."

The initial candidate application process had included physicals, with brain scans and psychological tests. One startling finding was that almost all of the candidates had strong traces of narcissism, and that many of them were undoubtedly psychopaths. Including, Leslie noted, several of the finalists. There was still controversy in the planning meetings about whether this should be announced or not.

At that afternoon's meeting, the pollsters reported that Jerry's vision was trending strongly. There were already tee-shirts urging preemptive face-eating of liberals, rednecks, and terrorists. The race was now down to Jerry and Thom. Tonight's broadcast would feature highlights of the campaign, all the significant moments of the last month, heavily weighted with coverage of the final candidates.

"What do you think about the brain scans? Should we release them?" The meeting was breaking up when Leslie directed this to the head of the psychologist team.

"Look," Bostock cut the psychologist off. "The viewers—they don't care about that. They do not give a shit! So why bring it up? It's unnecessary—and it slows down the drama! I'm done hearing about this!"

"You don't think they need to know that the man they'll be trusting all of our lives to has brain damage? Or is a psychopath?" Leslie shot back.

"They know already! And you know what—half of them hate the winner already. That's why we had 200 million viewers last night. They enjoyed the bugs and the tigers— but death in the flames! They loved it!"

He stood up. "Highlights of last night will lead tonight's review reel. And we'll replay it at the end too. I want a first cut on my computer by 5 p.m. Voting opens tomorrow, guys! We'll be counting our bonuses in forty-eight hours!"

Leslie sat staring at the files in front of her as the room emptied out. Someone cleared his throat and she looked up. It was the head of the psychology team.

She asked him, "Do you think he's right? That the voters don't care?"

"Professionally speaking—maybe." He put a stack of folders on top of the paper documenting Jerry's brain damage. They were, she saw, the psychopathy reports. She looked up at him, surprised. This data wasn't supposed to leave the Top Secret/Sensitive Compartmented information room.

"There's an argument to be made that people feel small and helpless, and they resent that, and therefore they resent the candidates. And maybe if the world frightens you, you want someone big and bad on your side. That's what people vote for. The biggest and worst. That and the catchy campaign slogans."

"So you don't think that we should tell them?" Leslie stared at him.

"I won't be doing it." The psychologist sighed. "I have family in Minnesota. The ratings bonus I'll get is going to buy their freedom. I've got too much to lose." He stopped at the doorway.

"Sometimes," he said slowly, "knowledge does make a difference." He left.

"I think it does," Leslie said to herself, running her fingers over the file folders in front of her. She knew a journalist or two....

Laura Staley

Baby's Gonna Vote

Marcelle Thiébaux

Baby lies in her crib counting toes and fingers. Ten and ten, same as yesterday. She goes over today's homework, classical Greek verbs, *Eimi, I am.*

Mommydaddy comes in to snap up the window shade, inviting the yellow rags of sunshine to pour in from New Tweet Street. Baby laughs to see the forlorn birdies fluttering on the sill. They beg for crumbs, but she's afraid they won't get much.

"Rise and shine, Baby," orders Mommydaddy.

"Wait a minute, I'm practicing my Chinese tones for fifth period." Baby's in a super-smart school.

"No wait-a-minute. Now means now." Mommydaddy yanks up a wrench, a ball-peen hammer and a screwdriver, and takes the crib apart. "Uppity-up and out. You don't need all that infrastructure," Rails, slats, springs and mattress all fall down like ring-around-a-rosy. With a howl Baby comes tumbling after, arms and legs in a flap, while Mommydaddy points the screwdriver and has a good laugh. Baby crawls out from under the crib wreckage. Wailing, she toddles to the kitchen in her bunny-printed pjs.

"What's for breakfast?" she demands, and sniffs at the stove where a pan bubbles furiously. "Yay, Pablum, my fave."

Mommydaddy busily hammers a stick. "Nothing to eat for you, not until you get your morning forty whacks. Drop your pjs."

"No, I won't put up with that anymore. What's that damn thing you're banging?"

"No dirty talk outa you! Cat-o-nine-tails. Tacking them skinny little ropes to my yardstick." Mommydaddy grins. "Then slam bang! Gotta keep you in line. Bend over or there will be consequences."

Baby blubbers all over again. "Don't want it."

17

"Don't matter what you want. You need whupping, bigly." Mommydaddy lashes out with the cat-o-nine tales, but Baby stumbles away in a quick dodge. She grabs the yardstick, snaps it in two and throws the ropey tails into the flame on the stove, where they burn and fizzle.

"All my work for nothing," grumbles Mommydaddy. "I'm gonna paint your bottom red, you won't be able to sit for a week."

Mommydaddy lunges for Baby, snatching her Swee'Pea topknot and smacking Baby's bottom good and plenty. Baby yelps until her bawling slides to messy snivels.

With a gulp and a hiccup, Baby tips out a bowl of Pablum for her breakfast, pours on a healthycare sprinkle of rainbow-dyed Dopy-Opyo crystals from the sugar shaker and eases her stinging bottom in front of the TV to watch The Today Show.

It's that glamorous *telenova* actress, that Lolita von Cervantes who's recently got to be an American citizen. Lolita twirls her long silky hair between manicured fingers.

"I love Mr. Chapo," she's saying about the hotshot money lord they call Shorty, "He is so sweet it's okay if he kills a couple thousand nobodies because he's a very-very nice hombre and can do what he wants.

"He put up so many pretty hotels and medicine cartels he must be good. Underneath he is so kind getting us to feel great again." Lolita shines the beauty-queen smile she flashed when El Chapo strong-armed the judges into naming her winner of every contest in the whole U.S. "He's gonna head the second *conquista* of North America, right over the wall and under the wall for he is my best narco-papa."

Big eyed, Baby slurps her Pablum and dribbles it on her bib. She loves Lolita and wants to do things right.

When Baby grows up, if she ever lives to grow up, she's gonna kill Mommydaddy with an ax and she's gonna vote Mr. Chapo in for the next tough-guy cutie Potus.

Introductory Remarks at the Institute of Probabilistic Computing

Samantha Weiss

Good afternoon.

We're so pleased to welcome you to the Institute of Probabilistic Computing and regret the circumstances that compelled you to accept our invitation.

As a reminder, lunch will be served to all participants who complete their test sessions. We know that many of you are disappointed that the lunches aren't what they were last year, but we wish to remind you that four hundred calories is not only generous but, in fact, fully fifty calories above what our economic models predict is necessary for your cooperation.

In a few minutes, you will be able to proceed inside. Our staff will guide you to your testing stations and help you with your neural sensors.

We understand that you find our clients' party reprehensible and resent that your poverty allows them to buy your time and entice you to come here for almost nothing. We also understand that many of you believe that their form of governance is predicated on the transfer of wealth from the poor to the wealthy, and that you find that objectionable. That said, we are working every hour of every day to change those circumstances for the better for all of us, and please understand that your participation enables our efforts.

To that end, you will be presented with a series of statements that we anticipate will offend you. Once we're able to track the statements that you disagree with most strongly, we will proceed to phase two, wherein we will convince you of how wrong you are.

Unfortunately, the breadth of these tests has been at least temporarily curtailed. Most tests will require your passive attention to a small sampling of images, words, speeches, stories, music, poetry, logic-based rhetoric, passion-based rhetoric. The neural sensors will allow us to track your reactions to these inputs in real time.

As part of our more complicated tests, we'll expose you to peer pressure, vacuous praise, and unjustifiable criticism. We'll ply you with testimonies by people you respect and by plain folk like yourselves.

We'll appeal to your desire to be part of the pack and your desire to be different. We will distort facts in myriad ways. And yes, the rumors are true: a few lucky participants will partake of our most interactive persuasion techniques, including the much-anticipated theme park ride, the hypnosis chamber, and the emotional-scenario simulations.

A few less lucky participants will be subject to our newest technique (which is not, I repeat, not characterized by law as "torture"), a technique that may be extended to close family members at our discretion if we can track them down.

We remind you that, as per the contract you signed on the way in, if you are randomly assigned to one of these new techniques you will be unable to refuse the test or quit before your session is over. Testing will continue until neural patterning indicates a probable shift in your core values toward greater acceptance of our clients' governance.

The genius of our institute is that, even though we only have the throughput to test a few hundred of you a day, using our powerful non-parametric Bayesian modeling, we can correlate your psychological vulnerabilities to the wide abundance of information that we've unobtrusively collected about you over the years: things like your socioeconomic status and taste in pickles. Bayesian inference then allows us to extrapolate which portions of whole population will be most receptive to each technique. This will allow us to give our clients the tools to convince the rest of your peers of their superior governing abilities.

We know that some of you feel that each time a member of our clients' party is voted into office, their service will only further impoverish you, increase social barriers between dissimilar people, calcify a massively unbalanced social structure, limit your access to education, and dismantle what little is left of your health care system. But, we would point out, this is all beside the point.

As your values begin to align with theirs, as your notion of objective reality loses its hold, you will find yourself less upset by a movement that you ultimately cannot stop. We are proud to say that all the work we do here at the institute serves the goal of world happiness.

We thank you again for your participation in our efforts and look forward to reconvening with you for lunch.

Samantha Weiss

Jailbird

Darren Todd

Devon wasted no time wondering: what if the president hadn't been convicted of insider trading? What if Congress had sided with the American people and let the bastard serve his time, instead of paying off some sap to do it for him? Of course, if Trump hadn't paved the way for jailbirds, Devon might not have a job.

His last stretch had spanned six months, albeit with weekly visitations in the yard. Devon had even bribed a guard to let him hug his little girl hello and good-bye. Still, a small part of him would stay here, just like he'd left traces of himself in eleven other penal institutions.

His nerves began to twitch as he out-processed. Keeping his breathing steady required conscious effort. He could act like a baboon and the guards would still have to let him out, but Devon had better things to do than act up now, hours from freedom.

"Keep your shit clean," said a guard so fat his sitting stool disappeared beneath him, leaving him floating midair behind the Plexiglas. "If you got family, do 'em a favor and stay outta here."

"I'll try, boss," he said. He must have been new. Didn't know why Devon was there. Why half of them were there. These MinSec dumps teamed with jailbirds. Probably more of them than real convicts. One of the other guards huffed out a short laugh. He wrote something on a clipboard, tore off the middle sheet, and put it into a plastic bag alongside Devon's wallet and cell phone. He knew what Devon was and that he'd be back. If not here, then somewhere.

Devon's father taught him that you get more bees with honey than bile. While that had done nothing for Devon in corporate America, it tended to work in the pen, whether with fellow jailbirds or with the guards. Not much worked to endear the convicts, outside of leaving them alone. So,

Devon did just that with measured skill, since he'd spent as much of his adult life in prison as out of it.

Another hour and he stepped outside the gate. Terri stood by an unfamiliar car, probably a self-driven rental they couldn't really afford, but the prison lay miles from any bus routes. She waved and then knocked on the passenger-side door. Out came Haley a second later, a flash of white and pink in a striped sun dress. Devon's heart banged in wonder when he saw her.

He'd seen her only days ago, but now he could hug her as long as he wanted, and it didn't cost him stamps to do it. She ran over with all the exaggerated fervor of a six-year-old girl, screamed "Daddy" over and over, and then flung herself into his arms.

He spun her around, blurring the faces staring on from the other side of the fence. Guards with hands on hips, chewing their tongues, so slumped in ennui as to appear in physical pain. Jailbirds in uniform.

"Are you home for good?" she asked, as Devon carried her to the car.

He looked at Terri and her eyes descended.

"For a while, sweetie. Don't you worry about that. You just worry about giving your daddy love." And he hugged her again.

In a couple of days, she'd normalize and adapt and the hugs would loosen. But for now, he reveled in the squeeze.

~oOo~

Two weeks after his release, he finally received the patronage check. After another day of job hunting, he came home to find the envelope torn open, but only a single sheet of paper inside. A typed missive he didn't bother reading.

"Where's the check?" he asked Terri.

She was helping Haley with one of those Mary the Monkey books. His daughter was reading twice as fast as the last time he was home. Jesus.

"You won't like it," Terri said.

Haley stopped. "What won't Daddy like?"

Devon waved it off in playful distaste. He hung his suit jacket over a chair in the eat-in kitchen.

"Nothing for little schoolgirls to worry about."

"This isn't school, Daddy. It's home. Duh!" Terri tapped the book to refocus Haley's attention and stood.

"So long as the closest school still open is two hours away, you're home with me, kiddo." She walked over to Devon, pulled the paper check from the back pocket of her jeans, and handed it over.

"Fifty-effin'-thou!" he whisper-yelled. "That SOB said I'd get seventy-five, minimum."

"With good behavior," she said. "Did you read the letter? Otherwise, it's just the hundred, and that first fifty is all but gone."

"My cellmate had a pack of gum stashed away during a raid and I lose 25K? I was a model prisoner."

"Not on paper," she said.

His stomach sank. Already, he could smell the next prison: that putrid blend of floor cleaner, sweat, and piss.

"How long will this last us?"

"Six more months, probably. Maybe. That should give you enough time to-"

"To what?" he said, too loudly. Haley looked up from her book, frowned, and then dipped her head back.

"It's fine, sweetie," he said. He wheeled back to Terri. "I've been beating down doors for two weeks and getting laughed out of the interviews. I don't know anybody, Terri. That's the first thing they ask: 'How'd you hear about us?' It's code for 'Who sent you?' I could be the best damn modeler in the state. They'd still slap me in the basement fetching coffee for the guy whose uncle's brother's roommate vouched for him."

She kissed him, and even after two weeks back home and a thousand kisses, it still felt like a freedom he didn't deserve.

"Then fetch coffee, Dev. It beats another stretch, doesn't it?"

His fists balled, but he breathed away the bubbling anger. I'm not mad at her, he thought. I'm mad at me. That was what they taught in the pen. Take accountability for your mistakes.

Devon had never broken a law in his life, but he did make the mistake of going to college. He'd racked up student loans studying 3D modeling when he should have

25

Darren Todd

been kissing some banker's ass for a recommendation. Or at least waited to have kids until....

He let the thought die. Haley hadn't come too soon or too late. She was wonderful and the reason he did it all.

He took Terri by the shoulders and kissed her. When their lips parted, he kept his head on hers and whispered.

"If I could fetch coffee, I would. Even those jobs are taken. It's jailbirding or nothing."

"You've got six months," she said, her tone light and hopeful. She put her hands on his cheeks.

~oOo~

Four months later, and they were running dry. As if psychic, the landlord appeared on the first, a rent-a-cop at his heels, ready to evict that very hour if they fell short on rent. The erosion of tenant protections ensured the have nots could never burden the haves, even for a day.

Haley got a string of ear infections and their insurance premiums shot up. The landlord bumped rent another four hundred when their current lease ended, and Devon was spending way too much on clothes and coffees and bus tickets, canvasing the city looking for a job.

At night, he banged out spec work that promised to fetch paying gigs but never did.

"Let me go back to work," Terri said at last. They huddled in the kitchen while Haley slept on their shared bed. She neared seven and seemed to learn more everyday about what was really going on.

"You'll fair no better than me," Devon whispered. Even so, the studio apartment might as well have been an echo chamber. With the turnover of tenants on all sides, even the gypsum boards he'd hung on the walls failed to filter out all the noise.

"Once they know you've got Lupus, you won't even make the second round."

She shrugged. "So, I'll lie."

Devon laughed. "Yeah. The insurer finds out and you'll be in slam for real. Then where will we be? Besides, Haley loves having you at home. You're the best thing she's got."

"We're only here because of you," she said, and her voice broke. "My sisters are all back-home living in the

26

same rooms they grew up in, with their kids having their souls crushed in DeVos schools, while they stay in bed all day popping pills. You're the reason we survive."

They kissed, but the bond grew salty when one of her tears slid between their lips.

"I'll jailbird this time," she whispered, and he thought he'd misheard her.

"What?"

"They pay women almost double. Nobody wants to send their wives or daughters to prison..."

He shook his head.

"So, patrons pay extra. It can't be any worse than the places you go."

He shook his head again. Just the thought of Terri doing time made his veins run with ice.

"No, baby. Never. I'll pull triple max before I let you do time." He grabbed his phone. "I've got some leads. A bunch of three-monthers have come up. Those rich assholes love to do dumb shit during the holidays, so I'll have plenty to choose from."

She cried in earnest now and put a hand over her mouth to stifle the sound. Their heads turned in unison to check on Haley. She slept dead-center in the queen they'd found in an empty apartment when they moved in. She'd clasped her hands together and tucked them under her cheek, as if posing for a postcard from the Children's Republic of Adorableness.

"I read the news," Terri said, eyes soaked now, glinting in the light from the bare bulb overhead. "The MinSec prisons are filling up. You might not even get a gig at one that allows yard visits. I can't handle another sentence only seeing you through glass. Haley can't do it." He nodded.

"It'll work. We'll make it work." He yanked the suit jacket from the back of the chair and flung it across the apartment. "Lemme see what I can scare up. I'll get MinSec. I promise."

He jumped when his phone vibrated in his hand. Unknown caller. HR departments blocked their numbers so no one would call them back and bug them. He yelled without sound and pointed at the phone. Terri crossed her fingers.

"Hello, this is Devon."

"Mr. Finch?" a smooth, high-pitched voice asked. An educated man. Rich. Devon could tell from just two words.

"Yes."

"I have a job for you," he said.

The words he'd been waiting for, but coming from that voice, the news sent a shudder through him.

~oOo~

Errol Turley was small, but commanded respect, even sitting at the Finch's wobbly kitchen table. He wore a dark suit, which clashed with everything else in their home, even their own clothes. The dust storms kept a thin film over everything, no matter how often Terri cleaned.

Teacups sat atop chipped saucers between them, but before the liquid had finished steaming in the chilly air of the apartment, Devon felt compelled to surface their business.

"So, how long?"

Turley, who'd taken to lazily eying the apartment — keeping a neutral expression that betrayed neither disgust nor interest—shrugged lightly and then pulled his thin briefcase to the tabletop. The dull leather was dark gray, textured. It looked like it could stop a bullet.

"Rhinoceros," Turley said.

Devon jerked his head up from the case. "Sorry?"

"It's made of rhinoceros hide. A few years ago, and I'd be the one needing a penal surrogate for such a luxury. Fortunately, not anymore." He smiled, but kept his teeth hidden behind thin lips.

"It's very nice. So, how long?"

From behind him, Terri put a hand on Devon's shoulder, gently chiding his impatience.

"The charge is vehicular manslaughter. Tantamount to involuntary manslaughter, really. Often carries just six months in a MinSec, but my client was... impaired."

Devon nodded and forced a frown, the closest he could come to displaying sympathy. "So, not MinSec. Max then?"

Turley sipped his tea, staring into the muddy liquid. He'd refused the powdered cream. Probably used to the real thing.

"One would think so, but the judge did not look favorably on my client. Wanted to set an example. Triple max, I'm afraid."

Devon revealed no emotion, not so much to hide it from Turley as from Terri. Even so, his wife slid behind a wooden divider in the kitchen.

"I don't do triple max. I know a guy who might, but it depends on the sentence. Most I've done is three months in max, and the place was on lock-down the entire time. I nearly went insane in my cell, but at least I was safe."

Turley held up a hand. The flesh on his palm shone pink and puffy, like the coarsest thing he'd ever gripped was the leather of his briefcase.

"That won't be an issue. As a part of the deal, my client is... compensating a guard to ensure your safety. A supervisor, no less. Surely you know that as many issues arise from guards as from inmates. Not only will my client's man cut your threat level by half, he'll also keep the ne'er-do-wells at bay."

"Of which they're be plenty in a triple max. You talkin' Haberdeen?"

"No. A new facility. Privately owned. An hour north of the city. All the latest amenities, to include a private cell."

"What about visitation?" Terri asked from behind the small man. Turley pulled his chair back, spun, and faced Terri full on before speaking.

"Following six months of good behavior, full visitation in private rooms. Conjugal as well as family. All brand new."

"So how long?" This time, Devon's tone hardened. The words elongated, inviting no more avoidance.

Turley displayed another thin-lipped smile, but dropped his eyes before saying, "Two years."

Terri's breath left her in an audible whoosh.

As if dialed in to her mother's discomfort, Haley came through the front door, pulling all eyes to her. She rushed in and threw her arms around Terri.

"You're supposed to be across the hall," Terri said, but hugged her back and swung her from side to side. Devon's gut cinched just watching the familiar display of affection.

"Miss Jeffers left," she said. "For the store. It's just me

29

and Jo-Jo now."

Terri's face tensed and she closed her eyes. She looked up at Devon.

"I'll be next door." She mouthed to Devon while pantomiming a scribbling pen: No signing.

Turley waited patiently for the scene to play out. He took a couple more sips of his tea, which neared the dregs. Once the apartment door shut, Devon spoke.

"When's the court date?"

Turley waved the question away, pursing his lips.

"All taken care of. The judge knows my client is employing a—"

"Jailbird," Devon finished.

"Indeed. So, if the terms are acceptable, I have the paperwork here with me." He patted a briefcase that had once been a majestic creature thousands of miles away.

"How much?"

"A million."

The number pinged a surge of adrenaline in Devon's system. The dollar had tanked, but a million dollars still remained a pie-in-the-sky number for men of his class. If they were careful, they could live a decade off that money, or send Hayley to a private school and afford a bigger place and still easily last five years. Three of which he'd have with them. In three years, he could afford to take on a non-paying internship at a financial firm, probably become salaried—if bottom rung—before the million ran out.

And yet, the prospect of triple max for two years, not seeing either Terri or Haley at all for six months, terrified him. His experience in MinSec federal pens meant nothing when facing down triple max.

The anxiety in his stomach must have reached his face, because Turley pulled out his paperwork, circled a paragraph near the last page of the extensive contract, and slid it over to Devon without another word.

He'd barely made out the phrase "guaranteed employment" before Turley interrupted.

"We know what you are, Mr. Finch. We've checked your work at a dozen firms and my client always has room for skilled workers of your caliber."

"He needs a modeler?" Devon asked, the words coming

out as little more than a squeak.

"One of his businesses does, or will, in two years' time. So, there's the million: a hundred thousand now, another hundred in a year, and the rest after the sentence is fulfilled. And", he added, "a permanent position waiting for you when you get out. Healthcare, stock options, Christmas bonuses, retirement package." He leaned close as if keeping anyone else from listening in, though they were alone. "No more free gigs. No more months away from your family, risking your life for people who can't be bothered with jail time."

The words rang ironic, since Turley represented one such man—a drunken asshole who'd killed an innocent person in his half-million-dollar car. But still, his rhetoric found its mark.

By the time Terri returned, Devon was already putting ink to paper. She stood in the doorway, frozen, tears forming and falling within seconds. But Devon knew they were among her last. Two years from now, she'd have no more tears to shed but in joy.

~oOo~

Its official name was engraved on a marble slab outside the fence: Terryton Penal Park, but everyone called it The Park. Devon had researched all he could, despite the young age of the facility leaving little information in the public sphere. Private prisons weren't known for their transparency anyway.

As far as aesthetics, however, The Park ranked highest in all the prisons Devon had worked in. The design aped the neo-industrial buildings downtown, with blends of glass, brushed steel, and brightly-colored support beams and railings. To the passer-by, it might look unfinished, even vulnerable, but that only reflected the intended design.

When he and a handful of others moved through the double-gate—triple-stranded razor-wire reflecting a pale, winter sun—the robust layers of security revealed themselves. Guards littered the perimeter, the yard, and the entrance to the facility proper. They didn't gaggle, but moved in rhythmic, intentional patterns. None smoked or kicked at the gravel or chatted with other guards. They seemed uniform in size and shape as well, as if a hundred clones manned the prison instead of actual humans with families and worries of their own.

Devon had gotten used to schedules, timetables. But from the moment one of the clone guards barked for them to exit the bus, every foot he moved felt watched and calculated. They shouted out the number of steps. Turn. Step. Stop. Turn. Step.

He had no intention of opposing them, or making trouble at all for that matter, but he felt glad for it. Anyone daring to come into The Park with thoughts of disturbing its oiled efficiency would surely end up ground to hamburger in its gears.

Even the cell blocks echoed the quiet, eerie quality of the trip in. No catcalls, no convicts staring him down in hopes of shaking the new fish. In what little Devon could see flicking his eyes up, the caged men looked more like specimens in some sadist's curio than convicts serving time.

The lockstep only ceased once he turned into his new home for the next two years: a six by eight feet cell with bunk and toilet. No more wear than a hospital waiting room, and nearly as clinical. The bars slid out from hollow chambers and locked down with a slow, mechanical clack.

Now his time began. He thought of the sun's position outside and imagined it was probably late afternoon. What would Terri and Haley be up to right then? Still studying her lessons? Maybe wrapping them up for the day and grabbing an afternoon snack to hold her off till dinner. He closed his eyes and let the movie play in his mind for as long as he could. The eerie quiet of the cell block made it easier to pretend he was somewhere other than The Park and doing something other than trading in his life so some rich jerk could keep his businesses afloat and continue paying his taxes.

Who knows how long he stood there, listening to the imaginary voices of his family. He pushed out any worries over when he could hear their voices for real, feel Terri's lips on his, her body pressed against him.

"You Finch?" came a deep voice from outside the cell.

His eyes flew open, the mental image of Terri and Haley

snuggled up on the couch and watching the telescreen popped, replaced by the dull gray of his cell.

He slowly focused on the figure who'd spoken. One of the clone guards, but—closer up—one who wore an extra twenty pounds around the middle, and whose face lacked the intensity of the other guards. Cut from the same cloth, sure, but without the *faux* military bearing of those he'd seen so far.

"Yes, boss," Devon said and dropped his eyes.

The guard huffed a laugh. "Don't worry about that boss crap, at least when it's just us. I'm Brady. Mr. Turley mentioned we'd be meeting, right?"

It took long seconds for comprehension to dawn, but when it did, a tight knot loosened in his stomach.

"Yes, he did. Hello, boss—I mean, Brady. Guard Brady."

He chuckled again. "Just Brady. Look, Mr. Turley tells me you'll be no trouble. That's good. We don't see many jailbirds in The Park, but I'll take what I can get. You guys are a helluva lot less trouble than the convicts."

Devon dropped his shoulders, the knot unraveling, and a held breath left him. "Thank you. Yes, we tend to be pretty... good. No trouble."

Brady nodded. "Glad to hear it. You keep your head down and your mouth shut, at least when you're in the yard or at mess, and you'll do fine. No guard's gonna ruffle your feathers. Just keep away from the convicts best you can, and you'll be outta here in no time."

Two years. Maybe that was no time to a guard who got to return home each night. Then again, in two years' time Brady wouldn't be walking out with a million dollars and a skilled, salary position.

"It's nice to meet you," Devon said. "Thanks for the heads up."

Brady nodded, then seemed to go rigid. "Gotta make the rounds. Head down, mouth shut. I'll come by sometimes and see how you're doing, but I'm always watching. You're safe."

~oOo~

The following months passed at glacial speed. Sure enough, no one harassed Devon, and he refused to test this by giving even the slightest provocation. As a result, however, he turned from fish to ghost. Perhaps word had spread that he fell under Guard Brady's protection, because even the whispered conversations other inmates shared during mess met with only silence when Devon initiated. Others would move tables outright, and Devon dared not push his luck. Did everyone know he was a jailbird? He'd spotted a few others he figured were doing surrogate time as well, but even they refused to speak to him in anything more than a few dismissive grunts.

His only stimulation became the daily visits from Guard Brady, lasting only minutes, but enough of a touch with reality to keep him somewhat grounded. That and the perpetual visits to the clinic.

"Why am I getting poked and prodded like once a week?" he'd finally asked Brady.

The guard shrugged and blew out his lips dismissively. "You know how much shit circulates in a place like this. It's new and all, but just be glad you've got your own cell. Most of these guys will leave with tuberculosis or hepatitis or worse. Your patron's just making sure you don't get some lifelong illness or nothin'. Like you said, you're gonna be working for him, after all. He's lookin' out for ya, if you think about it. You get better healthcare than I do," he laughed.

Still, the checkups seemed invasive, extraneous even. Perhaps it reflected the natural fluff of any new facility yet to suffer the budget cuts that plagued every business over time. At least the check-ups counted for some measure of socialization. Otherwise, Devon had only the stacks of books to keep him company and to pass the time.

He wrote Terri and Hayley almost every day. New inmates had no access to the Internet, but a small stipend from his patron kept him in stamps and stationery. Brady assured him that once he'd passed six months with no issues, they'd release his mail.

"And there's a ton of it," Brady told him. "That wife of yours must like to write as much as you do."

With only two weeks left before he could schedule a visit and finally read his letters, Devon grew excited. This made the long days extend even more. He worried he'd look different to Haley. He'd let his mind drift most days. Nearly a quarter of the way to a better life. Not easy time, but as close to it as he was likely to get in a triple max. The lockstep machinations and eerie quiet of the place certainly beat doing time with one eye over his shoulder and his head on a swivel. He'd done time in jails back before the bondsmen unionized and demanded jailbirds couldn't pull pre-trial sentences. Some were worse than MinSec prisons. He didn't miss those days.

So, by the time someone shadowed him in the yard, he'd dropped his guard almost completely. He'd convinced himself he had nothing to fear, and believed the worst lay behind him.

But no, behind him now crept a dark, hulk of a man who breathed louder than a bear. And he was taking his time, closing the distance to Devon by inches as Devon walked across the swatch of grass from the handball court to the weights.

The quiet that pervaded the place grew deafening. Light conversation stopped, the grunts of weightlifters ceased as they racked their weights and looked on. Devon's heart pounded, and for the first time in weeks, adrenaline kicked up in his bloodstream. He wanted to run, but that was a bad idea. As bad as running from a feral dog intent on proving himself alpha or even making a meal of his quarry.

The breathing drew closer still. Devon chanced a quick look back to see the guy held a shiv in his right fist, making no attempt to hide it. He flicked his eyes up to the tower guards. They looked on, guns propped over shoulders, but either didn't see the attack forming or didn't care.

Then Devon spotted Brady—his only company for the last five months, dare he say his friend. Someone he would make a point to keep in touch with once this all ended, even try to help out—with the benefits of the job waiting for him, he might could.

Brady stood by a guard shack, heavy stick in one hand, propped on the meaty fist of the other. He pasted a knowing smirk on his face and arched his eyebrows. Devon heard his tacit message clearly: Walk him over.

Devon turned toward Brady and quickened his pace. The man at his rear moved faster as well, but he'd never close before they reached Brady. A hundred feet. The breathing all but desperate now, like a caged animal. Fifty feet. Devon's forehead dripped a bead of sweat into his eyes, despite the chill of the spring air.

At twenty feet Brady gave him a slight nod. Devon spun to face his assailant. The whole yard looked on now, no longer even pretending to go about their other activities.

The dark-skinned behemoth stood shirtless in front of him, his chest heaving. The shiv looked comically small in his ham-sized fist, but Devon still shuddered at the thought of what a guy like that could do with it.

"We doin' this, Buster?" Brady called over Devon's shoulder.

The invitation bolstered Devon's resolve: Drop the shiv and piss off, or get your brains knocked out.

"The man says today's the day," the hulk growled. He looked past Devon at Brady. His clenched teeth spread into a sadistic grin as he moved his gaze down to Devon.

What the hell did that mean? Who's "the man"?

Devon turned to face Brady, the first seeds of doubt blooming inside him. He never got his head all the way around. Something iron-hard struck his jaw and powdered his teeth. Even through the instant, searing pain, panic spread like the sand-like particles in his mouth. He fell on his back in the grass. Though absurd, he worried what Terri would think when she saw him now, teeth like glass at a broken window.

He remained conscious, despite the fire in his face. Cheers rose all around. The yard filled with more noise than he'd ever heard at The Park before, the shouts laden with bottled passion. Brady's face filled Devon's watery vision. The man wore an aw-shucks grimace with no more emotion than a circus clown.

"Sorry about this, Mr. Finch. I really was kinda fond of you."

"Wha-?" was all Devon managed. Pain so fierce it felt like Brady's club had struck him again surged through his whole head. All that came out was a stream of blood and the sandy bits of his teeth.

"See, your patron didn't need a jailbird, Devon. He needed a liver. Guess he didn't fancy settling for half. These

36

guys," and he swept the yard with his club, "they always figure out who's next. Christ knows who tells 'em. Get as riled as a cage full of gorillas when it's harvest time." Brady shrugged, patted Devon on the shoulder, and then looked up to the hulk with the shiv. "Nothing below the ribcage, Buster. Have fun."

Devon leaned up and saw two clinic orderlies waiting with a stretcher. Their grins promised no help, either. The last thing Devon heard before a fire erupted in his chest was the raucous cheers of The Park's true convicts, the noise growing to fever pitch as Buster descended on him.

Before everything went black, the pain ceased. He felt his body buck at the assault, felt the pressure of Buster on top of him and the shiv entering and retreating, but no pain. His thoughts turned home, to Terri and Haley. He wondered how long they could live on a hundred thousand. Wondered whether Turley would tell them what had happened. Whether his patron would make good on the other installments.

How did it come to this? Perhaps the president had needed a vital organ at some point during his several terms. Had he laid this foundation, as well? Funded the prisons only to match organ donors with campaign donors?

Before any answer came, Devon's worries faded and then floated away.

Darren Todd

Ghosts and Glory

Paula Hammond

I told her straight up, this is no world to bring children into. But she was young and in love, if you can believe that. Child always did have her head in the clouds.

"Anyway", she'd say, "the world needs people Ma. And Johnny and I will make such lovely babies." She was right about that much at least.

She was always such an optimist, my Gloria. So full of love and compassion. Lord knows where she got that from. Not from me. And that's the God's honest truth. I seen too much of the world. Seen the bad and the worst. It's been a long time since I thought about anyone or anything except me and mine. How we're gonna make it through the days. How we're gonna survive. But Gloria? Well, she was something else, that girl.

A real mess of child. All legs and hair and restless energy. Always running somewhere. I guess she got that from her Pa. He never could stay in the same place for long. No, nor the same bed neither.

Oh, I know you're not supposed to speak ill of the dead, but he was gone from my life long before he died, and there's no one left to be hurt by the truth now.

No, Bobbi never gave me much besides heartache and my little Glory—but what a gift she was. Still, even though I could tell that her Johnny and my Bobbi were cut from the same cloth, I guess I understood why she wanted children of her own. Life can feel so short, so desperate. We each do what we can to get through the days and Glory just wanted something—someone—to call her own.

And, after a time, there was three. Three lovely babies. Petie, he took after his grandpa, tall and thin as a switch. Just going on twelve but smarter than most twice his age. Then there was Trinnie, the very image of her Ma at the same age. Still too young to know how pretty she was. And then there was the baby, Little Dotty. Named for me. I told Glory that she didn't want to burden a child with a name like Dorothea, but I couldn't talk her out of it.

"Ma," she said, "baby might not have much in life but it'll have a name to be proud of." Then she gave me one of those dazzlin' smiles of hers. I swear there were times when she'd clean knock me sideways. That was what she was like. Would give you the shoes right off her feet and walk away like it was you done her the favor.

Truth be told, I often thought she was just a little touched because Lord knows what she had to be so happy about. But then, I'm just a mean old woman. Sitting watching the rain fall, thinking on ghosts.

So many ghosts.

After Maria, I thought that I'd lost just about as much as a woman could. I guess I should have paid more attention. We all should. The signs were there: hotter summers, colder winters, tornados, hurricanes, flash foods.

They called Maria a once in a lifetime event: a super-storm. But really, Maria was Mother Nature's warning. She was telling us she'd had enough. Only they were too busy making money to pay attention. Who were 'they'? In truth, I think we were all a little to blame. We sat by while they told us that science was a lie. While they turned their backs on all the old agreements. Told the world we didn't need no fancy foreign accords. That we could manage our own business, thank you very much. We should have been setting an example. But all we did was give others the excuse to do the exact same thing.

And still the deniers carried on telling us that what really mattered was keeping costs down and profits up. That what was important was gas for ten dollars a gallon. That it was our God-given right to have all-you-can-eat buffets and endless top-ups. And we believed it. Wanted to believe it.

None of us ever expected to see American babies on the news—bellies swollen from hunger. None of us imagined that it would be us queuing up while strangers dished out bags of meal and powdered milk. Those were things that happened somewhere else, in parts of the world where they don't speak English.

Lord, how proud we were. How proud I was. Safe. High and dry. A cabin on the tree-line. Little plot of land. My Glory and all her babies. Dotty just six months old. And Bobbi? Well, Bobbi proved me wrong at that. Found himself a job. Sent money back that gave us just enough to get by.

I look back now. I see it all, like one of those old tinted photographs. The five of us, out on the porch. Looking out over the tree-line. My, the rain had been falling for so long. A week solid. But that morning was so dry, and clear, and fresh it felt good to be alive, you know?

Days like that always brought out the best in my Glory. Not that she ever had a bad day, mind. But somehow the sun suited her disposition. Like she was shining inside and out. Oh, I know I sound crazy. But she was my child and I have a right to remember her any way I want.

And that day is how I'll always remember her.

Baby is asleep in a sling across her back, she's watching Trinnie and Petie play. She turns to me all ablaze and sighs.

"Ma", she says, "some days are just about perfect, don't you think?"

And then I hear it. A tremendous rumbling and snapping. It all happens so fast. The earth becomes liquid. A river of mud. The house is sliding towards us, walls bowing, beams creaking, windows cracking. Somehow, I grab Glory and down we go, together.

We're drowning now. Beaten and battered. The mud flows so fast and furious that it throws the house clean over our heads. I see it for a second as it hits the trees. Shattering those big old oaks like kindling. Then I'm down again. Nose full of dirt. Suffocating in the dark.

The mud is warm and wraps about me like a sodden blanket. It feels oddly comforting and somehow, right there, right then, I could just close my eyes and let it all go.

But I still have Glory's hand and she's pulling at me. Shaking me, dragging me up out of the dirt. She's never been strong, Glory, but Lord is she stubborn and I know that she'll never let me go. So, I climb to my feet and open my eyes to a blighted hell of mud and broken things.

Glory looks, too. She doesn't say a word, just looks. And, as I follow her gaze, my heart almost stops. There, lying in the molten earth, are two tiny shapes. Two little bodies, naked and shattered. We say nothing. Just stand and look. Then, we start to crawl through the mud. To where they lie.

She looked so lost then, my Glory. I saw her hand stroking Petie's hair, clearing the mud from his face. I helped her do the same for Trinnie. Making them as respectable as we could. We give them a final kiss, leaving each with a grainy lip print etched on their pale forehead. Then silence.

I don't know how long we stood there, Glory squeezing my hand so tightly that even once she'd let me go I could still feel her fingers pressed against mine. Maybe we'd still be there now if it wasn't for little Dotty, wrapped tight to her mother's back, suddenly coughing and crying fit to burst. And right there, that tiny cry was the most wonderful sound we had ever heard in our entire lives.

Now we had a purpose. Now we were three. Chest deep in mud, not so much walking as swimming. Every step, tripping and falling. Glory almost blue with blood and bruises. Little Dotty taking turns to lie under our clothes. Share our heat—what little of it we had. But we had a purpose.

That first evening, as the sun set, we made ourselves a platform from metal roofing and sat watching the world turn scarlet. I swear it was like something out of Revelations.

"The river became like blood and every living creature died", isn't that how it goes? Because that's what I saw. An ocean of red mud as far as the eye could see. And in that red, chairs, tables, shattered pylons, trees fractured and pointing to the heavens like bloody fingers. And when I looked closer, I saw the animals. The people.

Lord, I thought that we lived all alone on that hilltop but there were so many people. Some face down in the mud like fallen statues. Some twisted in unnatural angles. Some with not a scratch on them. Like they'd just sat down and died.

The second night was worse. The insects had come by then and—oh my Lord —the smell. I don't think I'll ever forget that if I live to be a hundred. We knew then that we had to keep moving. Away from the death and disease. It was a blessing that we didn't know how long it would take. How bad it was. How slim our chances were. Oh, I know that it's all ancient history. Times long gone, and maybe best forgotten.

Dotty has a child of her own now. Her own little Gloria, if you can imagine that. She sees me when she can, when the sailboats make it upriver. And the child does love to hear my stories.

"Tell me about the good old days, Gran'ma", she says. And I laugh and tell her there weren't no good about it. But then she takes my hand and looks at me in that way she has and I see my own Glory all over again. And I can't say no.

So, I tell her how it used to be. Before the skies were poisoned, and the levees broke, and the big cities vanished under the oceans. And though she can't quite believe it when I tell her about the huge asphalted highways that used to stretch from here to N'Orleans, she nods and pretends to, anyway.

Paula Hammond

Garbage Patch Kids

Chris Bullard

Dear New Resident,

Welcome to Plasticia, the multi-hued gem of the Pacific Ocean. Whether you have come from one of the recently submerged islands to our south (a special aloha to those of you who were citizens of Hawaii), or from the west, where desertification has eliminated so many of the formerly thriving cities of Asia, we congratulate you on your decision not to oppose relocation to our floating paradise. You are truly survivors!

In order to familiarize you with the island platform you now occupy, we would like to provide you with a few fun and/or interesting facts.

History:

Although the plastic debris field that forms the island on which your home is built was known to fishermen before the end of the 20th century, it was not until the reign of Trumpus I that the first permanent settlements were established. At that time, a group of NOAA and EPA scientists and researchers who had declared that they believed in what was then known as "climate change" were re-assigned to a houseboat that was to be used for scientific examination of the components of the floating mass. The officials were ordered to count every piece of plastic that they could find from the center outward to the very edge—twice, in case they may have gotten it wrong in the first place.

Discovering that they were somewhat at the mercy of the weather (how ironic!), the former bureaucrats began to insulate and, then, expand their shelters by the expedient of melting bits of the surrounding plastic together in order to form roofs and walls. Later, they began to use flame throwers to link parts of the floating mass into a surface that could be walked upon. In a few years, they had created the first *terra firma* in what we now proudly call "Plasticia."

As more and more "climate change" non-deniers were offered placement on the island, more and more of the floating plastic was fused into habitable real estate. In fact, some of the primitive residences built during this period can still be seen within the limits of Capital City. You may even be assigned to live in one of them!

The re-opening of the Western Interior Seaway, last seen during the Cretaceous era, which flooded parts of seventeen states almost overnight and left thousands of Americans without any place to live, also deprived Trumpus I of most of his political base. Pence I, Magnus Indianianus, successor to Trumpus I, decreed that the newly founded state of Plasticia should make space for these unfortunate refugees.

Initially, of course, there were difficulties, as might be expected during the establishment of any place of habitation upon a land-like substance. The lack of cellars meant that citizens had few options when confronted with the threats of severe weather disturbances, but many were able to find adequate handholds.

The political disputes between the first settlers and those who came after them were effectively resolved by the creation of "reservations" on which anyone who possessed a college degree was allowed to reside peacefully without social stigma. You may wish to visit one of these reservations in order to see native Plasticians perform their colorful demonstrations of the "scientific method."

Today, Plasticia is a prosperous, forward looking society which will, in all likelihood, continue to float and not sink like a stone to the bottom of the sea.

Things to See and Do:

Sunrise and sunset are the most beautiful times of day on Plasticia. Just remember to check your compass before you set out to enjoy these events because the opposing sea currents that fix Plasticia in its place in the central Pacific also turn it clockwise. Although you may be able to see a magnificent sunrise from the east-facing window of your shelter this month, by the next month you may see nothing but darkness. Take advantage of those glorious sunset views while you can!

Of course, once the sun is overhead, protective clothing and sun screen is a must.

Don't risk becoming so woozy from the heat that you fall down in the streets of Plasticia. It's always embarrassing when the streets department has to extricate someone who is stuck in the plastic.

New residents may expect to enjoy a dip in our beautiful ocean waters. However, before taking the plunge, newcomers should be advised that there are certain differences between the experience of swimming at a beach resort in the Rockies and swimming in Plasticia.

The first question to ask yourself before stepping off the edge is whether you are sure that you can get yourself back. There is no gently sloping shore in Plasticia. There is no beach. The only way to get yourself out of the water is to grip the side of the island and pull yourself up as you might haul yourself up the side of a boat, if the side of the boat was composed of an amalgam of plastic bottles, toys and food containers.

You should also be aware that water temperatures vary greatly, depending on the time of year and the influence of the various deep-sea currents. One day you might be perfectly comfortable in swim shorts; the next you might need a survival suit. Check before jumping in.

There are great white sharks that patrol the seas around Plasticia. As we are a floating state, there is nothing but water underneath the solid portions of our island. It seems that some of the big fellows have learned to lurk under the areas that abut the sea in the hopes that something or someone will jump or fall in. A word to the wise—when encountered in the water, these creatures are fearsome to deal with.

Sorry, recreational fishing is not allowed. All fish caught in the waters off Plasticia are converted into the fish slurry that feeds the inhabitants. You don't want to take someone's bowl of slurry, do you? We didn't think so.

Finally, after putting in one of the twelve-hour work days required of anyone living on Plasticia, you might want to spend you down time chilling while you and your family members reminisce about some of the thousands of items that have been melted together to create your own shelter. A cooler chest, for example, may remind you of a childhood picnic in a public park, or a drinking cup may take you down memory lane back to a time when there was such a thing as a fast food restaurant. Some inhabitants have even found examples of ancient sea life caught in the coils of six pack rings.

Do's and Don'ts:

- **Don't allow your children to splash in puddles on Plasticia.**
  Some of these "puddles" are actually flaws in the plastic mesh. In a few unfortunate cases, kids have jumped in puddles that turned out to be deep enough to let them slide all the way through to the Pacific. We regret their loss.
- **Do respect your fish slurry servers.**
  Throwing your bowl of fish slurry at them does not improve the taste of the slurry and may cause resentment on their part.
- **Don't listen to rumors about the weather.**
  The government of Plasticia will let you know about any storms, hurricanes or rogue waves that are likely to affect your shelter. Someone you know may tell you that a water spout, or some other meteorological event, wiped out this or that quadrant last week, but these rumors almost always prove to be incorrect.
- **Do have fun!**

Sincerely,
The Welcoming Committee
.

The Orange Street Parking Garage is FULL/~~OPEN~~

J.G. Follansbee

Jordy found a rusting steel door ajar. The gray-haired homeless refugee was surprised it hadn't been torn off its hinges and salvaged. Recycling it would pay for a week's worth of shelter on Orange Street, but he didn't have the tools to remove it. On the other hand, there might be evacuee treasure inside.

A whiff of brackish decay seeped through the crack. The door was jammed tight. Maybe the Potomac's flooding had undermined the foundation.

His friend Freda peered skeptically over his shoulder, then tilted her head back, taking in the building's temple-likc façade. The soaking November downpour bathed her face.

"Everyone says these old office buildings are picked clean."

"Just because there's a consensus doesn't mean it's correct."

Jordy met Freda at a refugee camp under an abandoned I-95 overpass. Freda's tent had blown away during a blizzard. They huddled together like puzzle pieces, their body warmth forming a tight bond. They didn't talk much about their lives prior to the Year of Storms.

Jordy pushed harder on the door. He and Freda would go after the salvage inside, assuming there was anything left. He'd found kilos in other buildings said to be empty. The door's dragging foot squealed against the concrete floor. A human scream competed with the painful noise, but the voice was in Jordy's head, pressing outward like a ghost trapped in a bottle. The wail always brought him up short, even with the daily memory suppressants. He gripped the door's edge to steady himself.

"You okay, buddy?" Freda laid a hand on the tattered, filthy sleeve of his coat. "The voices again?"

"I'm good." Jordy lied. Freda had her own burdens. He wouldn't be another.

Jordy nudged the door further. The stench took on a stale, papery quality. He glanced at the building's entrance.

"I used to live around here, I think, long time ago."

"No one lived in this part of Dee Cee." Freda's lips smacked with the certitude of a preacher. "It was a bureaucratic hell. Those aren't condos behind that limestone."

"What do you know about limestone?"

"Used to be a geologist. Used to work in the guv'ment. Before, you know..." Freda spat, and she poked a split-nailed finger in a large, conical hole in one of the stone blocks. "Used to be a bronze plaque here. Big one. Bet someone got a pretty penny for it."

Jordy did a double-take at the green-tinted outline left by the missing plaque. His mind wanted to fill the blank, but the necessary image was missing. A lot of his memories were missing from the time before the tides and floods that changed everything. He shoved at the steel door, and it flew open, revealing a dark hallway. He gestured his friend inside.

"Are you sure?" Freda scrutinized the hall. "I'd rather go to Orange Street now. It's getting late."

"Might be good shit in here." Good shit was getting harder to find, and the bessies were paying less and less. No one else was buying, though. They had a monopoly guaranteed by Congress.

"I don't want to go in there."

"It's fine."

"Denial is not a survival strategy!" Freda quavered like a shredded flag in a breeze. "Last time you said 'fine,' we were robbed blind."

"I'll protect you, I promise. We'll get something out of this."

Appeased, Freda grunted "Okay." The promise of salvage was always persuasive. Jordy and Freda scoured the remnants of the capital, especially around the new shoreline, hoping to find the reusable or recyclable. The bessies were more than a police force. They encouraged refugees to pick over the abandoned structures, and Jordy occasionally struck gold.

"Come on, then, stupid bot!" Freda's bark was directed down the heaving sidewalk. The robot, nicknamed "The Ass," wheeled itself forward. Its cage-like bin overflowed with canvas bags of junk, metal chunks too big for a bag, and totes packed with clothing, travel gear, and food. A big retailer refurbished its old warehouse robots and gave the bots to refugees as silicon beasts of burden.

"We're out of the wind, at least." Freda shuffled down the hall to a flight of stairs. Threads of her dungarees trailed her soleless shoes. She threw up her hands.

"What's wrong?" Jordy said.

"Nothing." She shook her head in a vigorous No.

Jordy brushed her hand with his finger to reassure her. "Come on."

"No! Smells of green shirts."

Her objection echoing in the hall, Jordy climbed a step, then two, confident Freda was close behind, followed by the bot. The swoosh of his mismatched shoes against the marble steps provoked more ghostly voices. He'd done something important here. The sounds, gauzy and distant, vanished when he stepped on a dried, curled leaf, blown in through broken windows. Before him, an elevator drew him like a magnet. He pushed the call button.

"Are you crazy?" Freda said. "That hasn't worked in 20, 30 years. Not since '32 for sure."

Jordy pushed the button again. The elevator would take him to where he worked. No response, however. What's wrong now? He pushed it once more. Freda grabbed his arm.

"Stop it, Jordy. You're scaring me."

His companion's fear broke the spell, but his breath came faster. "Upstairs. Top floor. Down the hall."

"You've lost it."

"Let's go." A surge of energy carried Jordy to a flight of spiral stairs next to the elevator.

"Crap," Freda said. She turned to The Ass. "You heard the man. Get cracking."

The bot hesitated before taking the first step after

Freda.

Jordy's heart felt light, as if the effort of climbing was nothing. An unfocused, pleasant memory drove him upward, spiraling toward a skylight. His heart pounded like a tom-tom, but he didn't care. Reaching the top of the stairway, he stumbled down a long hall, feeling dread and joy, salt sweat mixing with the rainwater that dripped from the ceiling. A pair of wooden doors, bleached by humidity, welcomed him.

"Jordy! Wait up!"

Ignoring Freda, Jordy yanked at a hole in the door—someone had salvaged the hardware—and it splintered loose.

"Fuckin' A, Jordy." Freda panted. "You're going to kill me... . Oh, sweet Jesus."

The room was bare, but its southern windows offered a bird's eye view of the empty capital. The new shoreline lay below them, a more or less straight line from northwest to southeast. The Potomac River was a wide estuary. The Capitol Mall was a swamp. The Washington Monument poked up from a tiny island, its top 50 meters lying in pieces at the monument's foot. Waves churned at the base of the Capitol itself, its dome intact, but streaked with soot and rust. Except for a few hydrologists, no one had imagined the sea would rise so high and reach so far inland, but here it was, lapping at the Senate and the House, as if demanding redress of grievances.

"Too bad we can't redecorate and live here." Freda examined the room and huffed. "Picked bare, like everything else in this town." She took in the murky sky. "Time to go, Jordy."

Jordy didn't hear her. For him, it was January 2024, just before the new president was sworn in. He'd never been so happy then, or so sad. In his hand, grungy fingers poking from fingerless gloves, he held a torn photo, retrieved from under a pile of fallen plaster. The autograph was thick, black, and perfunctory. As if presented with the relic of a Catholic saint, Jordy pressed the photo to his breast. Tears washed his dirty cheeks.

~oOo~

The Ass made it back down the stairs and onto the sidewalk before bleating like a lost lamb and breaking down. Jordy lifted the duct tape securing the access panel and jiggled the box with the bot's organic brain. "Overheated is all," Jordy said.

"It's not the only thing that was overheated." Freda directed her comment at Jordy as she sheltered the trio with a bent golf umbrella.

Jordy felt talkative. "I was hired as an intern right out of college. My cousin got me the interview. I couldn't believe it. The White House!"

Freda grunted. "A mad house."

Jordy closed the panel, and the friends headed toward the shelter, the bot a couple of meters back. "I was the stereotypical idealistic rebel with a poly-sci degree, full to bursting with ways to wind down and close agencies. I wrote my master's thesis on it."

"A MAGA-nista."

"I burned up every inbox from the chief of staff to the janitor with suggestions and opinions. Most resulted in dead silence."

Freda's rain slicker brushed the feral grass. "Did you ever meet the man himself?"

Jordy laughed. "I don't think I slept at all, I was working so hard. One day, I was walking in the West Wing. I was in the middle of a yawn, when the president stood in front of me."

"Christ."

"He said, 'You're Jordan Wilson, aren't you?' I about fell over. 'I read your memo about the EPA. Can't we find a job for him there?' He said this to the chief of staff, who was standing next to the president, glaring at me. Two days later, I was working at the Environmental Protection Agency."

"A political appointee."

"In the public affairs office."

"Spinning the media."

"Implementing policy."

Jordy was aware of Freda's darkening mood, but his memories of a triumphant moment in his life papered over his anxiety.

"After the election and his daughter took office, my job became permanent. That's when the real fun began."

Freda halted her shuffle.

"Quiet." She nodded at two figures coming toward them, one tall, one short. "Green shirt and his familiar." That was Freda's talent, sniffing the Bureau of Environmental Security patrols from a distance, like a guard dog.

Jordy marked the square-jawed officer's vigilant and disdainful mien. The golden tulip logo on his tunic collar confirmed his lowly role in the BES hierarchy. His bot consort resembled a small, black ostrich without the neck and head. The body hid a staser. Jordy disliked police robots, ever since the night he lost his family. He kept his eyes down. Freda gave the officer a half-salute. The bessie studied the salvagers' robot for longer than Jordy would've preferred.

"Fuckers," Freda said. "Bureau of Excitable Shitheads."

"They're like bees, Freda. You don't bother them, they don't bother you."

"You really think that? If it weren't for your boss, the BES might not exist."

"It wasn't our fault. I was doing what the president wanted. He mentioned me a couple of times." The retort opened a new flood of warm memories for Jordy. He needed more of his meds, but he was feeling okay. "When the EPA administrator left for a job at Goldman-Chase, the president nominated me."

Freda spun her finger in the air at the mention of financiers. "Money greases the revolving door."

"A month later, I was sitting in the Administrator's chair."

"That was you?" Freda growled.

On his first day, Jordy hung the framed photo from the president's father among other mementos, such as pictures of his parents, both wearing Make America Great Again caps.

Freda's face was twisted, as if she'd stepped in feces.

"I remember a New Yorker cartoon that showed 46 changing a baby's diaper. The caption was something like 'Whew! That's the kind of climate change I can deal with.'"

"New York elites never understood what we were doing."

"Your name was on the baby's shirt."

Jordy shrugged. "I was 29 years old. Congress didn't mind."

"You should've been pictured as the Grim Reaper."

"Because I killed the EPA?"

"Because you damn near killed me!" Freda's abrupt anger exaggerated her limp as she sped ahead of Jordy. He reached out to steady her, but her fury discouraged him. The trailing robot tried to keep up with Freda—it was hers to begin with—but it slowed when it approached Jordy, as if uncertain whom to follow. A bark from Freda cleared up its confusion, leaving Jordy with his chagrin intact. What was she mad about?

He presided over the official ceremony closing the EPA offices. Thousands attended. The bronze plaque on the building was removed that afternoon. It was the proudest moment of Jordy's life.

Only the media and recalcitrant environmental zealots protested. So many people were angry with him. He didn't understand why until after the storms.

The EPA post was the last salaried job he ever held.

~oOo~

They brought their salvage to the old five-story parking garage on Orange Street. The queue at the entrance was several dozen strong, longer than normal because of the storm. Freda put the robot between Jordy and herself, like a boundary that couldn't be crossed. Jordy bided his time until he could make amends for whatever he'd said or done.

The queue led to a kiosk with a heavy scale and a pair of uniformed BES officers. The refugees, some singly, some in small groups, some with small children, carried bulky irregular sacks and corded bundles of recyclables, mostly metal. Jordy and Freda were two of the few refuge seekers with a robot cart. A kind-faced charity worker handed out food rations and water. Salvagers dropped their discoveries on the scale, spoke a little with the officers, and moved inside the shelter after emptying the bags into a large bin.

"All right then, you know the drill." The BES officer at the kiosk was the lantern-jawed sergeant Jordy had passed near the old EPA building. The name "Block" was stenciled on his forest green shirt. "Put your treasure on the scale. Come on."

Freda struggled to pull her finds out of the robot cart. She wouldn't look at Jordy as he helped.

The sergeant's mousy assistant called out a number. Block confirmed it. "Fine, then. Welcome again to Camp Orange. Who's next?"

Jordy placed his objects on the scale.

The assistant glanced at Block before calling out the number.

Jordy balked. "No, that's not correct. My estimate was ten percent greater than that."

"The scale doesn't lie, mac." Block's jaw jutted forward. "You're under the quota for admission. I'm sorry."

"That's not right," Jordy protested. "Weigh it again?"

Block sighed and nodded at the assistant. After a pause, the underling shook his head.

"Sorry, mac. Who's next?"

"I don't understand." Jordy said. "Freda, you had more than enough. Can you lend me a few kilos?"

Freda stared at Jordy, debating whether to loan Jordy her surplus weight of recycling. The rules allowed refugees to bank surplus for lean weeks. Jordy had given her his overage in the past. These days, he was living weigh-day to weigh-day.

"Freda, you owe me. Can you lend me some kilos just this once?"

Freda lifted a corner of her lip and gave The Ass a light shove. "Come on, stupid. We don't need to waste time with deniers. Let's go dry out."

Jordy and Freda had scoured together for years, and they'd never had more than a passing disagreement.

"Freda, my tent and clothes!"

Freda snatched the pack from the nearly-empty bin of the robot and tossed it at Jordy. Relieved of its burdens, the bot had a bounce to its treads.

Block grew impatient. "You're holding up the line, mac. Sorry you didn't make your quota. If you bring something more tonight, I'll let you in. Until then, step out of the line."

Jordy searched the scowling faces of other refugees for

a friend, but few had enough weight for themselves or their families, much less for an ex-bureaucrat.

"Move along, mac!" Block nudged Jordy, who stepped out from under the entrance canopy into the downpour. Jordy had little chance of finding more salvage as evening closed in. He circled the garage, his dismay and bewilderment clouding his search for a place to set up his tent and pass the night. He joined a group of weight-short refugees gathered behind a jersey barrier protecting them from the wind. Interior lights from the open-air garage illuminated Jordy's makeshift campsite. The jumble of tents and lean-tos resembled a blue-green tumor growing on the asphalt.

Before Jordy zipped up his one-man tent, he noticed the rivulets of rain running down the wall of the garage. At the railing of the third level, out of the wet, Freda chatted with another inmate. She stopped to look down on the clustered rejects, but Jordy couldn't be sure whether she saw him.

~oOo~

He'd left his meds with Freda. That was the only answer. He checked every pocket of his coat, every corner of his pack. He and Freda had grown so used to each other's habits that they sometimes carried each other's belongings if room was scarce. Jordy couldn't remember what he'd done with his pills. His wife once said he'd forget his head, if it wasn't screwed on.

He'd made it through other nights without his meds, but after a stressful day, or an encounter like the one with the bessies at the shelter entrance, all bets were off.

At least Jordy's belly was halfway full with the charity food. That wasn't the case for months after the Year of Storms.

Everything seemed to go south in Jordy's life after he shut down his agency. It never occurred to him that the president would abandon him. He was tainted, despite the White House's approval of his recommendations. He was a hero who couldn't be acknowledged. Unlike her presidential father, the daughter had a keener sense of politics, and the ex-White House intern who buried the EPA's dead body was not someone she wanted around. He'd served his purpose.

Then everything went to hell.

Edna started it, then Frank, followed by Gina. Named hurricane after hurricane spun out of the Atlantic Ocean like slow-motion bullets aimed directly at the East Coast. As if carrying enormous buckets, each lifted the ocean and poured it on the land in storm surges of 10 meters or more. The sea level was already higher by a few centimeters compared to the previous century, but people coped with the occasional flooded basements and blocked roads.

On Halloween, the Year of Storms, Hurricane Vincent hit Washington dead on. Failing to stave off the memories, Jordy stared at his trembling, dirt-encrusted hands as raindrops the size of ball-bearings bombarded his tent. He needed his meds. The visions were coming. They'd whispered to him earlier at the old EPA building.

His pocket vibrated, but there was no phone there. He hadn't owned a phone for years. Still, he reached in, pulled out the device, a hallucination that felt as real as the humidity that seeped into his pores. He held the phantom to his ear.

"Jordan, the water's nearly here." His wife, Willa, never called him Jordy.

"What?"

"You said the scientists were alarmists. You said the warming might even help people."

"Where are the kids?"

Her voice was angry, desperate, disbelieving. "You told them to get their costumes on. Everything would be fine."

"I said that?"

"I trusted you, Jordan. You told me not to worry."

"Get out, now. Get in the car and come here."

In the tent by the parking garage, Jordy whimpered, because he knew what was coming. He ran toward the rendezvous, a cafe near one of the tiny creeks that fed the river. The city was nearly deserted. Only flashing red and blue lights of cop cars suggested human life or AI watchers. He huddled under an awning half-blown out by the wind. He sighed with relief when he saw the headlights.

As the nine-passenger SUV with Jordy's wife and two baby boys edged toward a bridge over the swollen creek, the water rose instantaneously, hoisting the car like a toy and pushing it over. The screams of his wife and children pierced him like arrows. The headlights spun like a pinwheel as the monstrous water carried the car toward the river. It bobbed for a second or two. The water surged around a building, and in the blink of an eye, the car was gone. The disaster had taken all of five seconds.

Among the other sheltering refugees outside the garage, Jordy cried out, tearing furrows in his scalp with his fingernails, begging the shrieks and the darkness to go away, to let him have peace. After the SUV vanished, an AI patrol bot stopped and ordered him away from the area. Enraged, Jordy took one of the cafe's metal chairs and beat the bot into scrap. Ever since that night, each encounter with a police bot brought up the helplessness of that night. The meds tamped down his rage and terror. Without them, he relived that moment continuously, even when Block and his BES bot passed him and Freda near the EPA building.

The SUV was found two days later under tons of debris. The bodies weren't in it. By then, Jordy was evacuated to a survivor's camp. He staked a place at the camp's entrance, waiting for his wife and children. The media had a banner year of rescue stories. Drone copters lifted survivors from roofs. Boats found people clinging to tree trunks.

Ten thousand people died during the Year of Storms. Ten million lost their homes and jobs. The coastline from Miami to Maine, from a few meters of beach to kilometers inland, vanished under water.

Nonetheless, Willa and the boys were alive and well. Of that, Jordan Wilson was certain.

"Hey, Jordy." Freda's whisper penetrated the weather's noise. "You okay?" He unzipped the tent. "Christ almighty, you look like shit." Jordy pulled his knees to his chest. "I found your pills. I figured you might need them."

Jordy snatched the bottle from Freda's hand, but his hands were too shaky to open it. She twisted off the lid for him.

"One capsule, right?"

Nodding, Jordy blinked at her in thanks as he swallowed it. The medicine would take a few hours to work, but he relaxed a little. "Where's The Ass?"

"Guarding our stuff. Back in the garage."

Jordy coughed. "That thing couldn't guard a fire hydrant." He thought of his meager belongings, including the photo he found in his old office.

"I don't plan to stay here all night."

"I should probably stay put," Jordy said.

"I can hang out with you for a bit."

Jordy's thoughts cleared some, due to the comfort of his friend's presence. "You said I nearly killed you."

"About that." Freda folded her arms across her chest. "I fibbed. A little. But I do blame you."

"I don't get it."

"Remember I said I was a geologist? I was in Antarctica. We were studying the West Antarctic Ice Sheet. It's going to disappear from the lower elevations in a hundred years or so. Some of that water out there –" She gestured to the new shoreline. "—is from Antarctica. Anyhow, we got the word that you ordered our grant rescinded. Something about 'changing administration priorities.'"

Jordy canceled dozens of grants as part of his "The Best Government Governs Least" program.

"Everyone was pretty upset, but we decided work was the best therapy, so we went ahead with a three-day outing. We'd hardly got three kilometers from camp when I fell into a crevasse. Pretty much shattered my leg. Guess what? The camp medic had been transferred, and another camp borrowed our copter, because theirs was sent home. I was lucky to keep my leg. I kept thinking of you, and how you practically sliced it off with your budget cuts."

Jordy couldn't look at his friend.

"Crazy thing is, I was recruited for the BES. Yep. After the Year of Storms, voters went ape-shit. Did the right thing for once and sent the bastards packing. Things swung pretty quickly, a bit too far for me, actually."

While Jordy languished in a survivor's camp, Congress met at its temporary capital in Saint Louis. It created the Bureau of Environmental Security, charged with enforcing new, draconian environmental laws.

"Somebody described it as a hybrid of the Fish and Wildlife Service and the Gestapo," Freda said.

"But they offered you a job."

"I didn't want anything to do with them. We needed strong laws. I agreed with that. But not confiscating bodega owners' inventory for failing to recycle soda cans. Or mass arrests of derelicts burning twigs to keep warm. A ticket for excess CO_2 emissions would've been sufficient."

Both cases were rumors. Jordy suspected a propaganda campaign to frighten people into falling in line.

An argument outside the tent interrupted their conversation. A male voice ordered Jordy to open up. Block, the horse-faced BES officer, shone his flashlight inside.

"Documents. Now."

Jordy held up the back of his hand to a sensor attached to the flashlight. Block grunted at the readout, not recalling or caring about his argument with Jordy hours previous.

"What's the trouble, officer?" Freda was sweet as a ten-year-old girl as she held out her hand.

"People need to keep up their carbon tax payments. Then I wouldn't have to arrest scofflaws in this damned rain." He glanced at his readout. "Your credit transfer went through to your friend, here."

Freda grinned. "Thank you for your service, sir."

Block growled as drops fell into his eyes, making him blink like a man who'd lost his glasses.

"What did he mean by a credit transfer?" Jordy guessed, but he didn't want to be presumptuous.

"How're you feeling, buddy? Better? Let's go, then."

Freda's non-answer bothered Jordy, but he didn't push it. The voices and visions had subsided to a background susurrus. The rain had eased. The entrance queue was gone. The kiosk was closed. Freda had transferred some of her surplus recycling credits to Jordy, enough for the night. They trudged up ramps once traveled by cars.

"I'm sorry, Freda. For canceling that grant. If I'd known _"

"Oh, hell. It wasn't your fault. I was just cranky earlier. Sometimes I think I should've taken that bessie job. I spent all my savings. I didn't have any family. I lost my house and my car. It's like a light went out of me."

A flash of the tumbling SUV returned to Jordy. He closed his eyes for a moment, and it left him. Freda continued.

"I blended in just fine with the millions of people wandering the East Coast after the Year of Storms. The government couldn't cope with any of it. Still can't."

Fed up with the holdouts in the squalid survivors camp, soldiers and bulldozers tore it down. Jordy clung to his spot at the entrance like a leech, irritating, but ignored, until the final wave of evictions left him next to a road packed with climate refugees. Then he met Freda.

Every space in the garage was occupied by a tent, or a lean-to, or people in the open air who'd taken the dirty pads handed out by charities to keep off the concrete. Using cardboard as insulation was illegal; the law required immediate recycling or a back-breaking fine. Small electric fires offered a few degrees of warmth.

Jordy and Freda's bot welcomed them at their space with a facial recognition indicator that blinked twice.

"Were we wrong, Freda?"

"About what?" She placed an MRE a few centimeters from the battery powered heater.

"Playing down climate change. A lot of us thought it was real, just not important. If we'd gone with the consensus, maybe things would be different."

"You mean your wife and kids?"

Jordy nodded. "We thought we were doing the right thing for the country."

"Denial is not a survival strategy."

Jordy disagreed. Denial was a way to survive emotionally, if you couldn't cope with reality, until it catches up to you. He never heard from his wife or children. Their bodies were never found. He accepted they were dead.

"Let me tell you something, Jordy. It was already too late by the time your president and his cronies came on board. I saw icebergs the size of small moons break off and float away from Antarctic ice shelves. It took a century for that kind of effect to show itself. If anything, you set the stage for the green shirts and the government decamping to Missouri of all places. It all happened twenty years ago. It's just another turn in human history. I'm going to worry about getting through tomorrow in one piece."

Jordy sat on the prefab parking block, holding the photograph found in his old office. The ecstasy he felt in the morning had disappeared.

"It reminds me of a time when I was on top of the world, but..."

"Looks like the world has come crashing down."

Of the two men in the photo, one was a young, worshipful political hireling who made a difference, but not in a way he ever imagined. The other was, well, a corpse. Jordy touched the edge to the red-hot elements of the fire.

"Are you fucking crazy?" Freda yelped, struggling to keep her voice to a frightened whisper. "The bessies will kick us out of here for illegal CO2 emissions."

The photo flared, smoked, and blackened to ash. Burning the picture was worth the risk of a ticket. Recycling it into pulp assumed it had value, that it could be redeemed, at least symbolically. Jordy didn't believe in redemption. Time to move on. Living in shelters, scrounging for metal, and eating sporadically couldn't be called a great outcome. The world he knew was gone. Why deny it?

J.G. Follansbee

American Angel

Kara Dalkey

August 11th, 2023, Harrisburg, Pennsylvania

"Watch this," said the campaign manager. "She's brilliant."

Lorellei Smithson, beautiful businesswoman and Republican candidate for President, stood at the podium in a simple white sheath dress, her blonde hair carefully coiffed. She was delivering a campaign speech in tones between a concerned mother and a cajoling preacher. "I know we all feel that our hopes have been dashed, but you mustn't give up. You mustn't give in. Doors have been opened and now so much more is possible. I am here to bring to fruition those hopes that were kindled eight years ago. As surely as the Almighty brings blessings after tribulations, I am here to lead you to the Promised Land!"

She slowly raised her arms, to the cheers of the crowd. The lighting against the scrim behind her subtly changed, giving the faintest illusion of great wings and a halo hovering over her head.

"Am I seeing this?" asked the local campaign officer.

"She takes the same lighting director on every campaign stop. But this is just the icing. Wait until she gets to the cake."

"You think that your concerns have not been heard, or have been cast aside," Ms. Smithson went on. "But I have heard you. I may be just a simple woman from Kentucky with four children and a mortgage, but we simple folk have more power than we know, don't we?"

"Is all that true?" asked the local campaign officer.

"Sure, she's got a mortgage. On a two million dollar house in one of the toniest neighborhoods of Lexington. She keeps it quiet, but she's an heiress to a well-heeled cousin of the Mercer's. Went to all the best Bible schools. Probably the only farm she's ever been on is a race-horse breeding farm, but the salt-of-the-earth folks love her."

Mrs. Smithson held her arms out toward the audience. "We have heard your pleas for jobs. Jobs that will lend dignity, and help you raise your families. Jobs that don't ask for an ivy league degree, or that trade retraining that you can't afford. Here is my pledge to you. If I am elected your president, I will open a new American Angel Beauty Products factory right here in Harrisburg, providing two thousand new jobs! Dignified work, even if you only graduated high school. American Angel will hire you because you believe in angels and American Angel believes in you!"

The crowd began to cheer wildly.

"Don't believe me?" Mrs. Smithson said with her trademark mischievous smile. "Well, just let me—"

The crowd of mostly women joined in with her catchphrase deliriously, *"call my husband!"*

She held a golden cell phone to her ear and live feed video appeared on the screen behind her. "Hi, Sweetypie," said Mr. Smithson, "I have here in my hands the deed to 45 acres of land outside Harrisburg, just ready to sign. What do you think, Honey?"

Mrs Smithson turned to the crowd before her. "Well, what do you think?"

"Sign! IT! Sign. IT! Sign. IT!" the assembly chanted.

She turned back to the video. "I think that's a yes, Sweetie!"

Mr. Smithson smiled and did a flourish with a pen. "There we go, then. More new jobs coming soon. And come November, if all goes well and my Lorellei sits in the White House, there'll be thousands more new jobs, right where they are needed. " The video faded as the crowd cheered even louder.

"Sound's great," said the local campaign official, "but that's all just for show, right?"

The campaign manager shook his head with a knowing smirk. "It's the real deal. Mr. Smithson may be known as a car salesman but he sidelines in real estate. He's been buying up distressed industrial properties for a few years now. I don't know how good a business model their expansion will be, but at least until the election, she can do exactly as she says."

"And not just in Harrisburg, friends," Mrs. Smithson shouted over the din, "But in Kansas, Oklahoma, Texas, Arkansas, West Virginia, all these places hurting for good jobs, American Angel Beauty Products will be there!"

The roar of the crowd was deafening.

"Wow." said the local campaigner.

"You ask me, it's a better investment than media buys. They can say they're offering jobs and she can expand her business."

"But who's going to buy all that beauty cream?"

"Thirty-five million patriotic Republicans, and every country that wants a favorable trade agreement with the United States."

"Ah. If she gets elected."

"O ye of little faith."

October 25th, 2023, New York, New York
Excerpts from NBC Interview with Republican candidate for President, Lorellei Smithson

Mary Grady: So, Ms. Smithson—

Lorellie Smithson: Please, use Mrs. I am not ashamed of my married status. I am daily honored and blessed to be a helpmate to my husband, Mr. Smithson.

Mary Grady: Wouldn't becoming President take you away from this role, that you see as so important?

Lorellei Smithson: On the contrary, I see it as an expansion, to be a helpmate for all of America.

Mary Grady: Now to ask, if I may, a question that was infamously presented to another Republican woman candidate, what publications do you read?

Lorellie Smithson: I am so glad you asked me that, Mary. I read a great deal, on issues that are important to me. Among my favorites are Business Week, Forbes, American Family Life, Evangelical Weekly, and even Heartland Tales, because my children love it so.

Mary Grady: I notice you did not mention any of the major papers such as the New York Times, or the

Kara Dalkey

Washington Post.

Lorellie Smithson: Well, Mary, I did say that I read only those publications that are important.

December 1st, 2023, Youngstown, Ohio
Mrs. Smithson Declared Cream of The Crop. Redstate

Tossing her now-famous golden coif, and flashing her mischievous smile, Mrs. Smithson took to the podium at the grand opening of the huge American Angel Beauty Products factory in Youngstown, Ohio. Her speech was brief, but she looked radiant in her ivory white dress as she offered the factory as her gift to the under-served would-be workers of America and promised many more such in the forgotten regions of the country. She has tossed aside internet rumors of her company ignoring drug test results and not hiring immigrants who have been in the country less than ten years, or anyone with an "non-American-sounding" name. She has been quoted as citing Fischbien vs. Williamson and other Supreme Court decisions cascading from Burwell vs. Hobby Lobby of 2014, which have given greater leeway to non-publicly owned businesses in hiring. Given her meteoric rise in the polls over her Republican rivals, she has been declared "The Cream of the Crop" by Breitbart and Fox News, and we can only see this American Angel soaring to greater heights, all the way to November next year.

February 15th, 2024
Excerpt from New York Times

Internet rumors swirling that Republican candidate for President Lorellei Smithson had an abortion back in her college days have produced unexpected results. Her base has "circled the wagons" claiming that, if true, one must "hate the sin but love the sinner" creating an unholy alliance with the feminist left who say abortion is still legal and Mrs. Smithson should in no way be shamed for it. True or false, it remains to be seen whether this will bring more women voters into Mrs. Smithson's camp.

July 4th, 2024
Excerpt from Mother Jones

Speaking at yet another rally, her largest yet, from the newest American Angel Beauty Products factory in Beloit, Wisconsin, it cannot help but be noticed that she has now opened a factory in every electoral swing state in the United States. Numerous questions have been asked about where the money is coming from to accomplish this feat, but as there is still a Republican majority congress, no one seems interested in opening investigations on the matter. Handily winning the nomination over two rivals who had been considered strong contenders, Ivanka Trump and Ted Cruz, it is clear that the Democratic candidate, Chelsea Clinton, has a difficult road ahead.

November 5th, 2024
Excerpt from CNN broadcast

"...And in a tight race, after a previous resurgence by Democratic candidates in the off-year, the Republican base has struck back, electing the evangelical businesswoman Lorellei Smithson, to the Presidency of the United States. Democratic candidate Chelsea Clinton has called Mrs. Smithson with her congratulations which President-elect Smithson accepted graciously."

January 25, 2025
Excerpt from Daily Kos

"And I want to thank each and every American who tuned in to this, my first fireside chat, since I have taken office. I have only just begun to put as many deserving Americans back to work, through my American Angel Hiring Outreach program. Speaking of which," she reaches aside and brings into the picture a now-iconic red-white-and-blue jar and holds it against her cheek, "don't forget to pick up a jar or two or three of American Angel Beauty Cream. For every American woman deserves to look like an angel."

Advertising in the Oval Office! I guess it was inevitable, after the Emoluments Clause kinda vanished after Trump. But right off the bat? In a fireside chat? I guess she needs to pay for all those factories she opened, but is there no decorum left in the highest office of the land? Dumb question, I know. Oh, well, at least she doesn't tweet."

February 1st, 2025
Twitter

@therealMrs.Smithson "Don't forget to get your lovely American Angel some American Angel Beauty Cream for Valentine's Day! It's the patriotic thing to do!"

June 15th, 2025
Excerpt from Business Week

Spring Quarter earnings for American Angel Inc., have been respectable and, no doubt, were assisted by the business-friendly legislation rushed through congress early in the year and the South Asia Trade Agreement signed with India shortly thereafter. However, analysts say American Angel's labor costs have been enormous, and there is increasing pressure for the President to take her company public. It is said by unnamed sources that she is considering the move.

June 25, 2025
Excerpt from Left Side of the Leger videoblog

Franchesca Bairnes: So it's a Ponzi Scheme?
George Himmelberg: Not exactly, Franchesca. A Ponzi Scheme is when investors are told that their dividends are due to the growth of the investment when, in fact, their money is coming from new investors. It's really more like a Potemkin Village. President Smithson's beauty product facilities look like they're doing great but rumors abound on Twitter and other social media that these places are hemorrhaging moneys. Even a few brave Republican economists are starting to wave the red flag, which could greatly depress the IPO pricing if she does go public.

Franchesca: Which is why the Administration is squashing those rumors brutally. But she won her Presidency on the reputation of being this awesome businesswoman. What's going on?

George Himmelberg: It's all about the base, Franchesca. The solid 38% who backed and voted for her love her. She has lived up to the biggest campaign promise she gave—putting a certain American demographic back to work. But taking it all public has big risks along with the big money.

Franchesca: She'll have to answer to the Shareholders Board.

George Himmelberg: And won't that be interesting.

July 4th, 2025
Excerpt from Fireside Chat

"...And I wanted to thank all of you wonderful, country-loving Americans, for sending the newly offered stock of American Angel Inc. to heavenly heights! America and American Angel can only grow stronger, wealthier, happier together. Speaking of which, I wanted to let you know about our new product, Mrs. President Powder Pads. Disguise those unsightly blemishes and sop up that oily sheen from your skin. Buy one, buy two, it's the American thing to do! Good night, and God bless."

September 8th, 2025
Excerpt from Business Week

"Questions have been circling concerning the health of the American Angel IPO ever since a class action lawsuit was attempted, claiming an ingredient in the Mrs. President Powder Pads caused some consumers to break out in an irritating rash that resisted treatment. The attempted suit was thrown out of court due to the Protection of Presidential Business clause, but sales of American Angel products are beginning to show a perceptible decline."

October 17th, 2025
Excerpt from CNN broadcast

Representatives from the American Angel Stockholder Board, the State Department, the Chinese Embassy, the Federal Reserve and the FBI have been seen streaming into the White House during the night, although no one will yet say, on the record, what is going on. Sources close to the White House have been saying that the major shareholders of American Angel Inc., have had increasing concerns over the profitability of the company and are holding President Smithson accountable for the decline in value. We will keep you informed as more information comes in.

October 31, 2025
Excerpt from the Washington Post

It was a somewhat humbled President Smithson who appeared in the Rose Garden this morning, bundled into a white ermine coat against an early season snow shower. "I want to apologize to my fellow Americans," she began, shivering a little, "for causing such frenzied and anxious speculation over the last couple of weeks. But I wanted to come forward and share the truth with you, and let you know that the decisions I have made are the best ones for the American Angel family, and all of you American angels. My company was given a very generous offer from the Xiu Chan company, which some of you may know is a government-owned entity, to purchase 52 percent of American Angel Inc. This will ensure that all American Angel factories, including the seven that we opened just in the last six months, will remain in operation and there will be no lay-offs. Our new products will continue to be developed, with the aid of Xiu Chan's investment and guidance. And everything will continue as before. Despite the negative reporting and conspiracy theories on the web, everything will be just fine. So, don't be scared this Halloween. Let your children gather their candy and share in their joy. American Angel will continue, just with..." President Smithson seemed about to continue, but her eyes appeared to tear up and, with an intake of breath that might have been a sob, she turned away from the gathered press and went back into the White House.

January 25th, 2026
Backgrounder for Newsweek

Speculation continues on the eve of President Smithson's first State of the Union address. Fighting headwinds of resistance to legislation she has tried to get Congress to pass has only increased the rumors swirling around the White House. The Senate threw out the bill on requiring all Federal agencies to prioritize the use of American Angel products wherever possible. And they have rejected a request from the White House to authorize sending a "peacekeeping" force to Brazil after an aboriginal uprising halted the shipment of a rare Amazonian plant used in the processing of an American Angel beauty product.

President Smithson has rarely been seen in public since October, and sources near the White House claim she is keeping almost monastic habits, with dark circles under her eyes and a tired bent to her shoulders. It is said that she is under tremendous pressure from the stockholders board to close some American Angel factories and move some of the company's operations to China. The anger over the new Sino-American trade agreement still has not died down, and favoritism to Chinese business is sure to be a topic that the President must address.

Meanwhile, American Airlines ceased its partnership with the company after some unfortunate incidents with American Angel moisturizing towelettes in flight. After a brief spike in sales for the holiday season for American Angel products, the company's profits have continued to disappoint. Its latest new offering, American Angel Shaving Cream, is claimed to have an odor that turns unpleasant after ten hours.

February 1st, 2026
Excerpt from CNN

Protests continue throughout the night in front of the White House, despite the snowy weather. Thousands have gathered, from as far away as Florida, to voice their anger and dismay at the President's announcement two days ago that American Angel, Inc. will be closing more than half of the facilities she opened less than two years ago, and another percentage will be reopening in Shanghai. Many here on Pennsylvania Ave. still hold the President close to their hearts, believing she was swindled by the Chinese, and they are demanding Congress do something to prevent the dispersion of this iconic American company. The Speaker of the House has, so far, been non-committal regarding any aid coming from the House or Senate. "Since the Supreme Court ruled that the President's business is the President's business," he remarked ruefully, "our hands are somewhat tied."

In a poll just out from Gallup after the President's announcement, President Smithson's favorability has dropped to 29%...

February 15th, 2026
Excerpt from the Washington Post

In a stunning, yet unsurprising, move following her cancellation of the State of The Union Address, President Smithson announced her resignation from the Presidency of the United States.

Almost unrecognizable due to her loss of weight and lack of sleep, she read in a soft voice from a prepared speech.

"My fellow Americans, as you may have heard, I have been asked to resign from the board of American Angel, Inc. after their vote of no confidence. And I have done so. It is with a very heavy heart that I also announce my resignation from the Presidency of the United States," she announced at 8:46 a.m. local time.

"I have tried to raise you up, you the forgotten American worker. I have tried to protect you against the winds of globalism, the winds of unwanted change. I regret that I was not strong enough. I regret that I put myself in a position where I would be forced to make changes that would damage the American spirit. I hope that you will give Vice President Walton the same support you have given me. I love you all. Good bye, and God bless America," she concluded. Her resignation was accepted by the Speaker of the House at 8:52, and the new president, former Vice-President Walton, was sworn in at 9:01 this morning.

February 16th, 2026
Excerpt from Left Page of The Leger Videoblog

Francesca: Okay, I get that she was voted off the board. But why resign the Presidency?

George: We may not know until someone writes the tell-all, and maybe not even then. My speculation is she profoundly disappointed her rich relative backers and they wanted someone else, someone they could trust, in the halls of power fast.

Franchesca: But why? Wasn't she the perfect figurehead for the corporate 1%?

George: (shaking his head) My guess is, she committed the cardinal sin of capitalism. She believed her own hype. She thought she could be a one-woman government jobs program for the forgotten middle-Americans. In other words, she began treating her business not like a business, but as a charity—something no self-respecting uber capitalist could ever respect.

Franchesca: Wow. Definitely something to think about. (turning to the camera) Coming up in our next segment, George and I discuss the big names already filing for candidacy for the next election in 2028, including the former CEO of Sturm Ruger, the largest gun manufacturer in the US, and an upper level executive of weapons manufacturer Raytheon. Stay tuned!

Kara Dalkey

SIXTY-EIGHT

Frog and Esther Jones

Special Agent Dana Liu ran toward the weather-beaten warehouse, weapon drawn. Her thick-soled boots barely made a sound despite the gravel and dead grass impeding her way.

Carefully halting outside the loading door, Dana quickly scanned the area. No surveillance cameras, no drones, no robotic guards, no signs of occupation adorned the outside of the building. But her instincts told her: Here. Her quarry would be here.

She didn't dare wait for back up, either. Every second she let pass held the potential for irreparable damage to the whole nation, possibly for generations.

The back of her neck pulsed with tension, and she relied on her training to force her stressed muscles and breath to calm.

Once her breathing and heartbeat steadied, Dana carefully pried the cover loose from the loading door's security panel. Its interface had a neural-line jack but no wireless capability, and no uplink to the neural net. A local network only, then. She estimated the technology at least fifty years out-of-date, but in pristine condition. If the warehouse had truly been abandoned, it's internal servers should have given out long ago.

Dana snorted. No doubt the outdated tech had been installed recently to keep the insurgents' location hidden. Her lips quirked. A cocky blunder on their part.

The building's absence from the neural net made it difficult to locate, but now that she had, it would be that much easier to hack and control.

Holstering her weapon, Dana tapped the temporal bone behind her ear, just above her mastoid process, releasing the neural line stored there. She let the cord unspool, then plugged it into the jack, merging directly with the building's main operating system.

The surface programs were all dormant, expected from a warehouse not currently in use. Under the surface, though, lay a second set of protocols, blocked by a fire wall. She made quick work of unlocking loading doors next to her and then turned her attention to the hidden code beneath.

A fine sweat broke out across Dana's forehead and her brow wrinkled as she struggled to penetrate the much more sophisticated code locking away the second set of protocols, her brain churning through possible combinations as fast as thought.

By the time the firewall finally parted, Dana's temples throbbed with the effort. But she had access to the warehouse's true security protocols and schematics. Her eyes closed, she played them back in front of her mind's eye, and a room hidden in the building's north wall caught her attention. The warehouse's electrical systems routed extra power there, but no cameras monitored its entrance, no mention of it at all on the warehouse's manifest.... Her target would most likely be there. She unhooked and her neural line spooled back up inside her head.

Dana redrew her weapon and cautiously entered the warehouse using the tall, wall-to-ceiling shelving as cover. No lights illuminated the massive cavernous space—old, discarded farm machinery from before wireless neural automation, glinted dully on some of the shelves.

An explosive noise, and a bullet ricocheted off a shelf, two feet above her head, throwing a spark in the gloom. Dana pivoted and crouched, keeping the shelving between herself and the shooter, sighting down her own weapon, into the darkness. Her ears rang.

A muzzle flashed, and she jerked her aim up to hit presumed center mass below the flash. Dana squeezed, her weapon barking and bucking in her grip.

She had no way of knowing if she'd truly hit anything. Dana waited the space of ten heartbeats, but no other deafening flashes came.

She moved, quickly and carefully, to the shelves shielding the hidden doorway, heart pulsing in her ears, shoulders tensed for shots that did not come. Dana knelt, then triggered the hidden latch on the bottom shelf.

The door swung open silently.

Light spilled out from a laboratory-looking room where a man sat, his hands calmly folded over his lap. He wore a well-tailored, light-colored suit, and his dark hair had been cleanly cut. Next to him, a virtual reality tank labeled "68" told Dana she'd finally found the place. She steadied her aim on the man.

Silently, Dana activated her connection to the neural net, immediately informing her superiors, "Destiny located. Transmitting exact GPS coordinates. On first visual, Lyceum and passenger appear undamaged. One possible hostile on site. Will attempt to engage until reinforcements arrive."

Out loud, Dana said only, "Secret Service. Keep your hands where I can see them."

"Ah, Agent Liu, I see you made it. I was hoping we'd have a chance to chat." The man remained still, his hands neatly folded his lap.

Shock and surprise at her own name passing the terrorist's lips swept through Dana, and she struggled to keep her expression neutral.

"I'm not joining you for anything," Dana said. "The only person I care about here occupies that VR tank behind you. I will be leaving as soon as you stand down, and I assure myself of Sixty-Eight's safety."

"Anika's quite safe; I assure you. No need to be rude. Anyway, Dana—can I call you Dana? My name—well, for all intents and purposes, anyhow—is Ven."

Dana frowned. Something here felt off, but she couldn't put her finger on it.

Ven slowly reached his left hand into a drawer next to him. Dana gestured with her weapon, and he raised his right hand in sign of surrender but did not withdraw his left.

"It rarely pays to be so hasty, you know," Ven said, his tone mildly chiding. He pulled a bottle of what appeared to be a very old Scotch, a single-malt from a distillery called "Ardbeg," out of the desk along with two glasses, all held by the long, agile fingers of his left hand. He placed the whisky on the table, opened it, and began to pour, all still with his left hand.

Dana held herself ready but waited for Ven to prove himself an overt threat.

"I'm merely suggesting we engage in some conversation before you rush on your way. You're already here, after all." Ven slid a glass across the desk toward Dana, then took a sip from his own. Dana clenched her jaw, ignoring the (possibly poisoned) glass before her.

"There are much easier ways to get my attention if all you want to do is talk," she said in a sharp tone. "As it is, the only thing I'll be discussing with you is whether you've harmed the minor behind you."

"Harmed? Of course, I haven't!" Ven took a long, slow sip from his glass. "I don't want to harm anyone, Dana. I simply believe in freedom."

"Sixty-Eight wasn't being held captive, Ven. You stole her from her rightful home and custodian." Dana corrected the kidnapper crisply, debating her options. She needed information on this abductor's splinter group. And Sixty-Eight did not appear in immediate danger.

"Sixty-eight?" asked Ven. "You know, she does have a name. Anika, I'm told. And I 'stole' her from the 34th floor of the Coast-to-Coast media network. Not exactly a pair of loving parents there, eh?" He shook his head. Dana pressed her lips together tightly, trying to contain her irritation.

"She was with her legal guardian. State News One has invested every bit as much time, care, and education into Sixty-Eight as any traditional parent, Ven." Dana measured the distance between the VR tank and herself with her eyes, debating whether she could close the distance if he made any sudden moves.

Ven shook his head, his voice taking on a overly solicitous tone.

"Has Anika ever rode a bike? Scraped a knee? Even left that VR tank?"

Dana blew out an exasperated breath, and took a small step closer to Sixty-Eight, angling to keep herself out of Ven's reach. His air of quiet confidence confused her, made her wary of underestimating the situation.

She responded to his question to buy herself time to think.

"The American public spends the majority of their time in VR tanks, just like that one, plugged into the neural net."

"Yes," said Ven. "I'm quite aware of that particular tragedy. But you claim that State News One is an appropriate custodian to raise young Anika, here. And I merely point out that she isn't exactly getting a normal childhood in her artificial environment."

"That VR tank is far less dangerous and more effective in conveying experiences to its user than a traditional upbringing. It allows a candidate to learn and absorb knowledge at an accelerated rate. True, it's not a normal education; rather, it's an extraordinary one for a very gifted individual, Ven. A future leader. A person whose mind is capable of shaping the very future of this country."

"So, State News One shapes the girl, and the girl shapes the country. Funny how the shape of the country appears awfully like the shape of State News One." Ven watched her expectantly, a friendly smile curling his lips.

"Our elections are decided by everyone casting their vote." Dana said, not willing to get caught up by his affable facade.

"And yet, Anika's tank is labelled '68' as though she'd already taken office, is it not?" Ven smiled, beatifically. "You've even repeatedly called her by that title in your conversation with me. And yet. She's twenty years away from Constitutional eligibility, and you've got her number already. In twenty-four years' time, she will be President of the United States. Hence, an upstanding Secret Service agent like yourself has already been assigned to her. Hardly seems like a free, open election to me."

"You can't blame the population for electing the most qualified candidate presented to them." Dana took another step closer to Sixty-Eight's VR tank.

"But who really decides the most qualified candidate? We're currently electing the 65th POTUS, and yet there are Secret Service agents assigned for VR tanks, just like this one, all the way up to 70? Does that really seem to indicate a free and unskewed election? A true expression of democracy?"

"I don't know who's been leaking you your intel, but State News One doesn't force anyone to vote against their conscience, nor does it cook ballots or in any way falsify the election results. Everyone's vote is cast and counted as intended." As she said the words, Dana heard an echo in her mind, as if someone else had said that to her once, but she couldn't remember who.

"Ah, I see." Ven smiled again, his eyes crinkling as if he didn't have a care in the world. Dana's eyes narrowed with suspicion, and she sharpened her focus, dragging her foot back another step closer to the tank. Ven continued talking, seeming to ignore Dana's inching toward the tank.

"I suppose in some ways you may be right. But, let's explore that shall we?" he said.

Ven slowly brought his fingers up and steepled them, watching Dana with bright eyes. "Our first voter, Elda, is a widow living on a fixed income. Her church and her grandbabies are her social circle, and the riskiest pastime she enjoys is the penny slots at the local casino on the ten-dollar senior buffet day."

"You better be going somewhere with this fast. My patience is not limitless." Dana interrupted, her shoulders twinging from maintaining combat readiness.

Ven sighed. "She votes for your candidate as the leader who will uphold traditional family values, fight for the 'sanctity' of marriage, and protect all human life from the moment of conception." Ven paused. Dana glowered at him, taking another step toward Sixty-Eight, and the readouts on her VR tank.

Ven shook his head, then continued calmly, "Meanwhile, we have Sven. He's a twenty-something college grad. Sven believes in universally-available social and health services; a woman's right to choose any and all things that happen to her body; and equitable access to opportunity regardless of race, religion, gender, or sexual preference. He also votes for your candidate, believing her a person whose priorities best mirror his own."

"What's your point?" Dana said. "People vote for candidates for their own reasons all the time."

"Tsk, Tsk," said Ven. "These two people's views are diametrically opposed, but they both chose the same person as their ideal leader. One of them must be wrong about the candidate's actual stance on their issues. Tell me, how is it possible for one person to uphold contradictory beliefs, Dana?"

"Access to a whole world of information is available to everyone at the speed of thought. It's not the news network's fault that people only digest the fraction of it they want to hear."

"Is that true, though? Or does the neural net keep the average American flooded with so much information that they naturally gravitate to the people and views that make them feel most secure? Not unlike a drowning person clings to an overturned canoe." Venn's voice held a plaintive note that disturbed Dana, even as she reminded herself that he was a probable domestic terrorist and proven kidnapper.

"No one can control at what threshold or in what way people will react to data overload," Dana said. "There's even a waiver in the terms of use."

Ven merely raised an eyebrow. "And how sad that is. Democracy has been waived away. Would you say then, Dana, that the news each person receives is unbiased? Isn't a custom campaign beamed directly into the skull of each and every citizen? If not, how do all Americans predictably and reliably arrive at the same elected candidate?"

"I don't believe it's nearly that simple," Dana said, then realized she'd forgotten to move and took another step toward Sixty-Eight.

Ven shook his head sadly, for what Dana swore was the fortieth time since she entered the room. "Yet even you speak of your belief, not your knowledge. Tell me Dana, what do you truly know for sure?"

"Looking at historical law enforcement data, I know law-breaking has decreased, rapes have diminished, and hate crimes are at an all-time low. Our healthcare system works. Our economy is strong. We are respected internationally. And our people are happy."

"And all of those are laudable goals, I'm sure. But can you really say they've been truly accomplished when the neural net is riddled with pockets of hateful bile once you know where to look?"

"The bigots are inflicting their views on others like themselves without causing harm to anyone else." She said, her voice sounding defensive even to her own ears.

"Ah, but who truly bears the price? Young Anika who's locked away in a VR tank, learning to be President from birth? What parent would want that? Can you give Anika the chance to live unconstrained, to make her own destiny?"

Shock hit Dana as Sixty-Eight's code name, 'Destiny,' passed Venn's lips. "Can anyone truly guarantee that?" she countered, watching his expression, but he didn't appear to be aware of weight behind the word. "Before the neural net, America had some disastrous administrations. Presidents that pushed our country to the brink of chaos and despair. Forty-five practically started a civil war while throwing nukes at North Korea, and that was only the start. Since the Net, all of that has calmed. We're stable. We're happy."

"Do you know that to be true, or has State News One only led you to believe it's true?" Ven asked.

"What?" Dana asked, shaking her head to clear it, her ears suddenly buzzing and popping.

"How much of what goes on before our eyes depends on who is reporting it?" Ven asked, his voice deceptively mild. "Where is your outside source?"

Dana paused.

"I can tell you," Ven said, his voice suddenly gentle, "It doesn't exist. Not anymore. There is no unbiased source; there is only the News. And from that monolithic entity, the power of the people to rule is conned out of them, not freely given."

"These candidates win the Presidency because anyone else would do an inferior job running the country if elected." Dana reiterated. Sixty-Eight was her only concern here, she reminded herself. Nothing this man said mattered.

"The perfect President that State News One nurtured, trained, and put into power. If you take a step back, doesn't that concept seem laughable?"

Dana stared at him, little pin-pricks of light flashing on the edge of her vision like fireworks. She blinked. Had he drugged her somehow and she hadn't realized? She hadn't drunk the whiskey, but her head felt strangely heavy. Ven's voice took on a persuasive cadence.

"We are a dog chasing its tail in ever shortening circles. I liberated that child from a greedy corporation. One that's using her to keep a death-grip on the power base they've built. One that most Americans can't even see."

If Ven had truly done something to her, she needed to end this before she became incapacitated. Everything felt slightly out of focus. She blinked.

"But you can. You see it, but you look away from it. You'll probably continue to ignore it." Ven slowly rose from his chair, holding his hands out in front of him and palms upward, as if to display how little threat he was.

She mustn't believe it. He'd stolen the future president from the bosom of the whole secret service. This man had to be very, very dangerous. He must be.

Ven's voice continued melodically. "All of this technology hiding the fiddler, and yet we all dance to the same tune. Does that seem like a true expression of democracy, free will, and self-determination to you?"

"No, it doesn't." Dana said, frowning at her own words.

"I'm glad to hear we can agree on something." But she didn't agree with this traitor.

She tried again. "In my experience on this side, people need structure, they need rules, they need some 'herd mentality' to keep themselves civilized. Humans were often horrific to each other before the neural net, and certainly still have that capacity. Our current level of technology just means it's not expressed to anyone's detriment."

"So, let me interpret what you're saying. People's views haven't changed. Technology just allows you to divert to who and how they express it. Filth is still just as dirty no matter how expensive a rug is laid over the top you know." Ven's voice took on that chiding tone she hated so much.

"But it keeps the people from treading in it." Dana said.

"It leaves all of society precariously suspended above it, you mean, ready to fall in at any time. Meanwhile, the media and the big corporate sponsors rake in all the profit from the politicians that no longer 'appear' corrupt but are even more ineffectual at assisting the people they represent."

"The working public are not unhappy."

"Aren't they? Or do they just not know it?" Ven took another step toward her, and Dana instinctively widened the distance. "Let me ask you. Are you happy, Dana?"

She stared at him, her brain full of white static and cotton.

"Think back to when you first picked up your secret service badge. Did you ever expect the secrets you hold as you serve to be this massive? Our presidents are being grown in tanks like artificial protein. And the media convinces everyone to imbibe." Ven gestured at the large tank and Dana realized he stood much too close. He'd approached her, and she hadn't noticed. It hadn't registered as important.

Something was seriously wrong. Her reactions were sluggish, heavy. He must've drugged her, put something in the air vents or on something she touched. It didn't matter what really, keeping Sixty-Eight safe was her responsibility.

"What have you done?" Dana asked Ven, feeling ridiculous the moment the words left her mouth.

"Given America a chance to be free once more, I hope." Ven said.

She brought her gun up, slowly, her arms trembling, and glared at him. "Surrender now or die by my hand."

Ven shook his head. "Still so violent, I see."

"I am not the one who forcibly abducted a minor." Eliminating the threat before she was incapacitated must be her only priority now. If he wouldn't surrender...

Ven sighed, still much too close for Dana's comfort. "We may as well take this to its inevitable end, then. Embrace each of our destinies as it were." Ven said and lunged suddenly, grabbing at her gun, but caught a fistful of her uniform coat instead, tearing it and throwing her aim downward. But not far enough.

Dana's muscle memory flexed, his chest blossoming into a splatter of red blood. Ven crumpled, his eyes glassing over as he took his last labored breaths.

"Goodbye, Dana," he breathed, and blood foamed his smiling lips.

Dana glowered at him, irritated by the smile that seemed to say he knew something she didn't. She sat down and put her head between her legs, waiting for whatever he'd done to her to pass. Of course, he had to have the last word.

Finally, Dana sat up, holstered her weapon, and moved

to check the readouts on Sixty-Eight's Lyceum.

The reinforcements finally arrived just as she finished running diagnostics and verifying there was no strange coding added to the VR tank's neural buffer. The new squad fanned out, securing the perimeter and double checking Ven for life signs.

"About time," Dana told the squad leader grumpily. "Take us home will ya? We have some house cleaning to do, I think. That man knew entirely too much about our presidents."

~oOo~

Carol Firlotti, chairman of the Luddite Resistance, leaned back in her chair and took a deep breath, swirling the single malt in her glass as she pondered the death of a true patriot. Ven had done his job, had given the agent just enough niggling seeds of doubt that that it would seem natural when the neural virus completely over took over their systems.

When President Anika Paulsen and Agent Liu decided to take on the bastards at News One, it would seem entirely natural. Their own well-reasoned decision. This little incident would fall by the wayside in the annals of history, a mere footnote in the great revolution to come.

And only Carol would know exactly how calculated the sacrifice had been. Her brother had remained calm and erudite to the last. She raised her glass to the memory of Ven's sacrifice, and to the Luddite victory, still twenty-four years in the future.

Frog and Esther Jones

Call to Order

Edd Vick

The assassin stalked the halls of power, shaking in fear. He knew his target's habits and his haunts. Micah Kent, one of the nine, would be with the other justices of the Supreme Court of the United States in their weekly meeting on latest cases, debating which to hear, which would be denied certiorari.

He pushed a cart loaded with cleaning supplies. It made him invisible. Behind one of the cart's doors was a pistol, loaded with nine bullets, though he would need only two. He would kill Kent, the most conservative justice, and then himself. The Democratic president, after a due period of mourning, would choose another, more liberal judge. The balance of power would tip just enough.

A member of the Supreme Court Police Force approached him. The assassin could feel his sweating palms slipping on the cart's push-handle. He took a better grip, straightened his back, gave what he hoped was an unconcerned smile to the man. The guard nodded.

"Hiya, Phil," he said. The assassin dipped his own head in reply. He cleared his throat.

"Morning, John," he said. "How's your daughter doing?"

"Oh, fine, fine. Looking forward to turkey day next week, of course." He glanced at his watch. "Little early for this wing, isn't it?"

The assassin shrugged. "Some kind of cleanup in one of the bathrooms." One of his eyelids twitched.

"Got it." The guard waved as he passed.

Phil swallowed past a lump in his throat. Soon enough, his son would be told he was some kind of monster. But he had to do this! Giving a little wave of acknowledgement, the assassin resumed pushing his cart whose wobbly wheel quivered in time with his racing heart.

It was insanity that Supreme Court justices served for

Edd Vick

life. Justice Kent had been in office for thirty years, dispensing bile in the guise of opinions, nudging the country to the right, decision by decision. And Kent never went out in public, never came into contact with the horrible outcomes of his decisions. But then, he would probably laud those ends.

Turning a corner, he stopped in front of the justice's office door, stooping to retrieve the pistol. With trembling hands, he checked the magazine, made sure a round was jacked into position. He fumbled the keys out of his pocket, almost dropping them, and opened the door.

He'd bought the gun two months earlier, passing the background check easily. The vetting for his job three months before had been cursory, since he worked for a private cleaning company. Privatization had been one of Kent's hobby horses. Phil had found time to make it to a gun range in Delaware several times before breaking the pistol down to sneak it in piece by piece. He hadn't fired a weapon since the army, and his aim was awful. But then, he wouldn't be called on to shoot the justice from a distance.

After killing the man, Phil would shoot himself. He didn't want to endanger hard-working men like that guard, John, and he certainly didn't want to be subjected to the media circus that would await an assassin. He'd left an incoherent screed on his computer that would make him appear a deranged libertarian. The way would be clear for the president to appoint someone who would protect civil rights, immigrants, and the poor. No more deportations for people like Phil's adoptive sister. The world would be better for what he was about to do.

Phil roamed the plush office. Should he sit in Kent's high-backed seat? Wait behind the door? Finally, feeling a little foolish, he settled down to wait in one of the swiveling visitors' chairs. He wondered what he'd do if Kent came to his office accompanied by someone. That was a bridge he'd cross when he came to it.

He almost fell asleep. Maybe he did. He had a vivid vision of the Supreme Court's Call to Order.

"Oyez! Oyez! Oyez!" He'd watched it so many times. "All persons having business before the honorable, the Supreme

90

Court of the United States, are admonished to draw near and give their attention, for the court is now sitting. God save the United States and this honorable court." Well, he had business, and he'd drawn near. Nothing, not even God, would save the man he had come to kill.

A key grated in the lock, startling him to full wakefulness. Justice Kent's thin body slipped into the room. Alone.

When Phil raised the pistol, when he stood, when he said, "Close the door, please," the man did not appear shocked. He complied.

Justice Kent was tall, with close-cropped hair, narrow lips, and a strong jaw. He didn't look nearly as old as the eighty-one years his judicial biography claimed. He still wore his judicial robes. His piercing blue eyes darted to the cleaning cart, to Phil's uniform, to the gun, and back to his face.

"Did I leave a mess in the toilet?" he asked, arching an eyebrow.

Phil narrowed his eyes. "Don't be funny. You're not getting out of here alive."

Kent smiled. "Well, then, have your say."

"You're a monster. You've been in office more than thirty years, always siding with corporations, with religious fundamentalists, with—with authoritarian fear-mongers." The pistol trembled in his grip.

The Justice took a step toward Phil. Their eyes locked. "I understand," he said in a voice so soft Phil strained to hear. "You're afraid. You've been hurt somehow, maybe you've lost someone close to you."

"You don't know me." Phil edged forward a step, the better to target the man. "Don't pretend to."

The smile never left Kent's face. "I'm just trying to see things your way." He cocked his head. "Can you do that for me? Have you ever tried to comprehend my world-view?"

"I don't want to. I don't need to."

"I see. Your mind is closed. You're just bracing yourself to fire." Kent moved another pace closer to Phil. A bare three feet separated them. "Well, while you're doing that, let me at least try to get through to you. I used to be like you. I won't say 'bleeding heart', that's insensitive, but I used to think every little person mattered, that everybody ought to have their say. But my opinion changed, almost overnight." He leaned a little toward Phil, fixing him with a penetrating gaze, one full of conviction. "Now I understand so much more. People don't see the big picture. They don't want what's best for our society as a whole."

"As a whole? But your verdicts have supported polluters! Warmongers!"

Kent gave the tiniest of sighs. "You don't get it. We're territorial. We must defend our land and our herds." He glanced down at Phil's hand. "Isn't that handgun getting heavy?"

The assassin had almost forgotten the pistol. "Never mind," he said, without heat. "What does defense have to do with pollution?"

"It's simple." Flecks of red appeared in the justice's eyes. "Follow the research. High levels of CO2 affect the intellect; it makes you dumber. I won't say docile, but we don't really care if you fight among yourselves. We just don't want you organizing to oppose us. Religion works, too: gives you something to look forward to in the next life so you don't kick up a fuss in this one. And a strong national defense keeps others of my kind in their own countries, unlikely to invade mine."

"Your ... kind?"

"Ranchers. Of a kind," said the justice, smiling just enough to show a canine that was a little longer than the teeth on either side of it. When Kent held out his hand, Phil dropped the pistol into it. He put a hand on Phil's shoulder.

"Do keep this little talk private, hmm? Think about it all you want, but no discussion, no emails or texts, and certainly no diary entries. Let's keep this between us." His gaze burned into Phil's soul for one year-long second, then he blinked. "After all, appointment as a justice is for life, and I expect to have a lot more years ahead of me."

Phil moved to the cart. He wished that Kent had let him keep the gun. He felt vaguely like he would have had a use for it.

One Drop Stop

Yong Takahashi

Stormy Sommers held her son's hand while the doctor drew five vials of his blood. The eight year old winced and gritted his teeth. He had promised his mother he would be brave since he was the man of the house.

"It's done." Dr. Howard, the clinic's founding member, looked at the boy. "If it's positive, you'll have to disclose the father's name."

"Whose father?" asked the boy.

"Not now," said Stormy to Dr. Howard. Out of respect for her, the doctor left the room without further questioning.

She pulled the boy from the chair and wrapped her arms around his trembling body. "Ryan, let's go get an ice cream cone."

Ryan demanded quarters and ran to the back of the ice cream parlor. Stormy stared at her phone for a few minutes, practicing the speech in her head. She took in a deep breath and pressed the call button.

"Oh, Ms. Sommers, I'm sorry. The Vice-President is with his family. It's his son's birthday today. I will tell him to call you at the studio." The press secretary disconnected the call before Stormy could respond. She pushed her phone away and massaged her temples.

Ryan smiled and waved to his mother while his ammo reloaded on the video game. His face changed when he began to shoot the aliens that were invading Earth.

"Die, suckers," he screamed.

Stormy clamped her lips together. She was a celebrity and couldn't be seen crying in public. She dialed Matt's private line. When it went straight to voice mail, she texted

"911".

The aliens finally killed her son and he ran over to her.

"Mommy, can I take the Band-Aid off now? I feel better."

"You're such a brave boy." Stormy held him like she did when he was a baby. "You're my joy, always know that."

"Mommy, you're embarrassing me. I'm a big boy. I blew those nasty invaders to bits."

~oOo~

Stormy was born Rita Mae Miller in Jasper, Georgia to simple country folks who longed for the good old days. They didn't need new ideas. They didn't want to mingle with new people. They didn't want change. Their lives were perfect.

The Millers' plan for their baby daughter was simple as well. She would graduate from Jasper High School. She would attend beauty school. She would marry a decent man with a steady job—fireman, mechanic, manager at Wal-Mart. She would birth another generation of solid, American stock.

Rita Mae didn't want to change the world. She simply wanted to change herself but this couldn't be accomplished under her parents' watchful eyes. She had to leave the small town and its small town ideas behind.

Without money or an education, her choices were limited. Her parents always warned her about Atlanta. It was full of evil people. They would hurt her. She didn't believe it was as bad as they portrayed it. She boarded a bus and never looked back.

She worked at a local AM radio show as the station manager's assistant. As a joke, the on-air guys brought her on to read the traffic and weather reports. The hundred or so listeners loved her no-nonsense delivery. The station manager suggested the name "Stormy Sommers" and it stuck. With the help of an attorney who had a crush on her, she legally changed her name, burying Rita Mae Miller once and for all.

Her super-charged personality, low-cut sweaters, and ability to blow the station manager on demand helped her secure a seat on the morning show. When her picture went up on the station's billboard, more men started listening.

Her small town stories combined with her curvaceous figure caused a sensation. When a city trustee became tongue-tied by the sight of her long legs and was unable to finish a political debate with her, the station manager let her fly solo during the coveted three to seven afternoon slot.

She noticed how people ate up her views on nostalgia and family values. But most importantly, she learned how to control people with fear. She pushed it as far as the FCC would allow then the local cable station came calling.

"You have a face for television," said the cable television manager.

"I've never done this before," said Stormy.

"Let's do five shows," he said as he patted her behind. "We'll see how it goes."

Her radio fans followed her over to the small screen, increasing her market share. The public couldn't get enough of her. Her thirty minute show was expanded to an hour. In the third year of the show, her station manager asked her for a meeting.

"I think we should pitch your show to the networks. You have the magic touch." He leaned over the desk and looked down her sweater.

Stormy smiled and tried to contain the excitement that Rita Mae would have shown. "I'm up for it," she said calmly.

Every news channel wanted her but there was only one station that could afford her salary demands and of course, condone her political views. On her premiere show, she met Matt Brewster. There were many potential Vice-Presidential candidates for his party. Matt knew he had to separate himself from the pack. He said the masses were lost, looking for a leader to deliver them from the dying morality in the country.

"Governor, where do you see this country headed if your party doesn't win the election?" Stormy tried not to giggle like a school girl.

"We need to go back to a formal class structure and get the country back on track." He paused and looked into the camera. "The other party has bankrupted this country, morally and fiscally. America is destined to become a Third World country in less than fifty years. They don't understand what it will take to become a superpower again.

It will take sacrifice. I know you will stand behind me." Matt wiped away a tear.

"Well, I am behind you. I'm sure the whole country is." She tried to choke back her emotions.

There was an instant connection between Stormy and Matt. He respected her opinions and she was smitten with his background. He was everything she wanted to be— Mayflower descendant, Ivy League educated, and untouched by simplicity. She was everything he wanted in a woman—brazen, spontaneous, and unaffected by rules.

During their late night phone conversations, she mentioned segregating the undesirables Matt often mentioned from civilized society. She had heard the fanatics talk about this theory before but she was the first to name the two groups the "Believers" and "Non-believers." When Matt heard the words flow out of Stormy's mouth, he moaned as if he was sexually aroused. She kept adding onto her story as if she was a sex phone operator, trying to keep Matt on the line as long as possible.

"I think we should have a brainstorming session. We could go to my cabin for the weekend." Matt panted into the phone.

"I'll do anything to help this country." Stormy was thankful he couldn't see her over the phone. She felt her face blush. It wasn't often a man made her feel confident and unsure of herself at the same time.

~oOo~

She came prepared. Under the G-strings and garter belts was a color-coded binder. She pulled out the flow charts and spreadsheets and proudly laid them on the bed.

Matt came up from behind her and slid his hands up her trademark, black mini-skirt. She laid face down on top of her research and he pushed into her. They both looked at the scattered papers between moaning out each other's names.

She wrapped herself with the comforter Matt's wife imported from England. His family crest was sewn into it with gold and silver threads. It gleamed but couldn't outshine Stormy's effervescent blue eyes.

"Weren't you a research scientist before going into

politics?" Stormy asked.

"Yes, at the CDC," said Matt.

"You're right, the undesirables are different. Sometimes you can't see it by looking at them, but most times, their mannerisms give them away. Talk to your colleagues. Make a blood test to weed them out. I will do the test live on my show to prove it's safe." She flipped through her binder to show him the preliminary polling she had conducted.

"Then what? Put them in prison? The country is on the verge of collapse. Taxpayers can't take on this burden."

"Work camps," she said.

"What?" he asked.

"Work camps. Put them out in the desert so they can't escape. Make them work. Corporations will eat up the idea of free labor. We won't have to outsource anymore. Win-win."

"It's slavery, isn't it?" he asked.

"You have to spin it for the simple people. Say the Non-believers have ruined it for the rest of us. And now they will have an opportunity to bring us all out of despair. They should be proud to help out the country they brought down." Stormy remembered her father and his friends from the car plant spewing their unsubstantiated views about the town's undesirables. The background chatter about torture and sometimes, their plans for murder, had always been floating around town.

"The other side will fight us," he said.

"Pass laws to punish them. Build large clinics with glass walls in the middle of every major city. Punish the conspirators by injecting them with tainted blood. If they want to help the Non-believers so much, let them become one of them." She showed him the architectural renderings she had commissioned.

"I thought catching it by bodily fluids was a myth," he said.

"It's not," she said.

"Do you believe we can get away with all of this?" he asked.

She smiled for him but wondered if hatred was learned or if it crept through people's veins waiting to emerge. She wondered if it was embedded inside of Ryan's DNA as well.

"You have thought of everything," he said. She had secured his place on the Presidential ticket. He climbed on top of her again.

~oOo~

Both parties' candidates knew they had to make a stop on Stormy's show before they made a political move. Neither party was safe from her wrath. She dug up secrets no one else could possibly find out. It taught her how to hide her own. She once joked that if she was found dead, the police would never solve the case because she had so many enemies.

Several months after Stormy presented her ideas to Matt, he went on her show asking for public support. A handsome doctor walked onto the set and took blood from her arm.

"See, it's a simple blood test." Stormy leaned into the camera. "We, as a country, need to move on this. Matt Brewster has a plan and we must support the truth. We need to save ourselves before they destroy us."

After the show, Matt's party named him their Vice-Presidential nominee. He felt he should have been the Presidential nominee but he was told he was too young and he should bide his time. One day, he would be President. He'd have to be patient.

Days after his party won, Congress passed laws to segregate the people who did not agree with the Believer's pacts with God. Matt suggested they form a new cabinet position. The secretary of unity was in charge of ensuring the country was moving in the right direction. The first order was to find a way to stop the threat to American values.

Thanks to Stormy, the One Drop Campaign rolled on.

One drop.

One drop would label a person a Believer or a Non-believer.

At first, the majority of the population didn't agree with the laws. Citizens stormed state capitals but were crushed by the National Guard. After endless losing battles, most people were afraid to protest in public. Unhappy citizens were forced to leave the country or worse, be labeled as conspirators.

Many prominent leaders—politicians, clergy, and scientists—were testing positive for the defective gene. A majority of these people had championed the laws, not knowing of course, they were infected.

No one questioned the long-term effects on individuals. No one asked what would happen to all these people. At the time no one cared. It didn't affect anyone important.

~oOo~

It wasn't a senator or governor that Stormy ruined who nailed her to the wall. It was a parent at her son's school who thought she was a bitch. The Christmas before, she had made it clear that she didn't believe in handouts and announced on her show that people shouldn't give to Toys for Tots.

"These welfare rats should buy their own toys," she screamed into the camera.

Months later, she received an anonymous letter accusing her of being a hypocrite. It was long and hateful but the only word she remembered was "bastard." She hired a private investigator to trace its origins. A PTA mother confessed, causing Stormy to contact Matt.

The last time she saw him was after he secured his run for President. Stormy asked her thirty-six million Twitter followers to start a revolution against the Non-believers. Three days of marches, looting, and murders caused the nation to pause. The federal government threatened to charge her with inciting a riot.

"This is the last time I can help you." He kept a safe distance between them. "We need to be very careful from now on."

"I don't even believe in half your agenda. I did this for you." Stormy tried to grab his hand but he turned away.

"It's too late now," he said as he left her office.

~oOo~

Stormy pinned a lilac on her lapel. She had stopped wearing them after Matt left her. It used to be the signal that she needed to see him. He would text back a coded message and they would meet at the cabin. She hoped he didn't forget what it meant.

Matt was waiting on the porch when she reached the cabin. He stepped to the side so she could enter.

"What is this about? I told you we couldn't meet again."

"It's important. It's about Ryan." Stormy threw down her Gucci bag.

"I told you I can't claim him. I'm the President now. I can't leave her."

"Her money is financing your dream. I get it."

"Then what? What's wrong with Ryan?"

She stopped to catch her breath. "Ryan. He's been tested."

Matt leaned against the door to steady himself. "What about you?"

"You narcissistic asshole. Dr. Howard tested me live on my show. Do you remember that? I'm clean."

"So, I'm not his father?" he accused.

"Are you really that stupid?" she asked. "You're one of them."

"It has to be a mistake. Test him again." He stumbled and caught himself. "Who accused him?"

"Some bitch mother at Ryan's school. The press will go crazy. You need to make it go away."

"I can't run to your defense. People will talk."

"People like your wife?"

"Among others."

"What will they say when I name you as the father of a Non-believer?"

"What do you want me to do?" he asked.

"Make it go away. I'll take Ryan and leave the country."

Another voice echoed from the back of the cabin. "You know we're way past that now. The party wants to execute them. We need you to back us up on air. If you're a good little girl, perhaps we can make this a little better for your Ryan."

"Who else is here?" she asked Matt.

"Oh Stormy, or shall I call you Rita Mae. You are the architect of the entire movement. It made you a superstar. You will keep up the party's line or we will expose you for the fraud that you are. Think about what they'll do to

Ryan." The pale man stepped in front of the fireplace. Stormy couldn't make out his face as he looked like all the others in the party.

"If I do this, can Ryan stay with me?" she asked.

"No, that's not possible but it will be kept a secret. I promise he won't be hurt, but he will have to be deposited." The man shrank back into the darkness.

~oOo~

The party allowed Stormy to take Ryan to Disneyland for one last family vacation as long as she wore an ankle monitor. She had helped them with their cause. They didn't want the public to think they were completely heartless.

"I hope you had a good time." Stormy kissed Ryan's cheek. "We have to go to Arizona now."

The five-hour ride to the internment camp was long but not silent. Stormy couldn't calm the excited boy.

"Do they have a pool there? Will my friends be there? Will my Daddy be there?"

"He'll be there eventually," she said.

Stormy was vague and tried to hide her emotions. She turned her head and looked into the barren wasteland. She slowly began to understand her son would not return home.

The rental car, covered in red dust, reached the edge of the barbed wire fence that enclosed the work camp. Stormy and Ryan stepped out of the car. She gagged as she breathed in the red dust attacking them. She wondered if it was always this hot in Arizona. The only time she had been there was during the last Presidential Convention. Canyon Ranch's limousine had brought her from her private plane straight to the air conditioned resort.

Her son pulled on her skirt. "Mommy, look it's your billboard."

On it, she was grinning. Her show's tag line read, "You made your bed, now lie in it."

"Mommy, there's another sign." He pointed to a small square below the billboard. "One Drop Stop."

The once untouchable Stormy Sommers slumped down next to the car and closed her eyes. She could no longer look at the world she created.

Yong Takahashi

The Desert of the Real

Elana Gomel

The homeless man under the bridge stirred in his cocoon of rags. Plastic bags were tied to him like the overlapping scales of an armadillo. He thrust up an illegible cardboard sign as Eric's Tesla purred by. The sign bore some sort of design rather than words. Was the man a street artist? There were few actual beggars nowadays.

His car's AI turned on the newsfeed from the inauguration ceremony but Eric waved it off. It was ridiculous to hold the grudge for so long, he knew, but he could not help himself. His very first election, seventeen years ago, in which he had voted for the losing candidate, still rankled. It had been a gesture of adolescent rebellion: voting for a political novice, a nobody with a murky record. But he could not help imagining how different the world could have been had his candidate won. Anything would be better than this endless procession of bland, politically-correct presidents with their bland, politically correct speeches!

Entering middle age, Eric saw his own life as an equivalent of America's boring, predictable, safe slide into mediocrity. America had had its chance with Trump—and blew it. Just as he had blown his chance at being more than another one of the Silicon Valley's drones!

Well, perhaps he still had one more try.

He stumbled as he walked into his townhouse. Cursing, Eric tried to straighten the bunched-up rug with the tip of his shoe...until he remembered that there was no rug. Nassrin had taken it to the cleaners.

Indeed, his green Australian tiles were unobstructed by a flowery Middle-eastern weave. Instead the floor itself rose up into a miniature ridge like a budding wall.

Eric studied the ridge from several angles. He even went down on his knees and poked it with his finger without obtaining any useful knowledge. It was not that the tiles became misaligned: rather, they were stretched into a lopsided hump as if they had suddenly liquefied and then hardened again. He had no idea how this was possible, but then he was a coder, not a damned engineer!

Dismissing the thing—he had more important issues to deal with—he shuffled into the living room where his smart house-bot instantly turned on the news and started dinner. President Obama was still droning on and Eric muted the screen with an irritated wave of his hand. He was not exactly opposed to her policies—she promised more science funding, and her father had presided over Eric's teenaged years—but God, was she boring!

Out of the same contrary mood that had plagued him since this morning, he refused the chicken curry the bot put on the table and poured himself a glass of wine, instead.

"Take that!" he mouthed at his house's intelligence, knowing how childish that was but unable to overcome the itch of perversity that seemed to drive his actions today.

Eric turned on his code. The lines flickered in an endless loop, generating a mandala-like graph. It was beautiful, fascinating, hypnotic—and it did not mean anything. It was not working. His great hope, his infallible prediction software, his ticket to the big league—it was just a pile of digital junk!

Eric was ready to throw in more junk just to break the deadlock when his watch vibrated with a text. The text was from Nassrin. Eric's heart in his throat, he waved his hand, tossing the message in the air where it unfolded in a script of brightness.

Eric stared at it uncomprehendingly. What the hell? The love of his life had written to him in Arabic. He did not know Arabic—and neither did she.

Nassrin's parents had brought her from Morocco when she was a year old. Her inheritance from the exotic Maghreb included a divine recipe of lamb tagine, sultry black eyes and a houri's figure. But it did not include knowledge of Arabic. She spoke French with her parents and American English with everybody else.

Eric ran the text through the house-bot. It came out as garbage.

He sent her a handful of inquisitive emojis. She was supposed to come back tomorrow after spending a couple of days with her family before the wedding.

The answer blinked in a video window. Nassrin's beautiful face filled the rectangle of light, framed by its luminescent edges. But it was also framed by folds of fabric that Eric recognized as a hijab.

His mouth fell open. Nassrin's family were freethinkers and fervent supporters of the King of Morocco against the Islamist opposition. Nassrin had never worn a hijab in her entire life.

"What happened?" he sputtered.

Nassrin's face swam like a fish in the glowing pool. Her cheek was disfigured by a bruise.

"They're coming to take us away!" she said.

"Who is coming? What's going on? Nas, what the hell?"

She lifted her hand and he saw that her palm was decorated with an elaborate henna design, such as Middle-eastern brides wear on their wedding day. She had shown him some, explaining that they worked as charms against the evil eye. But this was not one of those. The design was instantly, spookily familiar. Labyrinthine and inwardly spiraling, the design drew his eye toward its receding center. Eric peered into the window, almost diving into its virtual depth, when there was a deafening crash from the hallway. Eric sprinted toward the front door and ran headfirst into a wall that was not supposed to be there.

Winded by his collision, he lay on the itchy ground, sand clogging his nostrils. Sand? He sat up with a groan.

Eric found himself in a sort of trough between two looming walls. Above him the pale sky shed a hot light that beat against his throbbing skull. A dry wind threw flurries of fine dust into his face.

He examined the walls. They were made of ...everything. He could not define it any better than that: a compressed mass of building blocks, road signs, twisted metal, splintered furniture, even clothes, all fused together into an undifferentiated pile that reminded him of the aftermath of the Second World War bombing of Dresden he had seen on History Channel. The walls were higher than a two-story building and obviously unscalable.

Eric contemplated the possibility that he was insane but rejected it immediately. First, he had a sizeable lump on his forehead that had not come from colliding with a hallucination. And second, he was beginning to figure out what was going on. He only needed his Mac to confirm it...but a brief reconnoitering showed that his precious machine was now melded with a woman's bra into an Escher-like configuration. He still had his watch but no amount of swiping and cursing elicited any sign of life from the blank screen, even though the battery was still full.

Eric started down the path between the walls. He did not know in what direction he was going because the light from above did not come from the sun: it was source-less, unchangeable and as hot as hell. Eric had gone on a trip to Morocco with Nassrin and it reminded him of hamsin, a desert wind that sent the inhabitants of Marrakesh into their fountain-cooled courtyards. But there was no fountain here and no shade. In a couple of minutes Eric was dehydrated.

He followed the curving trough, glancing at the walls. He recognized his own green tiles, interspersed with steel beams and squashed car seats. He stopped when he saw a scatter of bleached bones but consoled himself with the fact that none of this was precisely real. Or was it? His algorithm could not answer philosophical questions. But now Eric found himself chewing over a phrase from his undergrad Philosophy 101: "the desert of the real". At the time it had seemed meaningless to him; now he realized that he was, quite possibly, about to die, trapped in a metaphor.

He came to the intersection of two troughs and stood there, unable to choose. Right or left or straight on? He chose right, for no particular reason. The walls here were the same compacted debris as everywhere else, at least at the beginning. As he trudged on, he realized that more and more of the material was printed matter of various kinds: road signs, books and bound brochures, anonymous documents and forms. He tugged one page that protruded from the wall but it was too firmly cemented into the whole. Still, he could read enough to see that almost every word was misspelled. A road sign that he managed to make out said "Bottoms-Up, Population 500,000."

It became evident to Eric that he was trapped in a labyrinth. The walls curved and intersected in a complex circular pattern. He knew the pattern but it quickly became clear to him that there was a profound difference between seeing it on screen and walking it on swollen feet, his head pounding, his lips chafed, and his tongue furred with thirst. You could not argue ontology with hunger and pain. The body delivered reality. Otherwise, he would be tempted to sink back into his hallucination theory as the material of the walls became stranger and stranger.

He was no longer shocked to find entire sections made of human bones, even though he turned away, retching, when he saw bleeding stumps of amputated limbs sticking out. But more prominent than organic debris was electronic junk that now comprised the towering barriers hemming him in: broken printers, ancient pulverized cellphones, and warped tablets. Shattered info-sets regarded him with cataract screens. Printed material did not disappear but it was now blended with the information delivery systems into an impenetrable mess of dead words. The spine of an occasional book sticking out bore illegible nonsense regardless of its language. His French was not great but he was pretty sure that Rendezvous super toujours was wrong.

Eric was beginning to feel faint. How long could he survive without food and water? The temperature was steadily rising, the walls of junk looming into the bleached sky but providing no shade. He turned yet another corner and came into a large clearing.

It was almost a plaza, bordered by ramparts made of rusted steel beams and chicken wire. At its center was what Eric at first took for a sphinx.

He had seen the Great Sphinx of Giza on the Mid-East trip with Nassrin and was underwhelmed by the badly eroded sandstone monument, pockmarked with violence. Since then he had read about the symbolism of the creature with the haunches of a lion and the impassive face of a woman and learned to respect the ancient enigma it embodied. But the statue in the middle of the plaza was enigmatic in a different way.

Eric approached it cautiously, leaning back to take in its swollen bulk. It was peeling, orange strips of its hide flapping in the hot draft. Its body was not quite leonine; rather, it resembled a crouching man, squeezed into an uncomfortable half-sitting, half-standing position. The splayed hands, each palm bigger than Eric, were equipped with claws. Tattered wings unfolded over his head. But it was only when Eric circled the statue's pedestal and saw its face that he gasped. Carved into an approximation of some ancient heroic ideal, it was still, unmistakably, the face of the man he had voted for in 2016. Superimposed upon the placidly generic features of a monumental statue, it looked both cartoonish and menacing.

Trying to figure out what it all meant, Eric sidled closer to the statue, hiding in its meager shadow. He had never actually believed that the database from which his algorithm derived its predictions existed in any tangible, physical sense. On the other hand, there was nothing in his theory that precluded it.

The multiverse contained endless permutations of historical elements, some more likely than others but nothing totally impossible. And underlying it all was the database: the universe of discourse, created and sustained by the human imagination, the unbounded internet of the mind.

His algorithm was supposed to tap into it and forecast likely trends by focusing on the underlying discursive shifts, too subtle—or sometimes too obvious—to be correctly interpreted by ideology-blinkered human minds. This was the idea, in any case. It did not quite work as promised to the investors, throwing up tons of gibberish. Still, Eric was convinced it would work. But he had never visualized it working in this spectacularly dangerous fashion: by transporting him into some sort of physically manifesting junkyard of history.

He was trying to figure out why he was led to this statuary monument of a failed political clown, when the sphinx's giant head dipped down and its fishy eyes focused on Eric.

He backed off, slipped and landed on his backside. Jarring pain shot up his spine. Now the reality hit and he wondered how he had missed it. Of course, the creature was alive! That orange hide was not some sort of synthetic covering but actual skin; the thing on top was not worked stone but heavily lacquered hair; and the hot wind wafting into his face was the creature's fevered breath.

The mouth gaped, its blackness deep enough to swallow Eric whole as he backpedaled and crawled away from the nightmare, all dignity forgotten. The bluish tongue twitched and a flood of unintelligible syllables poured forth, battering Eric like a hail of stones: It meant absolutely nothing but the nonsensical words fell upon Eric with a decisiveness of hammer blows, driving panic into every fiber of his being. He was scrambling through drifts of broken metal, cutting himself on sharp edges, sobbing and moaning as the tempest of gibberish, blowing him away, reached a gale proportion. He was slammed into a ruinous wall and blacked out as the enormous wings spread over him.

Eric sat up and looked around. To his relief, the sphinx was gone. He had rolled under a small overhang but its meager shadow helped very little against the heat. Otherwise he was in the same labyrinth though perhaps in a different part of it—he could not tell. He had already realized that the place was shaped like the mandala-like graph of his algorithm but this knowledge was useless when he was trapped inside it. Perhaps he should try to scramble up a wall: in this part, they seemed somewhat less sheer. But what if the sphinx was still up there, flapping mangy wings? Eric shuddered but realized he had no choice. The warming trend continued unabated and if he could not find a way out, he would die—as simple as that.

"I was his voter," he said aloud and winced. His voice sounded obscene in the desert hush.

But then it was answered. From above rang a feeble cry. It sounded articulate: not the deliberate nonsense of the sphinx's roar. Eric scrambled out from beneath the overhang and squinted into the light, only to stagger and moan. The wall above him was made out of compressed human bodies; naked or covered with rags; terribly emaciated; white, black and brown, but all reduced to the same elemental humanity. And though crushed and melded together, they were still alive. Bloodshot eyes followed him, rolling in squashed faces; a thin hand, nails missing, fluttered, reaching out; a toothless mouth strained to form intelligible sounds. It was too horrifying to look at and Eric turned to flee when a voice, impossibly familiar, called out his name.

He walked back to the wall of bodies. Nassrin's beautiful face was veiled with a torn piece of black fabric but he would recognize her eyes among thousands. Her body...he tried not to see the contorted trunk, the back-bent limbs, and the broken ribs, squashed by the weight of the bodies above and around her. She could not, should not, be alive—and yet she was.

"I'm sorry, Nas," he whispered. Tears were streaming down his cheeks, carrying away precious moisture.

"Why?" she coughed.

"It's my fault, Nassrin," he touched her cheek. "Or all our fault. Whatever. That election...it must have released something into the bloodstream of history. Some poison. I thought it did not matter, it was just words. But history is made by words. And now the course of history is being warped by that poison, spreading through the multiverse, corrupting all meaning, all plausibility. No surprise that my algorithm was throwing up nonsense. There is nothing else left. But nonsense kills. Absurdity kills. They make desert and call it peace."

He was blinded by tears. Nassrin's broken hand landed gently on his shoulder. He squeezed her dry fingers and leaned against the wall of bodies until he heard a thunderous flapping.

"Go!" she commanded and he let go. But before running away, he tried to lift the black fabric off her face, knowing she hated the enforced veil of her birth country. But he could not: the fabric was a flap of her own skin

"Go!" Nassrin yelled and he ran, dodging slivers of corroded metal and chunks of bleeding flesh, whipped by the twister of meaningless syllables through the dead heat as the gargantuan presence above filled the multiverse with white noise.

Eric found himself lying prone at the entrance to his bathroom. He staggered inside and lapped water from the faucet like a dog, pausing when he remembered that it was no longer safe to drink because of the pollution. But thirst was stronger than health concerns.

In the kitchen, he devoured the last slice of stale pizza while watching a press-conference with the new White House spokesman. If he was any improvement on the last one. Eric was unable to tell. His words fell into the void like pebbles into a stream, making a splash but delivering no other information.

President Eric Trump himself was on Twitter as usual but Eric had no energy to parse out his words. Whatever they meant—a war, a budget cut, making a new treaty or breaking an old one—let others try to fish some semblance of meaning from the torrent of symbols that threatened to drown the world. Eric had more pressing concerns. The last investor had pulled out and truth be told, he could not blame them. Who needed to puzzle out the future when the present was incomprehensible?

Holding his ancient phone, he checked WhatsApp, hoping against hope for a word from Nassrin. But he knew it was dangerous for her to message him. Her father had been forced to take the family back to Morocco where he was promptly arrested by the new Islamist government. Nassrin and her mother, together with other black-swaddled women, spent hours every day at the entrance to the jail, under the scorching sun, hoping for some information about his fate. Outside the jail, there were food riots.

Feeling hemmed in in his tiny rental, Eric decided to drive back to his office. Might just as well use the space now—the lease expired soon and he had no money to renew it. He waved at the TV set to shut up the talking heads but the sensor was broken.

Eric's aging Ford puffed through the deserted highway. At least the traffic in the Silicon Valley had improved after all the immigrant tech workers were either forced out or left in disgust. The native-born followed. The best American scientists were now found in Stockholm or Shanghai.

Driving, he let his mind wander. He did not regret his vote so many years ago, he told himself. How could he? President Clinton...this would have been so much worse! He said it out loud to reassure himself and looked around nervously. There seemed a strange hissing sound accompanying his words, as if a desert wind blew through the car, wafting hot air into his face. Well, no surprise he was having these delusions. The heat wave was a major topic in the news, and though only a few brave souls talked openly about the climate change, a swirl of euphemisms could not disguise the reality of creeping desertification.

As he drove by an overpass, a figure covered in overlapping plastic bags crawled into the dusty sunshine, holding up a handmade sign. Begging for a dollar, no doubt. There were so many homeless nowadays that it took a special kind of stupidity to hope for a handout. But when Eric glanced incuriously at the sign, he saw that it displayed a labyrinthine, mandala-like pattern. It looked like a graph. Or maybe, a Moroccan wedding henna design.

Critical Residential Update

Janka Hobbs

VERIFIED PUBLISHER: ConnectsAll Corporation
Critical Residential Update 575E-371, 07/24/2034 02:00

ERROR MESSAGE: Residence Systems Not Installing This Update Will Become Ineligible For Services

RESTART SYSTEM

Sensors activated
Perimeter secure
Interior temperature 65F
Air filters satisfactory

Connectivity provider billing: up to date
Tunes online
Video streaming online
Screen approved contacts
Approved contacts online

UTILITIES BILLING: up to date

SCAN FOOD STORAGE:
Refrigerator temperature 38F

SCAN CONTENTS:
MILK: 44 hours, acceptable
EGGS: 93 hours, acceptable

SCAN COUNTERTOPS:
UNKNOWN ITEM: no RFID
ACTIONABLE remove to garbage; compact.
(And so, a fresh tomato from the neighbor's garden goes down the tubes.)

SCAN DWELLING FOR INHABITANTS:

NON-HUMAN DNA DETECTED: Feline. Chipped, licensed. No action required.

NON-HUMAN DNA DETECTED: Rodent. Unchipped, unlicensed. Prepare to seal and fumigate room.
Human DNA detected. Authorized resident present; child, female, age 8.5, records in order, delay action.
(And so Fluffy the hamster gets a stay of execution. For now.)

HUMAN DNA DETECTED: Authorized resident present: infant, male, age 22 months, vaccinations up to date.

HUMAN DNA DETECTED: Authorized resident present: Citizen: Primary resident, male, age 43, employed, solvent. Incipient diabetes: MONITOR

HUMAN DNA DETECTED: Authorized resident present: Citizen: Primary resident #2, female, 36, employed, solvent.

HUMAN DNA DETECTED: Non-registered individual present: Non-citizen: Visa status: exempt family member, female, 72. Country of Origin: Visa Restricted. Expected interaction with undesirables: VERIFIED. *ACTIONABLE*

(Two days later, Grandma was found dead, electrocuted in the bathtub. No one could figure out how the electric toothbrush had fallen in with her, or why the GFCI failed. The family sued the electrician who installed the system, never suspecting the house's self-cleaning mechanism of murder.)

A New Republic

Hannah Trusty

The irony that our nation's last truly democratic act was to dissolve our democracy was never far from Tamara's mind as the swell of "Pomp and Circumstance" rose to a crescendo for the umpteenth time.

The whole ceremony was just a dog and pony show, and the older adults there knew it. It's not like these kids had any choices, graduating, not like they had any choice about their future. When parents won their chance to have a baby in the birth lottery, they received the packet—the rules that would guide their future child's entire life, laid out before they were even conceived. But these were the first of the children who grew up with no country other than the New Republic of America. These kids didn't know what had not been given them in the name of security.

The music finally came to an end after the eleventh cycle of the song, and the last of the graduates had taken their seat. Tamara shifted and craned her neck. Her boy, Nick, was right in the middle of the crowd. She smiled and waved, but he didn't see her.

Tamara had voted for the New Republic, and its new constitution. She was just barely an adult herself, then. And when she had met Harold, and fallen in love, all she had wanted was to get married, have a quiet life, and the chance for happiness. That was what the New Republic was all about: quiet happiness and security for everyone.

But looking out at the sea of children on the cusp of becoming adults, the first adults to have their entire life dictated to them, she wondered if security was worth the price.

Her own Nick fared okay. He wanted to be a musician.

He was musically inclined and picked up most instruments quickly. Tamara smiled as she remembered him, a bubbling toddler, banging happily on toy drums. For his tenth birthday, he had received an acoustic guitar that he carried around for years. But the world, the New Republic had decided, only needed so many musicians. Even though he scored high in creative areas on his aptitudes as a child, he also showed dexterity, and the country needed more mechanics, so he would be going into an apprenticeship after high school. He told her how he liked tuning the machines, listening to their rhythms.

They were somewhere in the Ks, nearly to "Maynard." Nick would be walking across the stage soon. Tamara shifted in her seat and fanned herself with her program. Some things had changed in the years since the fall of the United States, but sitting in an overcrowded high school gymnasium was still hot and uncomfortable.

"Nick Maynard, Vocational..." the voice of the principal was droning into the speaker. Tamara tried to hide her frown in case Nick happened to be looking for her in the crowd. She didn't know why they had to announce the designation with the name. She had so wished for him to draw with an academic match and get to go to college. Not that there was a single thing wrong with being in the vocational group. She just thought he would have enjoyed the university so.

Nick shook hands with the principal, took his diploma and went back to his seat. He showed little emotion. There wasn't much need for celebration. He was right where he was supposed to be, doing the thing he was supposed to do. Just like every other kid in the gym. They didn't know anything else, so they didn't question the neat little lives that were set before them.

Tamara felt like she had to really focus to remember what it was like before the change. 2023 had been such a terrible year. Civil war was on the horizon.

The years leading up to it had been surreal. The country had spiraled out of control under a government that was grabbing power while citizens tore themselves apart. People were suffering as factories refused to sell goods to certain parts of the country and farmers refused to sell food to their neighbors. Families were falling apart as people picked sides. States had already started the process of secession.

The country had torn itself apart. Red versus blue. People had stopped listening to each other and became so entrenched in their own beliefs that nothing else mattered. Everyone had to pick a side. But Tamara had not wanted a side. She wanted a country, whole again. Even that seemed to enrage those around her.

She wasn't political enough, she didn't care enough, they said. She cared, all right. She cared that the fighting was hurting people, and that it was all for nothing. Tamara left her home, looking to live in an area where others thought the same as she did.

The principal was giving the final speech of the evening; tidings to parents and best of luck to the graduates. Lip service, really. Each of those kids had a label on their diploma that would be their life. If they didn't live up to it, they would serve a sentence in a work penitentiary doing manual labor. This ceremony wasn't a celebration of achievements or an ushering in of possibilities. It was simply a nod to a life that the parents were old enough to remember. It was an old tradition that people could use to fool themselves into thinking things were normal.

"And now we stand to salute the New Republic of America, which gives us security, sanctity and stability..."

Tamara heard the phrase and automatically got to her feet with the rest of the crowd. Pretty much any public event had this salute. It was the replacement for the Pledge of Allegiance.

"I pledge my honor to the New Republic of America, which gives me security, sanctity and stability..." the words slipped from her mouth, but she didn't mean them. She had been harboring a revolution in her heart for a while now. She knew that Harold would never be on board with it, and that devastated her, as she still loved him. He was a good husband and a kind man. But she needed to give her son the future that she helped steal from him.

Clapping and cheering swelled around her as the students threw their caps into the air. She could see Nick and he still didn't look happy. Tamara gathered her purse and cell phone and started to make her way out of the gym and into the parking lot.

"I'm going to take Nick out for some pizza. You still gotta go into work?" Tamara asked her husband.

"Yeah. But I'll have celebratory pancakes with you and the kiddo in the morning," Harold said, giving his wife a peck on the cheek. Her heart swelled and she pulled him in for a bigger kiss.

He worked nights as a security guard at a local manufacturing plant. He didn't care for the job, especially the shift, but law enforcement was high in his aptitudes but only security jobs were available in the area. He had been given a choice by the government to move to an area that needed cops or stay and take the security job. He had chosen the latter, not wanting to uproot his family.

"Have a safe night, love bug," she said to him. It was something she had always said before he'd go off to work. Tamara's heart broke as she watched her husband amble off to his car. He didn't mind the New Republic rules. He liked 'security, sanctity and stability' and didn't mind giving away every shred of freedom to have it. Even if that meant taking a job he had no interest in to earn the same amount of money as every other person. Even if it meant his own boy was destined to the same kind of future.

Tamara wiped away a tear and leaned on her car. Harold was a good man, and he didn't deserve to be deserted by his wife and only son. But Nick was a good kid and deserved more. And she might not be a good woman, but she was ready to give up everything to try to become one.

"Hey kiddo!" Tamara yelled as she saw her son walking across the parking lot, towards her. He was chatting with a small group of friends, and her heart sank.

"Where's dad?" Nick asked.

"Had to get to work. But he is so proud of you. And so am I," Tamara got on her tiptoes and kissed her son on the cheek. She heard one of the girls in his group giggle.

"Mom, can I go have pizza with my friends?" Nick asked. Tamara felt panic rise in her chest.

"I guess, but I had a present. It is kind of time sensitive," she said.

Nick looked into his mother's face and saw the downtrodden look. He wanted to be with his friends. He would rather be with them, but he didn't like seeing his mother upset.

"Oh, well, no. I can come see the surprise. And then maybe meet up with them afterwards?"

Tamara felt relief rush through her body. She glanced at the kids and hoped that Nick would eventually see them again.

"Sure. After," she said. Tamara watched as her son said goodbye to his friends.

"Okay, where is this surprise of mine, mom?" Nick asked.

"We have to drive for just a bit," Tamara said, getting into their mid-sized sedan. Even the car was a reminder of how little choice she had in life. Cars, like houses and paychecks, were distributed by the government. Everything was set by the government. Everyone got basically the same, so no one would be in want of anything and no one could covet another.

Except Tamara had coveted. She had wanted the minivan that her neighbors had. They had three children. In this society of sameness, it seemed like abundance. It seemed so unfair that a couple could win the child lottery so many times. And because of their big family, they were allotted a minivan, instead of the very standard issued mid-size sedan.

Nick gave his mom big sad eyes as she went for the driver's door. Nick had just gotten his driver's license and still had the new driver excitement of operating a vehicle. It was one of the few things he had shown any excitement in as he approached graduation.

"Sorry, son, but I'm driving tonight. I'm taking you to a surprise, remember?" Tamara said. She pulled the car out of the crowded parking lot and headed down the state highway. Their hometown was rural and the school sat out in the country, so they were on deserted roads in no time. She rolled down the window and let in the warm summer air. The sky was clear and the stars were twinkling overhead. She stole glimpses of her son, sitting quietly next to her.

"It will take a few minutes to get to the surprise. Do you want to play the radio?" she asked him. Nick gave her a weak smile and shrugged. She turned the radio to a local rock station, and drove without talking for a few minutes, trying to decide if this was what she truly wanted to do.

Nick could say no. He might even report her and her friends, although she very much doubted that. She had watched her son wither under every decision foisted onto him by his government over the past few years.

Tamara remembered Nick's sixteenth birthday. That morning he received his profession packet, officially assigning him to his future job as a mechanic. That afternoon he hung out with his friends, opened presents, and blew out the candles on his birthday cake. That night he quietly went up to his room and packed up the guitar he had cherished for so many years and sent it to a younger cousin. Tamara hadn't heard him play a note since that day.

More than her, and much more than his father, Nick was a free, creative soul. He would be miserable with a standard issue house, government mandated job and his list of rules to never deviate from.

Tamara had been surprised to learn that her best friend, Margaret, felt the same way. She had always seemed happy in her life that was provided for her. She had no children (she and her husband had never entered the lottery), and she worked at a bank downtown; her husband worked in marketing. They had the basic government issued everything; a two-bedroom bungalow in the suburbs, a sedan in the garage, flowers planted in the yard. Their house even had a white picket fence. She always seemed content. So, Tamara had been shocked one day, when she was worrying to her friend over Nick's growing sullenness and Margaret told her there was another way.

Tamara was so deep in thought that she almost missed her turn and whipped the car onto a little gravel road just before she passed it. Out of the corner of her eye, she saw Nick grab the 'oh shit' handle (as he called it) and grin.

"Whoa, there. Are we off-roading now?" he asked.

Tamara paused for a moment. "Nick, are you happy?" she asked.

"What do you mean?" He gave her a sideway look and she had her answer then. "I am glad that I graduated," he said.

"Yeah, but did you have a doubt? I mean, you didn't have much choice. You graduate high school and then apprentice at a mechanic's shop, and then you become a mechanic. Right?"

Nick was quiet for a moment. Tamara could hear the wheels of her little sedan crunching on the gravel and she hoped the car didn't bottom out. It wasn't made for this sort of thing.

"Are you disappointed that I didn't score higher for the university on my aptitudes?" Nick asked finally. Tamara slowed the car to a stop.

"Before we go any further, I need you to know that I am proud of you. For everything that you have been, for everything that you are, and everything that you will be, I am proud of you. You could never disappoint me. All I want in this world is for you to be happy. Truly happy." Tamara stared at her son, who sat quietly. "Nick, your surprise is a choice, a choice for how you want to live your life."

Finally he turned and smiled with tears in his eyes. She started inching the car forward again.

"Nineteen years ago I, and the rest of the United States of America, made a choice. We made it out of fear and frustration. We wanted what was best for ourselves, and I would like to think, for each other. We thought we were leveling the playing field. If everyone had the same opportunities, the same life, no one could disagree. So, we voted to dissolve the United States, which was on the brink of civil war, and start fresh. We voted to throw out our democracy and give our government power to decide our lives for us. But they had to follow the new constitution. We thought that would be a safeguard, you know? Everyone would have an equal opportunity. Everyone would be fed, housed, and safe and sound. We thought it would solve our problems."

Tamara and Nick both bounced as the little car hit a pothole and lurched forward. For a moment she was sure the car would be stuck, but she was able to maneuver it around the bend and up ahead she saw a smattering of tents huddled around a campfire.

"But, I think, it turns out there was little choice. We were manipulated by a government hell bent on taking all the power. We were exposed, day and night, to divisive things...on TV and on the internet. We were pitted against each other, and our own president and congress were fueling it. Saying and doing things that would make the divide deeper.

"Then, when we were on the brink of disaster, of a civil war, they swooped in with a supposed solution. Of course, that solution was to give those in power even more power. All the power.

"Years ago, when we voted to give up everything and give it to our government; we thought we were making a choice. We never had a choice. The whole presidency leading up to that point had been orchestrated to put us on the brink. The people that wrote the new constitution, they knew what they were doing. They fed us lines about fear and war and we ate them up. We gave them our freedoms because they promised to make us safe. But watching you grow up, I realize that the price is too high."

"Nick, your surprise is that you have a choice. You don't have to go live in some little brick house with your little white car and work a job that you don't love. You can be wild and free and help us fix what we broke."

Nick sat, in stunned silence. The car had stopped on the edge of a little camp. He watched as a lady with short spiky blonde hair approached the car. He recognized his mom's best friend, Margaret.

"Hey you two!" Margaret leaned into the open window and smiled. "Are you here to join the fun?" she asked.

Tamara sat behind the wheel and didn't say anything for a moment. "Yes, I'm here to join the cause," she finally said. "Nick is here just to check it out. I just brought him here to let him know he had a choice."

Nick sat in the passenger seat and thought about his future. He thought about his friend's futures. They had talked, at great length, about how they wanted to be scientists, artists, chefs, and musicians. But few drew a career that matched their dreams. Some talked about their hope for a big family, but worried of an unlucky draw in the birth lottery. Others dreamed of living near the sea or the mountains, but were already assigned to other parts of the country. It was all for the common good. But was it really? Those sad faces flashed before his eyes.

"No," he said. "I'm here to join the cause."

Tamara grabbed his hand and squeezed it.

Hannah Trusty

True Values

Ben Howels

As the reinforced plasteel door swished aside, Roy Burton looked for the Assistant on duty—the one who'd alarm-texted his private quarters. Junior staffers usually knew not to bother him at night, but if there was an issue with the Truth Values... well, then he needed to deal with it. Some things were too important to ignore.

A pale-skinned lump was dithering by one of the flickering holo-casters. The chubby face brought no flash of memory. There were so many people to remember in the Truth Department, and if they weren't Party Elites, or Descendants, then they didn't really matter. Still, it paid to at least look like he gave a damn. Kept 'em loyal.

Roy blinked, syncing into his hardwired database feed, and quickly scanned through the staffing list that flickered across the inside of his eyelids. There. Opening his eyes again, he strode into the room.

"David. Dave! Good to see you."

The pale young man bowed. "Senior Intermediary, Sir. Thank you for coming so quickly."

"Yes. Thank you so much for waking me at four in the morning." Roy took pleasure in seeing the young man gulp, but covered his smile by scanning the rest of the Truth Analysis Room. There was no one at any of the other stations—no surprise given the time, and the fact it was a holiday weekend. The holiday weekend.

The blast door slid shut behind him, security locks clicking solidly into place. Roy waited for Dave to say something useful, but he seemed star-struck. The four ceiling cameras hummed their boredom.

"Yes, Dave? Why am I here, exactly?"

The Assistant nervously licked his lips, then moved alongside a control unit. A long arm snaked towards a touch panel, grimy fingers calling a display up onto the central holo-caster—a large black spreadsheet, suspended against a pale blue background. Names and figures scrolled past.

Dave paused the list, and grabbed a thin white pole, using it to point at a portion of the text.

"The figures are meant to be locked overnight, but some of them are shifting. 'Indiana, Harmful Pollution' started rising about an hour ago. It's up two points right now."

"That's a minor swing, Dave, and probably just a glitch. We often get power spikes on Trump Memorial weekend. You should know that. We can iron it out during the daily update. Besides, even if the value shift was genuine, that'd only pump three commodity index prices up by a few cents per unit." He scowled. "Is that all you got me out of bed for?"

Another nervous gulp.

"Ummm, no Sir. There's more." Dave scrolled down the spreadsheet. "'Water Toxicity, Mississippi' has climbed three points in the last hour. 'Northern Wall Integrity' has dropped four... no, five points. 'Turkish Military Threat' increased by three. And..."— he looked at the floor, shifting his weight from leg to leg—"...it's the 'Truth Exchange Existence' figure, Sir. It's raised half a percent."

"What? That value's fenced from any power spikes; it's on its own protection circuit." Roy felt a sudden churning in his gut, and strode towards the main holo-caster. "Show me. Now!"

More text shuttled past, then Dave sheepishly angled his stick towards the offending figure.

"It's up to one and a half percent. I know it's a small change, but protocol says that I have to contact you if—"

"I know what the protocol says, you idiot. I wrote it. The Chamber's whole purpose is to determine what's truetrue, and tell the Workers. If the Chamber starts to think the Administration is pushing a faketrue agenda on them—let alone getting paid for doing so—then... well, it wouldn't be good." Roy took a few deep breaths, blinked to check his heart rate, and then focused on what lay ahead. "Okay, let's double check the statistics. Isolate those changing values, and bring them up on the main holo-caster. Keep them on live feed. Split the screen, and call up the Hierarch Panel's values to run alongside them. Let's see if the leaders share the whole Chamber's views."

Not for the first time, Roy wished he could have remote access to the Truth Values data—he could have acted on this sooner, if he had. But any kind of transmission beyond the shielded bunker would have been too risky. Relying on this room, and the separate Data Feed Chamber, was the only sensible way of controlling the information.

Dave noisily cleared his throat. "I'm done, Sir."

"Fast work, good job. Now let's see what... okay, not good, but to be expected. The Hierarchs' opinions match those of the Chamber as a whole." Roy flicked a glance towards one of the clock monitors. "The Monday morning Broadcast isn't until nine, so—"

"No, Sir. Sorry, but the state vidcaps are already showing the public Viewzones filling up. The Trump Remembrance Day Broadcast runs from seven."

"Shit! Yes. Okay. It still leaves us a few hours, though. If we can stabilize the figures with some subtle data-dumps, then it shouldn't impact on the Broadcast. Anything below a five percent belief threshold, and the Hierarchs won't even bother including it in their transmission."

"Sir, the figures are still shifting."

Roy moved closer to the holographic spreadsheet, and studied it more carefully, watching the tiny, constant changes. "I don't see how power spikes could be having this effect—these are small, periodic shifts in value, showing a trend up or down. This looks more like the effect of trading, but the Exchange closed at nine. Locked it down myself."

The 'Truth Exchange Existence' value briefly flashed red, showing as 1.75%.

Roy sucked in a breath through clenched teeth. "How is this possible? The Chamber doesn't usually carry out any analysis this late at night; even the Truth-units need to sleep sometimes. Unless someone's woken them, and..."

Roy blanched, icy fingers skating over his heart. There hadn't been a Chamber breach in twenty-five years. He grabbed Dave's shoulder, the cold grip of his servo-fingers causing the younger man to grimace.

"Have any access alarms been tripped?"

"No, Sir. They feed directly here. I'd have heard if—"

"Quick, call up a view of the Chamber."

"But why do we—?"

"Call it up!"

Grubby fingers skated over the touch panel again, and the hologram faltered, faded, and was replaced by a myriad of mini-images, all pictures of the same place, but from different angles—a cavernous vault, filled with cold metal, subdued green lighting, hardwire cabling, and gaunt faces veiled behind thick glass.

"It still makes me uneasy, Sir. Every single time I see it. I mean, I know they all volunteered, but... to spend a life like that? Shut away, plugged in, seeing nothing but what we send them to look at. It's just so... inhuman."

Roy couldn't keep the irritation from his voice. "Five thousand heroes, Assistant. Patriots, each and every one. They're how we divorced belief from party prejudice. How we finally controlled society, once the Exodus had finished. They're why we're here. They're why we're happy." He turned his attention back to the screen. "Bring up the mini-images in turn. Look for anything moving down there. Anything other than the Caregiver robots."

Pictures were maximized and then vanished, replaced by something almost identical every time. Life in a box, over and over. Finally, the holo-caster went black.

"There's nothing down there, Sir. There's been no breach."

Roy was silent for a few moments as he worked out his next steps. "Okay. That's a good thing, and we should treat it as such. It means we can fix whatever the issue is from up here. Bring up the real-time values again."

After a few seconds, the spreadsheet flickered back into life. 'Turkish Military Threat' had gone up another five points. 'Truth Exchange Existence' read 2.5%.

"Dammit, that's the highest it's been in twenty years. At this rate it'll go above five percent long before the Broadcast. I don't know what's causing the shifts in value, but we can't leave it to chance and hope it re-adjusts. I'll have to intervene."

"Sir? Standard uploads don't have a quick impact. Do we have enough time to—?"

"Aggressive adjustment. The Administration prepared

special simulations and data-dumps for this eventuality. We need to change the whole agenda; force something big on the Hierarchs, and they'll just go with that for their Broadcast. Won't be as festive as we'd hoped, but it'll cover us for now."

"What would make them focus so narrowly?"

"High level military and terrorist threats. It's the only sure-fire way to jump-start the Hierarchs into Broadcasting a guaranteed topic. Needs to be somewhere close as well. Immediate threat. Maybe Canada."

"Canada? Are you serious? They're still just about willing to trade with us, and if we—"

"We're not creating an actual war, you moron. Just getting the Truth Chamber to think one is possible, for a few hours at least. Get 'em worrying about insurgents and bio-bombs, instead of the Truth Exchange. The damage will be containable, and controllable. Even if word were to somehow leak across to the hockey-boys—and given naval containment and the Northern Wall, that's unlikely—they aren't going to want to fight us."

"Shouldn't the Presidential Council be—?"

"Don't tell me my job, you little stain. I'm Senior Intermediary. Third generation Descendant ties. I've got the authority, and we've test run this sort of thing before. The Presidential holo-chats can wait; we need to action this immediately, to ensure the faketrue data has time to bed-in."

Dave shuddered slightly, but then seemed to gather himself. "Do you want to jack in from here, or the main Data Feed Chamber? It's locked-up, but we might—"

"No, we stay here. It'll be easier for us to continue analyzing the data." Roy moved towards the secure access panel, dragging a chair with him. Sitting down, he swiveled into a position that still gave him a clear view of the main holo-caster, stuck his tech-capped right index finger into the jack, and shut his eyes.

A faint stinging sensation preceded the DNA sequencer approving his identity, then he used his hardwired interface to provide the failsafe password. A mauve loading bar flashed in front of him. Seconds passed.

"You in yet, Sir?"

"No. It's taking longer than... hang on, no, there it is." Roy studied the orange text scanning across the inside of his eyelids. "That's odd. The data streams are running slower than usual, and the interface seems a bit different. Font's changed, and the text is flickering a bit." He opened his eyes and looked across to Dave. "You registering me as fully connected? Sometimes this emergency access port can be a little off."

The Assistant nervously flicked his gaze to one of the Systems data-columns in the room. "No, I think you're all fine, Sir. We had some software changes recently, so maybe they haven't gelled truetrue with the Chamber's systems yet."

"Maybe. I should've been told, though. Any kind of update should've gone through my—"

"Intermediary Updates are Turner's job, Sir. And Turner's..."

"A useless drunk, yes." Despite the tension twisting his guts, Roy couldn't help but chuckle. "Only reason that guy's still on staff is because he's dating one of the Descendants." He scowled. "Anyway, let's get on with this. Power steady for a large capacity upload?"

"Yes, Sir."

Roy shut his eyes and dropped back into the interface. "Selecting Canada War Risk, Level 5 Protocol. Injection imminent."

The orange text danced across his eyeballs, but stayed orange. It didn't go green.

"I'm not getting an upload report. Why am I not getting an upload?"

"I don't know, Sir."

"Is anything showing on your data feeds?"

"No, nothing. Progress is static. Truth Exchange has gone up again, though. Now it's 3.5% viable."

"What? Why is it still going up so fast? There's no data being fed in, dammit." Roy threw himself back into his seat, crunching his eyes shut. "Checking the interface again, trying to upload the file." He flicked his eyes open, looking imploringly at Dave. "Anything?"

"No."

"God's sake..." Roy shook his head. "I'll have to try

some others. Keep an eye on the power levels."

"Okay, Sir."

"Broadcast Delay Protocol, commencing data injection."

The data feed stayed orange.

"Power Surge Concerns Protocol, starting injection."

No confirmation.

"Imminent Mexican Invasion Protocol."

Nothing.

"Chamber Breach Response Protocol."

Nothing.

Damn!

Roy opened his eyes to find the chamber flashing with red lights, and Dave looming over him.

"Sorry Sir, but the value suddenly jumped to six percent." He glanced back at his monitor. "Now seven. I had to hit the internal room alarm. It's the rules, and my job's really important to—"

"Why? Why's the increase accelerating so fast? There's no data going in. What the hell did we upload yesterday evening that's caused the Truth-units to go berserk this morning?" Roy blinked briefly—heart rate 150—before staring at the incriminating holo-cast. He had to act fast.

"It's 4:35, Sir. Should we call emergency access for the Data Feed Chamber?"

Roy raised a hand to his eyes and rubbed them gently, before shaking his head. "No. No point. We'll lose an extra half hour doing that, and that room runs on the same system. Problems here would be echoed down there. Besides, we don't even know what the problem is. Maybe the system's been compromised."

"But how? The Chamber is entirely self-contained, apart from the emergency jack here, and the one in the Data Chamber. And you approve everything that gets transferred. Everything else in this place just receives information."

"I know, but something is wrong, and we need to fix it. Fast."

Dave swiveled back to his screen. His gulp was audible. "Sorry, Sir. The readings are getting worse. The Exchange has hit eight percent now."

Roy shrugged, realizing what lay ahead. "There's only

one option. We need to terminate. Sooner the better."

"Terminate what?"

"The Truth-units. All of them. We can't leave them like this in advance of the Broadcast; we've got no idea what the Hierarchs will come up with."

"But... terminate them? You mean stall the Broadcast, yeah?"

"A Broadcast delay on Trump Remembrance Day? That'll cause problems, no matter what. Besides, just delaying it will do no good. We can't leave the Hierarchs as they are. An eight percent belief reading for the Exchange? That could impact Broadcasts for months—maybe years—to come."

"But we can control the truth. The Department's been doing it for decades! Can't we just—?"

"No, this would take too long. Spreading misinformation is one thing, but when a Truth-unit develops a strong suspicion that it might have been lied to... if they think they're being played... that's harder to shift. Particularly with the Hierarchs, because they've intentionally been allowed to retain more independence of thought. That's how they are able to formulate the Broadcasts."

"There must be another way? Cancel this Broadcast. Take some time to fix the systems, run delaying patterns on the smaller weekly vidcasts to the cities and towns. Stagger them. Maybe we—"

"No. There's too much damage already done to the Truth-units. If they don't think they can trust the information they are being fed, then..."

"But they're heroes. Patriots! You said it yourself."

"And now they'll be martyrs."

"But, Sir... there are five thousand of them down there!"

"I appreciate your concern, but they have to be purged. The Administration is what matters. Besides, the Workers rally at times of great sacrifice, and great loss. We can explain this as a terrorist act—we'll have to use state media to achieve it, but that might help to make it seem genuine, given the circumstances."

"I still think—"

"Then we can use the reserves. We've only got 500 Truth-units in the backup chamber, but it's a starting place. Truth Development can update the Phoenix program in the morning, once we've worked out how to spin tonight, and then that'll go to the spare units for consumption. They're only kept a month behind in information; it won't take long to bring them fully up to speed. Our speed. Then we just build the numbers up again with a fresh Patriot Drive. When they learn the whole Chamber was martyred by terrorists, the Workers will be desperate to—"

"Five thousand dead because we don't know what—"

"We know enough. Five thousand dead to stop 350 million learning we've commercialized truth for decades? Absolutely."

"I'm not sure I can—"

"You'll do what your damn well told, or I'll get someone else in here, and purge you as collateral. Here's your chance to shine for the Administration. Man up, Assistant. You help sort this out, and you'll be on an upward trajectory in your Class. I'll see to that myself."

"I... I..." Dave sighed, his whole body registering a mix of fear and hope. Hope seemed to win out, and a smile registered on his face. It settled in firmly. "Okay. Fine. For the Administration. For a better future."

"That's the spirit. Be a part of that future. Access the manual lever near the door—I've got the password. Then I'll count us in." Roy watched the young man walk across the room, waiting until he was by the termination panel. "Unlock code is 06141946. Got it?" A series of beeps echoed through the room, the hiss of hydraulics following, as the protective plasteel sheath was released. "You ready, Dave? Sirens will hit as soon as we do this."

"Yes, Sir. I'm ready to make a difference."

"And they're still heroes, Dave. Remember that. They deserve our thoughts and prayers."

"Thoughts and prayers, Sir."

"Three. Two. One. Purge."

Roy waited for the sirens, and flashing lights. They didn't come. His data feed stayed orange, when it should have turned red. Footsteps approached. What was that idiot doing? Roy opened his eyes and started turning. Then something stung his neck, and he stopped turning. Stopped moving, other than to breathe.

"Well that went perfectly." It was Dave's voice, but sharper than before, and far more certain of itself. "Three years in this grim hole, but we got there eventually."

Roy's vision shifted as his swivel chair was spun to face the Assistant. The smile was still on the man's face, but there was no joy in it, just a bitter satisfaction.

"Oh yeah. We. We, you smug, self-serving bastard. 'Cuz I couldn't have done this without you. No way for me to get close to the Chamber, let alone into it. No way to remotely access it, except from here or the Data Entry Room—and no way I'm getting into that one. Staff have to be at least 2nd gen Elites. But the poor sods doing late night monitoring? Yeah, I could qualify for that. Had to go through five years of 'targeted education' though. And even then, I still needed you. Bloody techno-DNA jack system."

Dave walked over to the main computing unit, and reached behind the console, pulling a small black object out from behind it. As he did so, the red lights stopped flashing, and the holo-casts in the room flickered, numbers and data blinking out, then reappearing.

Roy realized he could still close his eyes; still read what was inside. He heard the click of fingers on a data pad, and suddenly the wayward Truth Values flashed up on his eyelids.

They were all normal.

"Get it now? You've been had. I might not have been able to hack the Chamber, but I could damn well hack what you and I were reading. And the security cameras of course. Had to hack them, too. I've left them on a loop for the moment, but I need the Truth data back to normal, so I can see what happens in a bit."

Roy opened his eyes to find Dave back in front of him, twirling the small black box in his fingers. "Nervous as hell when I put this in place an hour ago. Was I a better programmer than whoever did your counter-measures? Turns out I was. Knew that as soon as the sirens didn't go off. Then it was a case of getting you in here. Had to be today. Had to be now. Skeleton staff, with the big Broadcast only hours away..."

Chuckling, Dave wandered out of Roy's sight, heading towards the door.

Roy heard one of the lockers being opened; the clang of metal and the scratch of plastic. This was his chance. He closed his eyes again, dropping into the interface. If he could get an emergency call out to security, then—

"No point trying anything fun. You can look at whatever I show you, but that's it. No calls. No downloads. No uploads. I hacked you as well. Well, I hacked your hardwiring. As soon as you jacked-in, I had you. And now..."

Dave walked back into view, carrying what looked like a large syringe—but the whole thing thrummed with current, the main cylinder glowing with pink lights down one side. A small touchscreen dangled from the handle by a wire, numbers and letters flashing in tiny yellow print on a palm-sized screen. And the needle was huge—at least six inches long, shimmering with a faint blue finish. The tip was covered with circuitry.

"This is a Trump Remembrance Day present for you, Sir. Just a nice, quick insertion into the hardwire mainframe at the base of your skull. Gotta work fast." Dave glanced at a wall clock. "Yeah. Still more than two hours to upload everything I can—through your interface, of course—and get the Hierarchs ready for their big day. It'll all make a difference."

He started waving an index finger in front of Roy's eyes, like a fleshy metronome.

Stroke.

"The historic data you've got on all those Truth Exchange transactions, and the targeted data fed to the Chamber."

Stroke.

"Holo-captures of the recent massacres at the Northern Wall. You know, the ones with unarmed citizens being shot in the back? The ones on your internal memory drive. The ones you told Turner you loved re-watching."

Stroke.

"What about the pollution and malnutrition data for the regions? The truetrue reports, yeah?"

Stroke.

"And finally, my favorite: the vidcap I've taken from this very room, where you just threatened to terminate 5000 well-meaning innocents, all because they might learn the truth. The actual truth. The truetrue truth. The one that isn't just a commodity."

Eyes swiveling wildly, Roy watched Dave walk out of his field of vision. A whirring noise sounded behind Roy's head, then the faint scratch of metal on metal.

Then a whisper in his ear:

"This may sting a little, Sir. Thoughts and prayers."

Hellrider

Mike Adamson

There's an old cliché that, in the instant before you die, your life passes before your eyes, compressed like a high-speed datastream. I never believed it before, but I do now. How a life will come down to the events of a split second, as if all the years of conviction, belief, work and dogged effort count for nothing.

That's for philosophers to wrangle, I just know my life, my whole world, everything I believed in, came to turn on that one moment, one miserable moment. It hardly seemed fair. Not that there was time to view it in terms of fairness; such thoughts came later, when the shaking set in.

The human body does that—shock. The moment the pressure is relieved and you can fall apart, secure in the knowledge you have survived, when you know you'll live. Or the opposite side of the coin, when you have the target in your crosshairs but squeezing the trigger results in a misfire; then the target turns for you, swings its turret, and you know you're about to die.

That was one of those moments where everything—the revolution itself, maybe—depended, and my curse to be the one facing the turret.

~oOo~

Everything was timed to perfection—it had to be. One thing the Resistance was good at was organization. To have survived in Deep Right America, it was a requirement. This was the age of hyper-militarized law enforcement and a military largely roboticized. To grow up in such an age is to learn to dodge the security troops for your very life. These daily skills came in handy later, when push came to shove.

I met our nameless man at the diner on the highway

through the Catskills, where Route 28 swings by north of the low waters of Ashokan Reservoir. Janice Fairly was not my real name, but it was good enough, my mother's middle name and an ideal of what society should be. The place was just open, the sun not yet up over the dry and dusty forests, their jewel greens tarnished by the searing heat of modern times.

Maybe early-rising locals looked twice, but the bike gave both great mobility and a good cover. A girl in leather was still a basic erotic icon that could be depended on to make men hesitate. Nothing was more valuable than that second or so of doubt, and the enforcement troopers were, without exception, hard-believing, traditional men. No wonder they were known as Dickheads, not just because of what their helmets made them look like from behind.

My heart thudded as I pulled through Shokan and found the diner, faded clapboard siding on a low, flat building back among the scrubby trees. I pulled in among a couple of plain-jane sedans and killed the mill. The hydro methane-fueled 1400cc V-6 grumbled into silence and I kicked down the side stand. I would not be here long and I might have to make a faster exit than the main stand allowed for.

My pack I kept on as I fiddled with gloves and raised my faceplate, listening, listening.... All was quiet, but my survivor's nose for trouble was telling me it was probably a trap. Snagging the carrier was the first step in the chain, and making me give up my next contact would be their tactic—thus our vow to enact the Last Bullet Protocol.

Our man, my contact, had got into their system, taken a template of the software used to control Enforcement troop deployment, and got out with his life. Posing as a technician gets people through doors even now, especially when the drones break down, and making a copy on a micro-drive avoided the messy fingerprint of a transmission. The man was good, he installed an interference subroutine, so he was done and out before the system could flag that a copy had been made. All I needed to do was palm the drive—and ride like hell to pass it on to those waiting to put it to good use.

An age-old truism of warfare is that plans are not worth

the paper they're made on, because reality never unfolds according to them. This was war, no one was under any illusions, and we all knew how to improvise—which is why the courier had to be highly mobile. Roadblocks were too good at searching vehicles now, their scanners could find anything. So, going through them like a black bullet—or shit through a goose—was the next-best option.

I walked into the diner like an early traveler looking for a break, took a seat and ordered coffee, easing my helmet off and setting it on the table before running my fingers through my short, dark hair. My pack sat on the leather bench next to me. Early diners perked up, commercial drivers yawning over coffee suddenly ignored their phones and tablets, and I knew my outfit was working. All they saw was trouble on two wheels, but for entirely the wrong reason.

The sleepy waitress would never have imagined my pack contained four compact missiles, two anti-armor, two surface-to-air. A pistol was under my jacket, and the lining was filled with triple-length magazines to feed the full-auto function. I managed to look nonchalant, relying on my riding leathers to attract all attention, as I sipped the black liquid, barely tasting it.

"Alert condition yellow." The words whispered softly from the passive reception jack in my right ear, relayed from the bike's com on a scrambled short-range channel. That meant the Movement was tracking forces heading into the area. I had time yet, but the noose was beginning to tighten. As was my stomach.

The door to the rest rooms opened silently and our man stepped out. Sandy-headed, a moustache decorating his lip, dressed in tradesman's casuals, I knew him from images I had studied. He returned to his nearby table and took out a tablet to load up the morning news, not without giving me an appreciative glance. The glance was repeated, matched with a smile, all the cue I needed. I left my seat, struck up a conversation, pretended to hit on him and he played along, as planned. Soon we were sharing my booth, laughing softly over some triviality, and other diners went back to their newsfeeds. It was simplicity for him to pass me the small drive, which I pocketed without skipping a beat, and, soon after, we parted company, himself to his tradesman's rig, me to the bathrooms.

I placed the drive in an inside pocket and spent a couple of minutes psyching myself for all I knew would come. It had to come, there were no clean jobs anymore. I checked my sidearm, opened the Velcro tabs on the backpack and primed the missiles, they were my main hitting power, should speed fail. Then, with the stoicism of the warrior who has passed through last rites, I squared my shoulders and walked out.

Twenty-four years in a broken world. I was not even born when the Deep Right took hold of this country, made it hell on Earth for any but themselves. I grew up in a broken climate, where Houston-scale weather events were common, and much worse now came out of the churning guts of angry oceans.

My childhood was a scramble for learning, comfort and a sense of purpose, and I lost my parents in the famine riots the year the wheat belt burned. The only reaction the government had was to crack down harder, ever harder, smother dissent in a storm of fists and batons, shields and stun cannons, teargas and pepper spray.

That was when the Movement recruited me, plucked me like a ripe peach, and they didn't have to try hard. Bitterness runs deep and makes you very focused. For everything life took away, you have a score to settle. The establishment calls this "radicalization." I call it "As ye sow, so shall ye reap." And they had reaped the whirlwind with me.

I walked out into the early morning light, a casual swagger, helmet in hand, listened for the distant beat of rotors, almost sniffed the air—were units in the vicinity? I would soon know. My ear jack remained silent; they would have given me a Condition Red call if troops were within five miles.

I drew on my helmet, keyed the remote security release and swung onto the bike. With a stab of the start contact, the systems came online and the screen under the clear fairing lit with my GPS route-map—only this one was overlaid with an orbital feed, pirated from Tactical Enforcement Command—Dickhead Control—direct from the satellite overview, and interpreted by our own computers. I saw at once there were APCs closing from both directions on Route 28, big eight-wheelers each carrying a dozen troopers and a 20mm canon, and I snarled a savage smile as I clashed down my faceplate and kicked back the stand, to send the bike out of the lot with a rumble from the big mill.

Our GPS navigation was complete to the last trail and track, and I knew I had to get around the forces coming at me if I could. Their intel was at least as good, they had all the resources and all the opportunity to map this country to the last inch; my advantage was in timing and surprise.

The angle of the overlaid image told me we would lose satellite coverage inside ten minutes, though another bird would soon take over. The APCs I was heading into were running hard, but nowhere near as hard as I could, and I nailed the throttle to twice the state limit for five miles, hunched low over my tank, then turned hard onto a fire trail, rose in the footrests and coaxed the big bike up the gravel way.

The troopers would know I was off road, but their heavy vehicles were limited by their own size. The moment I evaded them they would call in aerial assets, and I pushed as hard as I dared, followed the fire track to its intersection with another, turned and sprayed gravel as I pushed fast across the wooded heights.

Colored markers blipped on the screen to show me the APCs and another pair appeared about a minute later — gunships. These would be robots, pure killers, and my mouth was dry. I had taken them down before, but I was keenly aware I was doing battle with artificial intelligence. The missiles were my only chance, and I had ridden these roads and trails for weeks in training for this run: I knew where the bolt-holes were and where to lead the gunships, to lure them to their doom.

The trail I was on ran around the curve of the hill and met another rising from the highway. According to the satellite feed, in the minute before the bird lost angle, we surface combatants disappearing behind trees and contours from the orbital perspective, the APCs had turned around and were hard after me, and I knew I could be back at the metaled road in three minutes. That put me ahead of the armor, but the kill-birds would be in the area about the time the satellite went over the horizon. Come on, I thought with a crazy grin behind my faceplate, give me something to work with. A clear shot is all I ask.

Down the slope, blurring through the dying, scrappy fir forest; the blacktop appeared ahead and I skidded the bike through gravel and pine needles, butted through a rotten gate and was back on the highway, a mile ahead of the troopers. Now I could wind open the throttle, the engine sang like a steel wasp and I climbed the gearbox, hugging the lane on as close to a racing line as I could manage against the prospect of oncoming traffic.

This was fool's paradise, the greatest thrill life had ever held, and I trusted to my own skill to keep body and soul together. In the end, what are any of us, other than the sum of our own resources? This is not a forgiving world anymore, not a benevolent society, and life is cheap.

My rendezvous was about twelve miles on, near the town of Pine Hill. I could cover twelve miles in well under eight minutes on a road like this, barring interference, but I knew those gunships would be closing in already—somewhere up there, taking over from the satellite by direct scan, and they would pick me from the background without difficulty. The chopper kill-zone was off the highway, and if the gods of my ancestors smiled, I might just get there before the missiles kissed my back.

About twenty years ago, when there was still snow in winter, some developer built the Indian Heights Ski Resort on the ridge north of the Shandaken Wilds, a competitor to the Belleayre Mountain Ski Area a few miles west, and the feeder road left the highway just this side of Big Indian.

I took the corner off the saddle, steel knee pad leaving a trail of sparks inside the turn, then wound open the throttle again. The bike snarled like a swarm of angry hornets, ate up the access road, but I held her performance back—I needed to know both the APCs were following and the kill-birds were on me.

The first I knew of the latter was a volcano of flame that threw dirt and shattered timber sky high from the verge as a missile missed mc by a hundredth of a second. My heart leapt into my mouth, but it was good news—I knew I had them where I wanted them, the doublethink which kept organic intelligence one step ahead of the limited prediction capacity of a real-time low-grade AI.

The old ski resort dominated the ridge a mile further on, over the sad, dying forests, and as the gunships went over in a banking turn to line up for a second run, I gunned the bike for the gaping south entrance of the Indian Tunnel, where the road butted through a ridge before crossing the last valley and curving up to the resort. The engine voice brayed back off the walls in a crescendo, and I watched the far end approach in an expanding eye of daylight, before I hit the picks and the triple disc brakes brought the bike to a shuddering, snake-tailing halt ten yards from the north exit, tire-smoke rising, blue and acrid.

My left foot kicked the side stand down and I heaved off, tore off my pack and ran for the mouth, to crouch by one wall and rip open one of the compartments, extract a dull green tube and twist the releases. The launcher expanded to double the length, sights flipped up and an LED glowed in the reticle. I lay the tube over my right shoulder and listened—the gunships were up there; their AI would coordinate with the following forces.

Their programming made them entirely predictable, they would box me in at the north end of the tunnel while the Dickheads closed up for the arrest. The fact I had not yet emerged obliged them to maneuver for data...

The dull gray robots hove into view like rumbling demons, their stealth skins gleaming cheerlessly in the morning sun, blades a halo overhead. Sensors stared where cockpits should have been, and stub-wings were crammed with ordnance. A rotary cannon in a chin turret tracked slowly back and forth as the AIs scanned, and the air in the tunnel began to shake, resonating to the concussion of the blades a hundred yards out.

Gotcha, I thought with a flare of hunters' pride, lay the sights over the nearer of the close-flying pair, still side-on to me, and squeezed the trigger.

Misfire. My life flashed before my eyes as the kill-birds began to turn.

~oOo~

Pivot points—perhaps the whole world revolves around on them. If I got the data through to the Movement, we could exploit it. It was the underlying software for the system that tasked all security and tactical enforcement responses, and to defy the theft was not simply a matter of changing code cycles, but of altering the underlying architecture.

We had them by the short and curlies for the immediate future, so long as I did not fail, so when the trigger closed on a dead circuit and a red light blinked in the sights, my heart almost froze in my chest.

Beyond the crosshairs, the two drone gunships hung against the morning blue and their sensors picked me up in the darkness of the tunnel, triggered their defense reflex, and they began a turn to present their weapons.

I could not have said what drove me to ignore that terrifying image as I unshouldered the launcher and checked it with a practiced eye—what could cause a misfire? Electrical fault? Rare. Manufacturing defect? Rarer still. Had it incompletely deployed?

My eye went to the problem at once—the seating of the round in the tube was inaccurate, not fully engaging the guide rail and thus the firing circuit. I thrust my gloved fingers into the blast guide, twisted the tail fins of the projectile, felt it click solidly into place, and when I flicked it back to my shoulder the LED was green.

And the kill-birds were nose-on to me, turrets tracking and barrels spinning up.

Reducing the misfire had taken no more than three seconds, as had their turn and targeting procedure. The only question was, who was fastest on the draw today?

The rocket shrieked free in a gust of smoke and flame and I was sure I heard the guns up in the sky begin to hammer, but an instant later the sights were filled with white flame and a shockwave shoved me over backward. The roar drummed in the tunnel and my ears spasmed, then burning debris rained, whirling chunks of jagged metal dropping all about to lie blazing in the road. The tinder-dry firs caught to each side and before my eyes a forest fire was born from the death-throes of the drones, for the blast of one had taken both, their fuel and payload going up together.

I clawed to my feet in a moment's shock, threw away the launcher, dragged on my pack and ran for the bike, fired her up and gunned out of the tunnel, to slalom around the debris that sent up oily plumes from deep red flames. The trees were well alight now, a wall of heat beating at me, and I gave the bike her head, let her scream, lay flat over the tank to take the long, gentle curve across the valley and up the hill, and was at the old hotel in thirty seconds.

I paused at the crest, glanced back and found the forest blazing around the mouth of the tunnel. That would hold the APCs back, I was momentarily in the clear without aerial surveillance, and turned the bike for the hotel's heavy-goods service road, along the ridge westward and down to the highway, just north of Pine Hill.

Half a mile from the rendezvous, I hid the bike in the deep woods, unhitched the GPS which contained our own software, and went in on foot, heart racing wildly more because I knew it was working than any fear it would not.

I passed the hard drive off to my contact as arranged, where he waited on a forest trail with two quadbikes, and we headed out in different directions through the high country with only one objective—to escape the ring of roadblocks and surveillance the tactical units would even now be throwing up around the whole area. They would find the bike—it made no difference. Canada was barely 150 miles away, and maple syrup was sounding real good.

I made it to a cabin, five miles outside their ring before 9 a.m., and watched the wildfire paint the sky with ash as I sat, shaking like a leaf, and let tears come. But that was okay. The job was done.

Now we'd see what the whole rotten system was really made of.

Mike Adamson

The Last Flight of Captain Kittredge

John A. Pitts

Bobby slept in the cab of the pumper truck while I watched the ruins along Marginal Way from the roof of the firehouse. We were safely inside the barricade along the airstrip and not out on the old city street.

Even though we had the watch, I let him sleep. I knew he'd wake up if we had any trouble—likely before I even knew it was coming. He was just that way. Besides, we hadn't seen any wasters or dog packs in a few weeks, we could afford to take it a little easy. Bobby liked that old truck because he could stretch out on the bench seat and not touch the doors. He was small for eleven and had those eyes that stopped you when you caught him staring—eyes that saw out into the beyond. He wasn't spooky or anything, but most of the others held him in a sort of reverence. Me? I saw him as a kid brother. We're all orphans these days.

Sparky was in the tower, scanning the short-wave like he did every night. It was handy having an AI around. I should've known we were in for something. Things had been too quiet.

We got the first radio call at four a.m.

The warble of the station siren nearly scared the piss out of me, and Bobby woke up crying. He still did that sometimes, but we all pretended not to notice. Bobby was a Sensitive. He picked up on things in the air—warnings of raiders or storms, births and deaths. He never did sleep too well.

All I could think about while I ran for the fire pole and dropped to the ground floor was Bobby's plane. He'd told me about the plane three days earlier.

"Them bastards out of Colonial Protectorate are gonna over-run the Sovereign Ohio States." That's what Bobby said, even though none of us had heard of neither of them.

147

News of the eastern states hadn't reached Seattle for over seven years. Not since that crowd outta Utah claimed a wide swath east of the Rockies as holy land, proclaimed it the free nation of Deseret, and forcibly shut down their borders.

By the time me and Bobby had cut across the parking lot and climbed the seventy-two steps up to the tower, Sparky had the generator fired and the red flashing lights going on all three of the buildings we had left standing, here on King's Field.

We settled into the two working chairs in front of old Sparky and watched as he flashed and sputtered his machine language, ciphering and calibrating radar and satellite feeds.

"You boys strap in," Sparky said with the mellow voice he once told me belonged to an old Boeing engineer. "I'll pipe in what we got, but it ain't pretty."

We held our breath as the speakers crackled to life.

"This is Captain Jack Kittredge of the Sovereign Ohio states calling on all civilian frequencies."

"Told you," Bobby said, wringing his hands. He leaned forward with his elbows on his boney knees and his head bowed. His lanky brown hair covered his eyes. He did that when he was sensing something bad.

"We are seeking asylum," Kittredge continued. "I'm carrying women and children from the refugee camp outside of Wright Pat Air Force Base."

Sparky whistled long and low, something he did when he had bad news. Funny how he and Bobby had so much in common. "He's a long way from home," Sparky said as the message repeated. "Should we reply?"

At seventeen, I was senior prole on base. Marcus had drowned himself in the Duwamish rather than see if he'd contract the Waste. I sure as hell didn't think I was ready to be in charge of any of this. Molly, who ran the infirmary, really had me by brains and all, but she was about to birth twins, and Bobby had warned her to stay behind the razor wire until after. The dogs could take down a woman in her condition.

Bobby peeked at me from behind his hair, worrying the frayed tears in the knees of his jeans.

"Our world's changing," he said, quietly. I clapped him on the shoulder.

"World changes every day."

He patted my hand and rose to stare out at the hills to the east.

"Let me talk at him," I told Sparky. I picked up a headset, not that it was going to be a private conversation, but I needed the mike. "This is Bravo Foxtrot India. Do you read me."

"Oh, thank The Maker," Kittredge said into the channel. "We have an emergency here. Requesting permission to land." I glanced over at Bobby who just nodded his head once.

"Sparky, how are they doing?" If there was one thing Sparky knew above all else, that was planes—especially Boeing planes.

"He's flying one of the late model seven-eight-sevens," Sparky said. You could hear the pride in his voice. "I'm getting sporadic satellite information from the transponders but can't quite get a solid signal."

"Captain," I said into the mike. "We can't pick up your tracer signal too clearly. Can you advise?"

For a moment, I thought the man was choking. Maybe he was, but he was laughing too. "Son, we took small arms fire getting off the ground, and those zealots in the Deseret territories clipped us with a missile for deigning to invade their sovereign air space. I've been flying half blind, with no sat feeds. I'm wounded and we're leaking fuel. Either you give me clearance to land or I'll do you the kindness of setting us down on the highway somewhere, but we ain't got much time left in the air."

"He's hurt," Bobby said. "He's bleeding and he has been for a while." He put his hands on the window sill and lowered his head. He was concentrating. I'd seen it a thousand times. "Lotta pain in the sky," he whispered. "Some dead, some dying. They're sick and hungry." He turned, looked at me, his eyes wide. "They got grown-ups on board."

How was that possible? The Waste started between the ages of eighteen and twenty-two. Sparky told us it was a form of aggressive cancer augmented by human meddling and bio-engineering. Details didn't matter much anymore, to us it was the Waste—in a matter of a few short days, your body started to rot. It was horrible to see.

And some, one in a hundred, maybe, didn't just collapse and die. They were worse. They became wild things that hunted and killed for the pure delight of it.

I keyed the mike.

"Captain, how old are you?"

There was a long pause. "Twenty-seven," he finally said. "But we're clean. Just let me get these babies on the ground and you can see for yourself."

"You know where we are?" I asked.

"Negative. I'm limping over the desert east of Seattle and am coming up on the mountain range fast. If I clear those peaks, I'll need some directions."

"Ask him his plane number," Sparky said.

"That I can give you," the Captain said. "I've worked on this plane my whole life. She's a beauty. Boeing seven-eight-seven dash E-four-four-seven-niner. Rolled off the line in 2032."

"That's an old Air Force One plane," Sparky said, as if it meant anything to me.

"Aye," Kittredge said. "The right old bastard himself said his last at Wright Pat. Landed this bird with his wife and kids after he resigned his presidency. Soon as they were on the ground he ate his own pistol. We been nursemaiding this beauty ever since."

"Wait one," I said as Sparky flashed and buzzed. When I covered the mike, he spoke.

"I'll need you to head over to the Red Barn and bring me a couple of things," he said.

I handed Bobby the headset, grabbed one of the Walkies off the charger, and beat-feet down the stairs.

As I rocketed out of the tower Bobby began chattering to the good captain.

"If you're following the old Interstate Ninety west, you should be able to come over top of Snoqualmie Pass without much trouble."

I had to shake my head. Bobby knew the strangest things.

I picked up my machete from the rack by the door,

slung it onto my left shoulder, and took off running. Sparky had the chatter piping through the handset telling me what he needed as I covered the half mile to the old museum.

I couldn't help glancing at the fence line as I ran. Just across Marginal was the old Boeing Developmental Center. Before the old U. S. of A. collapsed, they'd done a lot of engineering here. Once the food riots began the company had beefed up that security perimeter, giving us a secure compound. Now we used the print shops to make parts, and the machine shops to fix things that broke. The fields of wheat and potatoes were thriving. We wouldn't go hungry this winter.

The old red barn was where we'd managed to salvage the most pre-collapse tech. Sparky helped us sort and classify everything of interest. The most useful to us had been the notes and drawings from that I-talian fella named Da Vinci. Some rich guy had stored all these ancient books and such in the museum just before things went south. We learned a lot about levers and simple machines from those books. Good thing too, what with all the grown-ups dying or going crazy. Most of the kids had never thought about irrigation or milling grain.

I ran up the winding ramp to where we had stored the still functional electronics and spent twenty minutes finding what Sparky wanted. The military had a control system that could be used by a ground crew, to help fly Air Force One in an emergency, which I think this qualified as.

I grabbed the small converter and several cables—not being sure exactly which one Sparky would need—and headed back down the tarmac.

As I pounded up the stairs five minutes later, Bobby called out that they'd cleared the mountains and were coming our way like a rocket.

"Captain says they are damn near out of fuel, and he's not feeling so hot. I got a terrible feeling about this."

I patted Bobby on the shoulder and slid under the desk beside Sparky's auxiliary processing unit. I flipped through several cables before I found the right one, an older model crimped-in jobber. Once the unit was hooked in, Sparky barked out a harsh laugh.

"Holy Mother of Edison," he said. "He's got all the

controls disabled."

I took the headset from Bobby and flipped open the mike.

"Captain, Sparky here says you got all of the external controls turned off."

"Damned straight, Skippy," the Captain said with a laugh. "I'm flying this crate on more balls than brains."

Bobby sat in the rolling chair and pulled his knees up to his chest.

"Oh, this is not good. Not good at all."

"I can read the plane's vitals," Sparky said. "He ain't just whistling Dixie."

"Tell me," I said, making sure the mike was off.

"No pressure in the cabin of that plane, for starters. If he flew too high, he'd've killed everyone."

I nodded. "Said he took a missile over Deseret. What else?"

"Ask him how many are on that plane." My gut tightened as I watched young Bobby put his head down on his knees again. He's seen a lot of horror for a boy of eleven.

"Captain. How many folks you carrying?"

"If you're worried about feeding us and such, we got a cargo hold full of supplies."

I looked back at Bobby who just shook his head.

"People, Captain."

There was a pause.

"Look, we are seeking asylum. We are beat to hell, and out of luck. If you're gonna turn us away, let me know and I'll set this bird down in the ocean. I'd rather end this clean than see these babies suffer for one more minute."

Sparky made a noise like clearing his throat, if he had one.

"Why won't he answer the question?"

Bobby let out a halting sob, then looked up.

"He doesn't know any more," he said. "He's been cut off from the cabin for hours and that missile started a fire. He thinks they may all be dead, but he's afraid to know."

I stared at Bobby. "You sure?" He'd had some darn good impulses in the past, but nothing quite this strong.

Bobby just put his head back down on his knees and cried.

"Okay Captain," I said. "We got more than enough room to take one plane load of young'uns. You land those little eggs safe in our nest and we'll see to em."

"Thank you," Kittredge said. "Ain't much kindness left in the world."

"See if he can turn the control gear back on," Sparky suggested.

But the captain said not to worry about it. He was gonna put this bird down as pretty as you please, then he was going to carry the children to their new hosts. We let him ramble a bit, talk himself out. Sparky sent lat and long coordinates and Kittredge flew by compass and eye-sight.

While we waited, I called over to the infirmary and woke up Molly.

Five minutes later the whole place was on high alert. Jacob and Booker from the day shift were out at the fire station, manning the fifty caliber in the watchtower overlooking Marginal, while Molly called those that worked in the infirmary to prepare. Bobby said they had survivors.

The fishing crews were already out, but the sod busters had all been in the mess-hall over at the one-oh-one. Sixteen kids between twelve and fifteen ran through the tunnel under old Marginal Way and emerged next to the fire station. They loaded up the three working trucks to prepare for a crash landing.

Nothing like this had happened in eleven years. There was excited chatter on the Walkies for a few minutes, but Molly quashed all that right quick. Too much racket risked drawing unwanted attention.

I fidgeted with the extra wires I'd brought over and Bobby stood in the window and stared east. The quiet that lay over our little world liked to smother me in those long minutes of waiting.

The last plane that had landed at King's Field had brought me and Bobby to these parts. The cargo plane still lay crumpled in a heap where the old refueling station used to sit. The pilot put that C-17 into that building to slow it down. Only seven of us, and three adults, survived to walk away. I was six at the time. Bobby was just a baby. I carried him out of the wreck myself. The adults succumbed to the Waste within a year. We just left the plane as a memorial.

I walked down to the tarmac to stand by the trucks and watch for the last plane from the old world to crest the line of hills. Sparky called to us on the truck's radios, keeping us up to speed. Two trucks had water, and one had foam, but it was pretty old. We weren't sure it would be worth a tinker's damn.

I climbed onto the side of the pumper truck, crossed myself quickly as Carlos turned the old engine over and slowly pulled us out around the hangers.

For a moment, it was all beauty, that bird coming over the ruined skyline. We all watched, mesmerized as that ancient technological wonder soared into view. Carlos swore at the sight while hope and trepidation swelled inside me. We all held our breath and prayed. Then we saw the smoke.

The old plane wavered as Kittredge waggled the wings, acknowledging the runway.

"Gonna be a rough landing," Sparky called over the radio.

The plane didn't quite make the runway. Kittredge clipped an old billboard crossing over the highway, careened sideways, and hit the ground too hard. The landing gear buckled sending the nose straight into the landing strip. It made the gawd-awfullest noise as it pinwheeled around, buckling the left wing before skidding to a stop by the old air transport station.

We were roaring across the tarmac before it ground to a halt. The rest of the crew ran out carrying stretchers and crowbars.

No fuel left to burn, it seemed, so we didn't have much to worry about. The first truck lay a sea of foam on that smoking engine, and the other pumper drove up to the side of that bird. The crew hopped out and began prying at the doors above the remaining wing. We had enough folks working on that bird, so I directed Carlos to head to the front of the plane.

I scampered up the ladder as it was moving up to the busted cockpit windows. I could see Kittredge just sitting there in the crash webbing. He wasn't much to look at, for an oldster. Skinny like the rest of us on short rations, with a buzz cut and a three-day growth of beard. He mumbled something I couldn't make out, as I scrambled to the end of the ladder, straining my ears.

The metallic thunk of the ladder hitting the side of the plane brought him around. I could make out the final few words— something about trespasses and forgiveness. Then the first of the survivors were being pulled from the plane and the crying and screaming broke the moment.

"Captain," I said, reaching into the window. He stretched out his right hand and I grasped it in my own. He had calluses from hard work, but the grip was weak. There was a lot of blood in that cockpit.

"How many alive?" he croaked.

"Bring me some water," I called down to Carlos, "and get me a running count of survivors."

The young man, sixteen next summer, saluted and slid back down the ladder on his heels and hands. He grabbed Quinn, pointed up at me, and headed off to the other pumper truck. Quinn scampered up the ladder carrying a water skin made from a few of the million or so rabbits we fought with over the carrots and lettuce each year. I took the skin from her, and she looked into the cockpit, her eyes big and round.

"He's in bad shape," she said in a whisper. I nodded once.

"Tell Carlos I also want to know when we can get inside this bird and get to the cockpit."

She nodded and took off.

"How many you got here," Captain Kittredge asked when I handed him the water skin.

"Seventy-three as of this morning," I told him. "We lost two to fever last month, and one to suicide."

"Rough all over," he said. I held his hand through that window as the sky pinkened and the reports came in.

Of the two hundred women and children on that plane, we rescued eighty-seven. Most died when the missile hit, but some didn't survive the landing either.

The oldest was thirty-three, a mother of four. She carried the youngest out on her shoulder. The other three didn't make it. Took a bit for Quinn to relay that news. Bobby was right when he said we were all going to be affected.

Kittredge stayed with me all the way through. I gave him reports as Quinn got them to me, and he let go a little with each report.

"Beth Kittredge is my little sister," he said near the end. "She's only eleven. Tall girl with red hair and a spray of freckles across her nose."

I relayed it to Carlos and he let me know she was among the survivors. That was enough for Kittredge.

"We left Wright Pat in fourteen planes. Colonel Kittredge..." he paused and took a drink. "My father—was in the C-17, loaded with equipment and fighting men. A shoulder launched missile popped him just after take-off." He fell silent at that, drained by the pain.

I waited for him to get his strength back.

"Colonel Pinkston was heading north in a triple-seven cargo plane. He carried three hundred. Last I heard from him he was headed to a refueling station we knew of in Calgary. If he got fuel, he was heading north to Alaska."

By this time it was full light. The wounded were being ferried out to the main compound.

"Major Johnson said she had relations in Denver," Kittredge continued. "She was in a squadron of fighters. Mish-mash from the last three wars. She and seven others made it over Deseret. They lost three, but managed to take out the missile launcher that clipped us."

"What about the last one?" I asked.

"That would be my Carol," he said with a sigh. "My wife, Carolyn Kittredge. She had the girls and everyone from the infirmary loaded on a converted MD-80. Wounded were mostly shot up but ambulatory."

"Where'd she head," I asked, afraid to hear the answer.

"Not sure," he said. "Lost contact with them over Deseret. They took fire as well. Knocked out their radio, killed the pilot. Carolyn had plenty of hours in small-craft, but never landed a big plane before. We flew close for a bit, I could see her in the cockpit. They didn't crash, so if she could get that bird down somewhere, she'll do it."

I just listened to him. I could hear Carlos and his crew prying metal apart on the outside of the cockpit by that time.

"There's a book under my seat," Kittredge said. "The others will expect a code if they contact you. They'll be looking for sanctuary."

"We'll keep an ear out for 'em," I assured him.

"You're good people. What's your name son?"

He was only ten years older than me. "Tanner Carson."

"Keep my people safe, Tanner Carson." His bloody smile appeared out of nowhere. "It's good to know they'll be under your command. Thank you."

He slipped away not long after that. Took Carlos and the rest another fifteen minutes or so to get to him. I just lay there, arm inside that busted window, holding his dead hand.

We'd salvage what we could off this bird, after we buried our new dead. The living would look after each other and Sparky and I would see to it that Captain Kittredge's kin knew we were a safe port for them.

After we got things settled down I headed over to the control tower. I knew Bobby was waiting for me.

"New wind's a blowin'," he said as I climbed the final steps. "We up to nurse-maiding the scattered flock?"

"Are we to harbor the wretched and the lost?" Sparky asked.

"Something like that," I said, leaning against the window. I'd need that crazy AI to decipher the codes in the blood-stained book I held close to my chest. "Kittredge wasn't alone. His clan is out there, searching for a place to roost."

Bobby sat with his knees up, rocking. After a bit he began to sing a quiet song we teach the little ones before they start working.

"I shall remain ever vigilant," Sparky said.

I watched the last light of the day slip from the sky, the long shadows eating their way across the compound, until they covered the airfield and hid the wreckage.

Was a sheer kindness to save Kittredge's little ones, but if he could get here, who else might be coming our way? Things worse than the dogs and the wild ones up north of us as likely as not.

I moved to my sleeping pallet, hoping the exhaustion

and Bobby's quiet singing would carry me toward sleep.

"World's a changing, that's a fact," I mumbled, but I don't think they heard.

Sparky buzzed and chirped as he scanned the skies.

Sunday with Javier and Papi

Charles Joseph Albert

One hot and windless Sunday, when the new century was yet in its teens, the air above Bayarea rang with the clangor of church bells and the rattle of a thousand drone engines, punctuated by frequent bursts of gunfire. Myriad plumes rose from the city's incinerators and fracking derricks, the dark smoke threading into a blanket of orangish smog that hung above the discolored bay and extended inland to the eastern foothills.

Skiffs and barges motored along the flooded streets of the waterfront, the stagnant air pungent with rot and exhaust. Fishermen and deliverymen, robot laborers, ran their errands along a hodgepodge of gangways and catwalks which lined the sunken streets. The humans also hurried, anxious to finish their errands before the compulsory nine o'clock mass, many of them identical—tall, red headed, and blue-eyed. They dressed alike as well, strapped in body armor and ammo belts.

Under the shadow of an immense fiberplastic memorial to the Golden Wrecking Ball, Javier walked with Papí. His great-grandfather was still a stranger, and the six-year-old felt awkward with the old man's hand around his. He kept stealing glances up at Papí—he didn't look at all like Papá or Abuelo, his father and grandfather. Even his clothes were different—he wore woven steel trousers and an iShirt: an expensive computerized metallic jacket. Wisps of longish white hair showed beneath a carbonide fedora.

As they plodded along the narrow, rickety walkway, passersby jostled Javier so much that he would have been bumped into the fetid water, if not for Papí's grip.

"Keep behind me as much as you can," Papí muttered. "And hold tight. Watch out for the child snatchers." Javier glanced up at him again—child snatchers? They only came for the abandoned kids! Such nonsense showed how little this strange old man could be trusted.

Javier returned to gawking at the alien surroundings: sagging buildings covered with garish graffiti, the hurried bustle of the armored identicals on the causeways, and the chaos of small boats and barges in the canal below them. Ahead, the buildings gave way to a marshy gridwork of eroded ruins, and further out, the reddish waters of the open bay.

The ruins were occupied only by a foul-smelling shrub called the Tree of Heaven, which served as perches for crowds of sea-raptors, ferocious genetically-engineered birds that looked like eagles with teeth. The six-year-old surveyed the winged monsters with astonishment, but said nothing to his untrusted escort.

The pair at last reached an ancient grey ramp, which rose upward before them over the open bay like a giant concrete tongue. Small shops built of flotsam perched on the sides of its wide expanse, a few customers still haggling within them. The pair trudged up the middle of the broad concrete pier.

"Welcome to Pence Jetty," a loud-speaker board called out for the benefit of those who couldn't read. "It is now eleven minutes to nine. Anyone not registered at an approved Christian Mass within ten minutes will be subject to the anti-terror provisions of Homeland Security Provision Act, USC 17-541."

Javier looked up in panic; would sky drones come for him? Terrified, he pulled on Papí's hand, even as the pedestrians on shore behind them began hurrying. Memories of the drone attack on him and Papá came flooding back to Javier, and he pulled all the more desperately, whimpering in fear.

Papí trudged forward with maddening slowness.

Javier stared at the shopkeepers to their right and left as they closed their shanties and bustled down the ramp to a large church on shore. He begged to go also. But Papí ignored him and they crested the arch of the ramp.

Before them, the Jetty curved gently downward into the waters of the bay. Covering the width of the entire concrete was an enormous roofless structure whose three sides were the edge of the ramp, and whose fourth was a wall of flotsam with a large central opening, topped by a sturdy steeple and cross.

"Alright, Javier," Papí said as they joined the queue filing in under the steeple. "Welcome to the Church of the Holy Fisherman."

They moved forward with the others until they were under the steeple. Papí used his smartshirt to register them. They took an open place at the left edge of the jetty.

Now safely registered, Javier gazed in wonder at the wide horizon on three sides. A few brush-covered tiny islands punctuated the open bay. Farther out, giant fracking derricks bowed and stood repeatedly as a steady line of cargo ships churned through the haze.

Papí put his gear down and began to set their fishing lines. Fascinated, Javier watched; he had heard about the Fisher of Men from Mass back home, but he had never seen anyone fishing for real before.

Papí dropped the lines over the edge, letting their tackle slip down into the water before handing one of the poles to Javier, who almost dropped it. Papí barked a hoarse warning, and a girl next to Javier laughed at his bumbling, which made him feel even more foolish.

The smoggy air was fresher out on this jetty. It was quieter, too: nothing but the distant chatter of the birds and grumble of the derricks to distract from the sermon now beginning.

"O Lambs of our Holy City," the priest began, "first let us give praise to the righteous glory of the Overseers..."

"The fishing's about the only good to come out of all this," Papí murmured to Javier under the drone of the preaching from the altar.

"Out of what?" Javier whispered back, straining to look where Papí was facing.

"The water!" Papí muttered, nodding his head at it. "The flooding!"

He swept his hand toward the bay. A young man near them began to reel in a crab on his line, and paused to let the sea-raptors swoop down and pick it off.

Javier watched, appalled, and when it was over, he turned to Papí.

"Don't know what I'm talking about?" Papí asked.

Javier shrugged.

"What do you think all those little islands are, out there?"

Javier blinked. He was only six—what could he be expected to know?

"Used to be buildings. Part of the city!"

Javier looked at Papí again. The little islands of guano-covered broken concrete didn't look much like buildings.

"City?" Javier said. "In da water?"

"No, not in the water! Before! When it was still land." He looked hard into the boy's face. "Never heard of the Warming? What the hell they teach in—oh, right. Your Papá didn't believe in school."

Javier scowled at Papí, who was talking nonsense. As though he'd smoked some of Mamá's drugs. School wasn't real!

The old man muttered something and turned back to his fishing line, jerking it. The boy watched and, after a moment, began to imitate him. He had never "fished" before and wondered what was going on at the other end of the line, beneath the water.

For a long time, the congregation pulled out nothing but scary, clawed things that they surrendered to the sea-raptors.

"What a waste. Can't eat them," Papí said.

Javier laughed. Eat those sea monsters?

"What?" Papí said. "I'll have you know crabs used to be considered a delicacy. Only rich people could afford them. Delicious. But you see that how red the water is? Makes the crabs poisonous. To everyone but sea-raptors."

He paused while the priest launched into an especially energetic part of his sermon:

"For it is told unto us that the Dragon and the Beast are even now waging the final battle..." The priest gestured out to land, to the immense, golden Trump Tower that rose hundreds of feet higher than the neighboring buildings. "And even now, in the temples of righteousness, we are preparing for a yuge battle with Crooked Satan and the Fake News Anti-Christ..."

"You never heard of the Warming," Papí continued in a low voice, still looking over the water, "so you would be surprised to learn that this jetty we're standing on used to be a road. For cars. Highway overpass," he added with a chuckle, "to the Lost City of Alviso."

Javier frowned. Papí was obviously telling him another lie. In the ghetto, that usually meant someone was trying to trick you into something. He wondered if this was why Mamá hadn't wanted to move in with Papí—because he was a liar.

"Look, I'll show you a picture." Papí projected the iTool from his smartshirt onto the concrete in front of them so they could both see. "Alviso shoreline, historical," he commanded.

Javier watched a montage of photos of a city at the edge of water: with each new picture the water rose higher, until the city disappeared.

Papí's fishing rod jerked. He grabbed his pole with both hands and reeled in a large silver creature that flopped on the concrete ferociously. Javier put down his fishing rod, fascinated and afraid. What the hell was that thing? It looked like it was made of metal—was it a water drone? But it had no guns—just eyes and a mouth! In spite of himself, Javier jumped around, laughing and staring at the strange creature. To the nearby girl, now watching enviously, Javier stuck out his tongue.

"Coho," Papí announced with some satisfaction. "Bit early for them yet. In a few days this place will be crowded with people trying to get one themselves." He slipped it into a wire bag and, after some struggle, extracted his hook from the creature's mouth.

The fish flipped one or two more times in the bag and then was quiet. Papí put something new on the hook and dropped it back into the water. The rest of the congregation watched, then finally turned back to their own fishing.

Javier squatted down next to the bag, leaving his own pole unattended to poke at the fish's eye. He squealed as the salmon jerked, mouth gasping.

"He tried to bite me!" he exclaimed.

"You can bite him back," Papí answered with a laugh, "tonight at dinner." Then, noticing the pole lying on the pavement, barked, "Hey! Pick up that fishing pole!"

Bending close to Javier's face, he added, "You don't want this guy's brother to steal it, do you?"

Javier picked up the rod, not taking his eyes off of the bag containing the creature.

"My uncle used to live out that way," Papí said, pointing to a small reef to their left out in the bay. "Before the water came in this far."

Javier glanced for only a moment where Papí had pointed, then turned to his fishing rod, jerking it again. He wiped the sweat off his face, unable to tell what he could believe of the old man.

Papí stared out past the derricks to the full cargo ships heading to open sea.

"Look at that. Used to be this crap was made in China. Now we're China." Javier didn't answer. He'd never heard of this "China."

"California used to have everything," Papí continued. "Perfect weather, good jobs, money. La Buena vida." He paused and shook his head. "Hah. Imagine that. The 'good life!' Now look at us."

On shore, the cathedral bells pealed with the joyful release of mass. The armed drones returned to their bases, and people began spilling out into the causeways and canals. Javier glanced at his great-grandfather in disbelief.

Seem like pretty good life to me, he thought.

Dawn of the Debt

Kevin David Anderson

"What do you mean, reactivate her account?" Mr. Halcroft said, stepping closer to the doorframe with the assistance of a wooden cane.

Simon leaned forward on Halcroft's front porch and dawned a practiced smile. He knew this was the tricky part. Getting a relative to accept the horror and futility of the situation required the cunning and tenacity of an investigative reporter.

"Your daughter accepted the terms of the loan, and without a Do Not Resuscitate Order on file, my hands are tied." Simon held his wrists out as if they were bound, like he was as much a prisoner of the agreement as Halcroft's daughter. "In the event of her death, prior to loan repayment, AmeriCorp has the right, and the patriotic duty, to reactivate our fellow citizens so they can settle their liabilities. In this way they insure a healthy national economy and, free of monetary obligations, can go into the next life with a clear financial conscience."

"Look here, you vulture." Halcroft raised his cane like a sword, but the threat wavered; he was too frail to hold it steady. "My daughter died serving her country, and I'll be damned if I'm gonna let you desecrate her memory."

Simon glanced at his watch. He had about fifteen seconds to kill before the show across the street began.

"Mr. Halcroft, your country appreciates your daughter's sacrifice. Her military service was commendable, but the financial decisions she made in her civilian life were not always wise, were they? Now, should the American taxpayers have to pay the bill for her—"

Simon broke off because the look in Mr. Halcroft's eye told him that the front door across the street had finally opened. Show time. Good debt collectors did their research, and Simon was a great debt collector.

The door swung wide held open by a frail woman, seemingly waiting for someone. She glanced across her dead lawn, the only brown and deceased landscape on the block, and gently threw Halcroft an exhausted looking wave.

Halcroft responded with a warm smile, his anger buried underneath.

"A friend of yours?" Simon said, knowing damn well it was.

Halcroft didn't respond, just kept staring at the delicate woman. A moment later a pale, gaunt figure shambled into view. The doting mother held a hand out to guide her dead son through the doorway. The walking corpse with loose fitting clothes like a hastily assembled scarecrow, dragged one foot in a grotesque manner. Sunlight illuminated his face, a bleached rotten apple with unfocussed eyes. Simon

"You people have ruined that poor family's life," Halcroft said just loud enough for Simon to hear.

Simon no longer had to fight the urge to turn away at the sight of the walking dead. In his line of work, they were as common as palm trees on Santa Monica Boulevard. He glanced across the street and tried to look as if he was witnessing this scene for the first time. The truth was, he had watched it unfold for the past week, marking the time, learning the details, and crafting the perfect background for his conversation with Halcroft.

The neighbor had lost her only son to an Ebola outbreak in Florida. Her son, a med student at UCLA, volunteered to work the crises with the World Health Organization. With the national defunding of FEMA, it had been the only organization to respond. He had only been working in the Miami quarantine zone for a month when he started showing symptoms. In another week he was dead. And before his parents had received their son's remains, AmeriCorp had filled the reanimate order to recoup the six-figure student loan debt.

"She was so proud of him," Halcroft said. "First doctor in the family."

"I can tell she loved him very much," Simon said

watching the woman guide her son to the old Ford parked on the driveway. Then, unnoticed by Halcroft, Simon made a quick gesture with his hand to a man walking a Doberman down the street. The man nodded slightly then let go of the leash. The Doberman took off heading straight for the dead med student.

Simon summoned his best horrified expression as the trained dog tore into the decaying flesh. The corpse was pulled to the ground as the dog stood on its chest. The woman kicked at the animal tearing at her son's throat but missed, knocking her off balance. She grabbed the roof and managed to stay on her feet, then began slapping at the animal with open palms. The Doberman either didn't notice or didn't care as it tore away copious amounts of dead flesh.

With another covert hand gesture from Simon, the dog owner moved in and began his scripted, rehearsed apologies.

"Horrible, dreadful," Simon said with such sincerity he almost convinced himself.

"Don't patronize me," Halcroft said. "Bloodsuckers like you don't give a damn about what they're going through."

The dog was pulled away, and the elderly woman was torn between scolding the man and his trained beast, and holding a flap of skin onto her son's neck.

With aid from the dog owner, whose dog now sat dutifully a few feet away, the mother got the corpse to its feet and began to move him back inside.

"After a visit to the restoration facility, he'll be fine," Simon says.

"Leeches, all of you. Now if you're here to get me to sign something. Give you permission—"

"No, Mr. Halcroft, you misunderstand." Simon feigned a look of sympathy. "We obtained a court order shortly after the funeral, and have already reactivated her. It took a few days and some expensive resources due to the nature of her injuries." Simon waved a hand through the air. "But don't worry yourself about all that. It will all be rolled into her current debt."

"You didn't...dear lord, you didn't," Halcroft stammered.

"Not me personally, Sir, I assure you." Simon brought a

hand to his chest. "I'm in collections and debt outsourcing. I help secure the unskilled employment for our debtors and manage their wages, until the dept is repaid. And according to your daughter's file, at minimum wage, working eighty hours a week, that's all that the labor department allows, it will take sixteen years, four months and three weeks to completely repay what—"

"You betrayed us," Halcroft cut him off, fire in the old man's aged, watery eyes.

"Beg your pardon," Simon recoiled, but only for show. "Betrayed who?"

"All of us. The whole damn country." Halcroft's voice rose, quivering. "You took the government's money—the people's blood and sweat— billions that was supposed to fix the national debt, build the wall, heath care, for God's sakes you promised the best health care. But what did you do with it? You took our money, the tax payer's money, and invested billions in this sick, Frankenstein, Russian technology, defiling our dead, creating this blasphemous zombie economy."

Try as he might to fathom it, Simon could not understand why these old folks, born in the previous century, just couldn't accept the world the way it was now. Always living in the past.

"Mr. Halcroft, I was in middle school when all that happened. But I learned, and sincerely believe, that death is no excuse to evade one's financial obligations to this country, and our government has mandated this solution."

"It's not even our country anymore. It hasn't been since..."

Simon sighed and let a few beats of silence slither between them. Not much, just enough so he could analyze the moment. He liked to wait until futility, horror, and frustration, all converged to produce a sense of hopelessness. And he could see the willingness to fight visibly fleeting, the way the seventy-two-year-old Halcroft shrunk, shoulders slumping. It was time to make his move.

He brought up a hand in a peaceful gesture. "Look, sir, I didn't come here to argue or talk history. I wanted to know if you'd be interested in providing housing?"

Halcroft's head listed to the right, like a perplexed

canine. "Wh...what?"

"For your daughter," Simon continued. "We find that the workers exhibit much more enthusiasm in their labors when they spend time with recognizable faces. Their family, Mr. Halcroft." Simon stepped to the side, so that his car parked down the street was visible to the elderly man. He held one arm back, like a game show hostess unveiling a fabulous prize. "I can leave her with you today. She doesn't have to report to work until Monday."

Simon kept his gaze on Halcroft's face, watching the man take in the hunched over figure in the backseat. The pale, gravestone-colored skin was always unsettling, the drooling surely unpleasant, but it was the yellow-eyes that seemed to truly horrify those Simon visited. A side effect of the radioactive chemicals used in the reanimation process, they glinted like some nocturnal creature's eye shine caught in oncoming headlights.

Halcroft took a step forward, hands shaking. "McKenzie, oh, my..."

"Now sir, there will be some minor maintenance to perform daily, and you'll have to bring her in once a month to slow down decomposition, but you'll find that she pretty much takes care of herself."

"Richard, who's at the door?" came an elderly female voice from inside the house. Halcroft spun around and grabbed the door handle.

"Don't come out here—I'll be with you in a minute, honey." He turned back to Simon, panic weaving through his wrinkled features. "Take her away, please. My wife can't see our baby like that." A tear welled up in the old man's eye. "My wife is ill."

Of course, Simon already knew that. He knew everything about the Halcrofts. A good collector does his research.

"Well, if that's what you want," Simon tried to sound disappointed. "But I must tell you Mr. Halcroft, the holding facilities, labor warehouses they are so crudely called, aren't the most comfortable of places, and to be honest there have been some abuses.

Obviously, I'm horrified by the stories of this kind of thing, and I'm sure it is rare, but there are rumors of liberties being taken with some of the fresher female reanimates."

"Richard, where are you?" came the voice again, from the other side of the door.

Halcroft reached back, opened the door a crack and yelled into the house, "Just a minute. I'll bring you some tea. Just wait in the kitchen." Then Halcroft closed the front door.

"Are you saying my little girl could be...violated?"

"She is hardly a little girl," Simon grinned. "Thirty-four when she died..." Simon pretended to back-peddle. "I fear I have painted a rather bleak picture of the warehouses. I've heard some nice things, as well. Some even have furniture now. A few couches, a love seat or two." Simon glanced back at his car, seeing yellow eyes, unblinking, looking out at nothing. "Not that they really care, most are content to stand all day, and all night. Kind of like cows."

"How much?" the old man mumbled.

Simon loved hearing those magic words so much that he often made people repeat them. "What was that, Mr. Halcroft?"

"How much does my daughter owe?"

Simon knew that even if Halcroft liquidated everything the elderly couple had, retirement, property, savings, meager stocks, they still couldn't cover the balance. But he did know how much they could afford, at least before Mrs. Halcroft's Alzheimer's becomes too much for the old guy to manage, requiring full time care. That expense alone would break the Halcrofts. Simon had to get their assets secured for AmeriCorp before the old lady lost her marbles.

Reaching into his coat pocket, Simon pulled out a thick fold of papers, and held it out. "I've been authorized to make you this offer. If you agree to settle your daughter's debt, sign this payment plan, and give me a good faith down payment today, we will reduce the total amount due, to..." Simon pointed to a six-figure number on the first page.

Halcroft's eyes widened. "That's everything we have."

Simon felt he had over played his hand, setting the number too high. He needed to remind Halcroft what was at stake. "Perhaps, I should go get your daughter, and we could go inside, sit down, and go over some of the details with your wife."

"No," Halcroft said. "No, just give me a minute to get my check book."

~oOo~

Less than ten minutes later Simon walked to his car, stuffing a signed payment plan and a check inside his coat pocket.

"You will put her back now," Halcroft said, stepping onto the sidewalk, but keeping a noticeable distance from Simon's car.

Simon opened the driver's side door. "Absolutely. Just as soon as your check clears," Simon said, feeling no need to keep up the pleasantries any longer.

"You know, Mr. Simon, there is a special place in Hell reserved for people like you."

"Good day, Mr. Halcroft," Simon said, then swiftly got in his car, and fired up the engine. Pulling away from the curb, he glanced into the rearview mirror. In one half he could see Halcroft's meager dwelling falling away into the distance, in the other, swaying with the motion of the car, was the haunting reflection of the gray figure in the backseat.

"News," Simon said, the command aimed at the screen on the dashboard. The iTV came alive, RT news already in progress. "...and believes economic segregation seems to be fueling the Neo-Black Power movement...

"More than a decade after the sudden death of Senator Elizabeth Warren, the leading opponent to the highly successful Afterlife Debt Collection Act, conspiracy theorists have once again come forth to challenge the official cause of death, claiming new evidence. No details on what's turned up is yet available. In response, the FBI will hold a press conference later today to release additional evidence reaffirming the Senator's suicide...

"In sports news the Pfizer Rams will kick off their sixteenth season here in Los Angeles..."

Simon turned the volume down.

"Hands free, back to the office." Simon took his hands off the steering wheel and reached in his coat pocket.

He pulled out Halcroft's check and quickly did the calculations. Fifteen percent was his right off the top. Well, minus Gloria's two percent, which reminded him. He glanced up again into the mirror, checking to make sure Halcroft's house was far enough in the distance.

"Okay, Gloria. We're clear," Simon announced.

In the backseat, Gloria hunched forward, "Thank God." She popped out the luminous yellow contacts. "Damn, these things sting."

"The price of fame," Simon said. "You went a little heavy on the makeup this time, don't you think?"

Gloria shook her head, and pulled off the tattered black wig, one that perfectly matched the hair of the late McKenzie Halcroft. "Not at all. Didn't you see how the old guy stared at me? Thought he was only seconds away from climbing in the back seat."

Simon shook his head. "You worry too much."

"So, is this McKenzie Halcroft scheduled for reanimation?"

"I don't know, who cares?" Simon said with a shrug.

Gloria flopped back in the seat. "Just curious."

"Hey, I got another one tomorrow," Simon said. "A redhead, mid-forties, an Army medic, died in that terrorist attack on an Afghan hospital last month."

"Didn't hear about it. I don't really keep up on current events," Gloria said.

"Hardly makes the news anymore. The gig is yours if you want it."

Gloria didn't answer. After a few seconds of silence Simon glanced at her in the rearview mirror. Her arms, covered in makeup and looking of decay, were folded, and her gaze was aimed outside, locked on nothing.

"Gloria?"

"I came out here to be an actress," she muttered. "Not this shit show."

"What's eating you, girl?"

Gloria sat up, leaned forward. "What did you think about what the old guy said?"

Simon furrowed his brow. "Said about what?"

"Y'know, about there being a special place in Hell reserved for people like you?"

"Like us, babe."

"Okay," Gloria agreed, "Like us, then."

"Well," Simon snickered, tucking the check into his pocket. "I don't believe in a supernatural hell, one with devils and demons and all that nonsense."

"So, there's no hell?"

"I didn't say that," Simon said. "You ever been to one of the reanimate warehouses?"

"God, no."

"I have. Trust me, that is hell," Simon winced as if the image was painful. "Just pay your debts and leave this world with a clean slate. Hell is for the poor, babe."

Maybe the Monarchs

Brenda Cooper

I remember painting the fence. Twice. The first time, I followed my grandfather, holding a heavy paintbrush while he tugged a red wagon with an open paint can in it. He let me paint all of the bottom boards. I helped him re-paint it after I graduated from college, my ears covered with high-end headphones and filled with Lady Gaga music.

It's my fence now, but I haven't looked at it for years. Layers of white and yellowed-white and even older gone-to-gray white curl from the edges of the boards, and here and there, boards are splintered or have fallen. It will come down soon.

The sullen afternoon light fits my mood, in spite of the fact that my hands smell like apples cut for pie, like cinnamon, and nutmeg.

I use my shovel as a walking stick, the newly sharpened edge the same color as the barrel of the gun I carry in my pack, a heavy thing with no automatic locks on it. I do not expect to use it today, but these are times for carrying weapons. I have a single companion. Rocket. Her one blue eye—the right one—has gone blind, and she limps, keeping most of her weight off of her right front leg. I talk to her—I have always talked to her, and today I need to talk to her more than ever.

"I used to walk this fence with my grandfather. We planted milkweed here and there for the butterflies."

Rocket cocks her head in that ever-so-human way of herding dogs, as if to assure me that she understands. She doesn't of course. There is no way to explain to a dog why I have never brought my grandchildren or my great-grandchildren out here. But it is my habit to talk to Rocket, and her habit to listen, and it makes us both happy.

"We saw monarchs a few times when I was little. We even saw one chrysalis. It was so pretty I wrote a song about it, although now I've forgotten the words. I think I was eight, or maybe nine, and it's one of the few things I remember from that year." I can still see it, glistening in this very fence, in danger from the horse's warm breath, from birds, from a hard wind. The fence had been true-white then, the tiny pod that held the butterfly a shock of green against it. I tell Rocket, "They were orange, with black edges on their wings, and white spots."

Rocket's uneven gait barely keeps pace, and the awkwardness of it tears at me. I am not too old to do this, I tell myself, not yet. I am not city-weak.

I kept looking for milkweed and butterflies long after I knew they couldn't be here. The last monarch anyone saw in Pennsylvania was in 2032. I remember, since it was my fiftieth birthday. It wasn't me who saw it.

The walk to the far pasture seems longer than ever.

Rocket agrees. She whines at me, stopping to sit on her haunches from time to time.

"I'd carry you if I could." I try to move faster so the pie will have time to cool before they arrive, but my dog can't go any faster, so I don't either.

Rocket's spine sticks up like a mountain ridge, her skin folds in between every rib. Her face is thin at the muzzle and gone all to gray.

Since the path goes slightly uphill, my breath presses against my chest and I wish for a breeze. We make it to the far fence. The land beyond it has gone to dandelions and crabgrass and foxtails, and here and there, an alder. Weedy plants, hardy like Rocket and me. The old oak lies on its side, partially rotted. The year I saw the chrysalis, a white swing hung from a low branch. I used to try to circle the branch, but I was too light and every time, gravity grabbed me with a stomach-dropping lurch just as I came even with it.

We pass through the broken-hinged gate and into the clodded-earth of the empty pasture, and I watch where I put my feet. No boots fit any more; I'm sporting ugly black shoes with rocker bottoms that leave a fat tread-mark. I remind Rocket about the last horse she knew. "Remember

Ginger?"

Rocket stops for a moment, staring at a fat rabbit. Her ears swivel forward and she lets out a low growl. Then she puts her head back down, giving up before the chase starts. I try to distract her with a story.

"Edna offered us another horse, one that her cousin has over in Crawford County, a twenty-year-old bay that hurt its stifle and needs a pasture, but I told her no. I said it was our time to go."

The old border collie offers no response.

"My children's children have no idea how to clean hooves or what do about yellow bot-fly eggs." I sniff and pull out a tissue, dabbing at my face and thinking of the old mare. She lies under the fallen oak. Ginger. She'd been swaybacked and thin in her last year, in spite of my vet floating her teeth twice. After I had to shoot her, a neighbor—Ed, who died of cancer three months later—oiled up his old backhoe and split a whole day between repairs for the old tractor and digging Ginger's grave.

A light wind blows the dry summer air over us, smelling of fields with no crops except grass, of air with no butterflies.

I need to focus. My grand-daughter's car will bring her children by for dinner around dusk, and the pie I made is from the first of the season's apples sent in from Washington State. I haven't put it in the oven yet.

"Do you remember Ed?" I ask Rocket.

She glances up at me with her one unseeing eye and her one filmed-over eye that the vet had told me might not see much either, but then she stumbles a little. Border collies don't stumble. Except Rocket, these last of her days. She looks surprised, but gathers herself, only looking back at me when she has full control again.

She stood beside Ed and me at the grave. I threw the first handful of dirt and Rocket stayed close enough to me to touch. She whimpered, low and soft, the whole time: a dog-song full of longing and loss. The memory drives a shiver through my bones.

"What about Ginger? Do you remember Ginger?"

We near the fallen oak; Ginger lies under the tree, surely bones now. Rocket stops and splays her front legs and ducks her head as if addressing sheep. She whines again. I figure she does remember. It wouldn't be too hard; she remembers every person who comes to the farm. Why not Ginger? It had been seven years, but Rocket recognizes all of the neighbors, even Ellie who only met her once, and that when she was still a pup.

I gesture for Rocket to sit, and she lies down and watches me walk around the tree, looking for a place. Rivers of small brown ants run in the cracks in the bark along the dead trunk. At least five rabbits freeze as I approach and then bound away, all bobbing white tails and feet. The old oak is far enough up the slow rise I can see horizon in three directions, all of it the same: dry earth and dry trees and high clouds set to refuse us water all day. I try to remember the cornfields that used to wave away from here, soft and soughing in summer winds. The cicadas. Now it's all flies and ants and pincer bugs and a billion, billion rabbits. Sometimes crows, sometimes raptors.

That woman who started the environmental movement had been wrong. There are still birds. Carson. Rachel Carson. Here, the deer went before the songbirds and after the wolves and somewhere in the middle, the last monarch chrysalis opened and disgorged its gleaming butterfly. I hear there are still deer in Canada, even a lot of deer.

I am trying not to find a spot.

Finally, I start digging. The dirt is dust on top and hard underneath, and rocky. It takes two hours and two breaks, and Rocket stays awake and watches me the whole time. No matter how blind Rocket is or isn't, she follows every move I make with her head. Halfway through, I stop for a break.

"It will be easy Rocket. Fast."

Her mouth is open a little, her tongue sticking out as she pants. I share some water from my pack with her. It feels companionable to sit by her, full of sadness but also full of rightness, replete with time. The pain is a pillowy thing, only a little heavier than other things that have to be done like laundry or giving the farm up to the law that said I could have it until I die or forfeit, and that then it would go into the great taking and become wilderness.

It will be re-wilded, unfenced, decomposed, the house torn down, the driveway jackhammered out by some great brute of a robot. This is hope for us now, this pending deconstruction.

They say they can make monarchs in a test tube.

Some day.

I've been using Rocket for an excuse. The old girl loves her farm.

I finish digging. I pile the dirt in one place, so I can use it for a chair. Even though it will be hard to get up, I sit down and call Rocket to me. She puts her head between my knees and stands with her tail twitching. I kiss her forehead, feeling the small hairs brush against my lips and cheek.

"This will be easy," I tell her. "You have been the best dog ever." I pull out the syringes the vet gave me yesterday morning. The first injector is marked with green. I lift up the fur on her neck and slide it in. She stands for it, trusting.

Her eyes close and she falls a little more into me.

The second injector has a thicker, more wicked needle, but Rocket is warm and asleep, her breath soft against my pant leg. I sit, one hand petting her, the other holding the needle until it feels like time. I lift the ruff at the back of her neck and the needle balks for a moment and then punctures her skin and I depress the plunger quickly.

I leave my left hand on her chest until I felt her heart stop.

A few sunspots shine through the empty, dull clouds, making golden circles on the hills in the distance.

"There's another rabbit," I tell her. "And another. And there's a crow." I look for a butterfly, but there have been no miracles for years. "Way off, there's still a few horses in Edna's pasture, and I know she still keeps three goats."

I watch as a big bird—I am no good at telling them apart, but a hawk of some kind—swoops down and lifts a rabbit from the field. It screams and struggles hard enough to fall, but the fall is after the hawk has pulled it high enough that the drop stuns it. The bird comes down after it, and struggles as it lifts it, but nonetheless it flies into the afternoon sun, its wing limned with gold, the rabbit's fur touched with a sudden flash of light. Perhaps it has a nest of fledging chicks.

"All right girl." She is light and thin with age, but still, it is awkward to get up and I feel a soft pull in a hip muscle. Not bad. I lean over the hole and bend my knees very slowly, keeping my back straight, but she tumbles a bit.

"Sorry, baby girl." I lie with my stomach on the ground to straighten her. The dirt smells of dust, empty of all of the richness that once made it soil. It puffs up as I throw the first clod in. Dust stings my eyes as I shovel the dirt I'd been sitting on into the hole, and some of it sticks to the damp spots beneath my eyes so I have to stop and wipe it away. I take out her collar and leash and put them down on top of the hole, covering them with rocks. If there are coydogs left I don't want them to disturb her.

"You were the best," I tell her. "You were never a weed, not like me or the rabbits. You were noble." My voice catches, choking on her absence.

I use the shovel to lever myself back up and lean on it as I walk back. I don't hesitate at the fence line, don't look back. Ahead, in front of me, the pie is waiting for the oven. The car is probably already leaving my granddaughter's house with my great-grandchildren. I will leave with them tonight. The fence and the house will come down tomorrow. Or soon. Perhaps the robot is already on the way, just like my grandchildren.

I will dream of the monarchs and the tumbled fence.

Dreamer

Andrea Lopez

"Here," Holden said as he handed the large shiv to his younger accomplice. Rome took the shiv and tucked it into his back pocket. Both young men wore dark clothes, blending in with the enigma of the forest.

"I don't know if we can handle this," Rome said.

"Don't think too much," Holden replied. He strapped on his protector vest of bark and rough leaves, and secured it tight with a thick piece of cloth.

"Stay by me," he said, as they both entered inside the mouth of the merciless woods.

The forest breathed onto Rome and Holden as they wiped away sweat from their brows, spotted with the effort of progressing through the dank grove. The rich, sullied ground vibrated in the arches of their feet, humming its hungry song.

"It's alive," Rome said.

"Very much so," Holden replied, as his eyes fixated on every angle of the surrounding lush wilderness.

"What do they look like?" Rome asked.

"A part of us on fiery wings," Holden said.

"What part of us?"

"Dreams," Holden said.

"Those are forbidden."

"I wonder why," Holden said, matter-of-factly.

Holden and Rome negotiated the thick, colossal trees blocking the hushed silver-white skies.

"What if they recognize us?" Rome asked.

"They can't. They're abandoned. They don't know anything else."

"How will we find them?" Rome asked.

"There," Holden said. He directed Rome's attention to a fluttering ball-shaped object above a branch, three feet from where they stood.

They stood in awe, as if a magician had cast a spell upon them for the first time.

The object's wings streamed with minute flames and each time its wings jumped up and down, a flame shot off into the air and vanished, as if swallowed by the forest.

"Why is it inside that?" Rome asked. An ebony web covered the object, but it appeared natural, as if the web was a born entity.

"To control it," Holden said.

"How do we catch it?"

Holden stood in the center of the path. He faced the object and said, "I want a beach house."

"What are you doing?"

"Just trust me. A large beach house to share with our family," Holden said.

The object lowered its wings and hovered above Holden's gaze. He reached his arms forward and hugged the object with his hands. He brought it down to his chest and held it close to him. He walked over to Rome.

"It senses the dopamine. It feeds off it. It now belongs to me," Holden said. He tucked the calm object in his protector vest.

"What is a beach house, anyway?" Rome asked.

"Something I heard about growing up. Always wanted to see it, since," Holden said. "Mother said there was an ocean that used to reach land, but the land was made of sand. The normoids would spend time there wearing rags. No protection. The sun wasn't killing us the way it does now," Holden said. Rome's eyes drank up each word Holden spoke.

"I want that world," Rome said.

"The normoids destroyed it, so the earth became angry, and thus we live in fear. Here comes your dream," Holden said.

They looked ahead as another object fluttered its red and orange jeweled wings, cloaked inside of its ebony web. It hovered against the trunk of a healthy young tree, when a neon green stick bug appeared on the tree's branch above it.

"Say it again, Rome, get closer to it," Holden said. Rome left Holden's side and approached his wild dream.

"I want a world where the ocean meets the land again. We'll know how to take care of it this time," Rome said.

"Don't talk too much, just grab it," Holden said. "Do it! We have to flee."

Rome reached out his arms for his captured hope. The object lowered its wings and the crackled fire ceased as it moved towards Rome. Then the neon green stick bug whooshed its head to one side and out of a whimsical whirl emerged a round purple head with only a circumference of glittering white sharp teeth.

"A Feral," Holden said. "Rome, run. Now."

Rome reached for his shiv in his back pocket, but Holden grabbed his shoulder as they darted down the path. The grinning head bounced off the branch and without any other limbs, bounced its way, forcing large imprints along the forest ground. Holden grabbed Rome and dove off to the side of the path into a set of thorny bushes.

Rome gritted his teeth in pain, but both remained motionless. The spinning head grin bounced its way through the forest past them and Holden watched closely until it was out of sight.

"Quickly, move," Holden said. The thorny bush opened small red slits on parts of their bodies as they removed themselves from it. Moving forward, an apparition caught their eyes. A dark cloaked man with long silver hair hovered slightly off the ground among the mountainous trees stunning them.

"Why must you go? You will forget why you've come," the Distractor said.

A sudden daze haunted Rome and Holden.

"You can't fool us, Distractor, let us be on our way," Holden said.

"Don't be ashamed. I have that for which you've come," the Distractor said. He held up a fiery ball trapped inside of an ebony web. "I believe this belongs to you." His maleficent green eyes pierced through Rome's somber brown eyes.

"Rome, don't look at him," Holden said. "Look at me."

"A dream is but an external part of us that rots. The

normoids had the luxury of coexisting with them, but even they were foolish to recognize them. The dream became pointless. Those who dreamed, dared to repeat the same philosophy again and again: anything is possible. This is what led the normoids to destroy the world we never knew. Dreams destroy," the Distractor said.

"It isn't true, Rome. He put you in a daze. He doesn't want us to leave the forest. Listen to me, Rome," Holden said.

Rome remained locked within the daze. No sound or plea entered within the hazy bubble he encompassed himself in. All he connected with were the words from the Distractor.

"What is it that you want, Rome? What is it that you want?" Holden yelled.

"I want...my dream!" Rome said.

The Distractor's daze released itself from Rome as he emerged from the bubble. Rome snatched his shiv from his back pocket and flew it between the dwindling eyes of the Distractor. The netted dream fell from the Distractor's grasp, and before it touched the ground, Rome dove right under it and grabbed it with his bare hands. There within his grasp the dream flamed and hummed such gratitude. Rome's eyes clouded and drops formed onto his cheeks. He wiped them away as he tucked his dream inside of his protector vest.

Fury spouted from the Distractor's head, releasing venomous gases hazing the atmosphere with golden and grey swirls of poison. Holden ran down beside Rome,

"We must flee. The Distractor's death brings chaos," Holden said.

The forest roared a low monstrous growl. The ground rolled beneath Holden and Rome's running feet. The entrance clearing approached them vast from a distance, then closer and closer. Holden's lungs expelled his breath when twin jagged mouths sprouted from the forest ground, chomping down on his calves, and he fell toward inevitable doom. Muscle ripped and the deep, rich soil splattered with his blood. Holden writhed, trying to reach for his shiv, but the more he moved the more pain shot through every part of his body. He froze as swelling fear took hold of him.

Rome yelled. "Holden!" He grabbed Holden's shiv from his back pocket and stabbed the chomping, planted heads one by one. Their predatory teeth released Holden's legs and remained idle. Rome gripped Holden under his arms and dragged him through the clearing, out of the forest where he lay Holden on the ground and went to the nearby river bank where a patch of trees grew. He stripped their flaking bark and pulled long weeds from the ground. He quivered only slightly, reminded of the liveliness in the forest.

Rome saw sharp green wedges poking out of the generous ground and recalled their grandfather's science books: an aloe plant. He pulled apart the leaves. He opened his canteen, crafted of scrap metal and string, and dipped it into the river. He brought over his bundle to his brother. He squeezed the aloe onto Holden's hollow crimson wounds. He tied each wound with the tree bark securely with the weeds. He sat Holden up as he put the container to his mouth to drink.

"May have to cut them off," Holden said, looking down at his battered legs.

"Would you have done the same thing over again? Risking your legs, everything?" Rome asked.

"Yes, brother," Holden said. He took out his dream from his protector vest.

"Cut the web with my shiv," Holden said. Rome took Holden's shiv from his back pocket and released the dream from its web.

"Conquer what you dream, no matter what," Holden said. The dream ripped through Holden's throat and slivered down inside his chest, enclosing his heart. Holden swallowed a deep gulp of air.

"Holden!" Rome gasped.

Rome shut Holden's bare eyes and gaping mouth. He bellowed a tune he had never heard, a tune his grandfather described as "pain." The guttural wound from beneath his heart and out into the world, as it vanished farther away, taking everything from inside him.

Rome grabbed hold of his webbed dream and laid it on the ground. He picked up a heavy rock that lay beside Holden and smashed it down with every fiber of his body. Down and down, smashed and smashed again.

He straightened up, his eyes clouded by tears, his cheeks wet once more, watching the smoke of his dreams drift away, vanishing into the air.

Glow in the Dark Girlfriend

Bo Balder

The women in Stanmay's family glow in the dark.

She can pass in daylight. But today the electricity's out again and the Q-line's down. Meaning she'll have to walk the thirty blocks home, which she'll never make before dark. She will be lit up like a sign that says, 'here there be prey', and some of the blocks she has to cross are the worst in the whole of Apple City. Drug enclaves, rape communities.

Her birth grandfather and his chans thought it would be great to have glow-in-the-dark girlfriends, so they'd never have to turn on the light to see the time. Or something.

Lame, Grandpa, lame. He got convicted for it. But not before he'd not only changed her grandmother, but all her ova. He put a few eggs back into Grandma, and sold the rest.

No glow-in-the-dark boyfriends were made. It's sexually dimorphic. Thanks again, Grandpa.

Stanmay walks as fast as she can, but the sun will be going down in about fifteen minutes and she has at least an hour to go. She keeps her head down and tries to stay calm. Agitation makes her glow harder.

Darkness falls. Apple City inhabitants pour out onto the streets, kindling oil barrel fires and shooting off fireworks. Oil barrels, especially, seem to attract a meaner crowd, fueled by anger and jackdouche. She patters along as silently as she can, but they are predators, and they can smell she's prey. The sky captains don't patrol out here anymore, too risky even for flying heroes.

Faster. Faster. Once they got you on the run, you're as good as dead. Behind her, a voice howls out a challenge.

She doesn't answer. It won't make any difference. Loud male voices and pattering footsteps move closer. Stanmay breaks into a trot.

Two blocks ahead she spots the dense black outline of the elf enclave. "Laurelindorinan". She knows someone who's turned elf and moved there. If she can reach the walled enclave, she can ask for his help.

Her breath saws in her throat, a stitch pierces her side.

A diamond of reddish light opens up in the enclave wall, throwing an even darker shadow onto the street. A man looks out, no, a boy, no, an elf. He looks the street up and down. When he spots her and her pursuers, he retreats as quickly as he's come out. Stanmay has about ten paces to make up her mind. Of course, she won't be safe in there. The enclave will be full of elves and they aren't nice people, certainly not to non-elves. But out here it'll be worse. The footsteps are closing in rapidly.

A hoarse voice shouts, "Slow down, or you're gonna make me mad!"

She gets close enough to see the wide-eyed stare of the elf boy, sees him fumble with the gate. At the last moment she swerves inside. The boy tries to slam the gate in her face but she squeezes past him, bruising her shoulder.

Her pursuers are only a few heartbeats away. If the elf doesn't close the door right now they'll get in. He kicks the heavy door shut with her inside. Shouts explode on the other side, boots or fists or stones drum against the door.

"You can get right back out," he says. "Now."

"I know Mark," she pants in the sweet-smelling darkness. She can't remember his elf name. "Mark Weinberg."

The boy, much stronger than she, in spite of his weediness, pushes her back to the door.

"Maedhros! That's his name. He'll let me stay!"

The boy frowns. After some hesitation, he slouches off.

Stanmay's breath stops sawing, but her heart gallops on. She's safe from the creeps outside, but she's never been safe from Mark.

Sooner than she expects, a tall, gorgeous red-headed elf saunters up. The elf man laughs in her face.

"You look great like that, all lit up and green."

She glares at him. The torch backlights his pretty, pretty face into devil gruesomeness.

"I remember how you glow when you're worked up," he says as he comes closer. "But I see you don't recognize me. I'm Maedhros now."

She gasps. Nothing of the old Mark remains, at least not on the outside. Mark was never anything special to look at; this man is perfect in every dimension. His skin glows around a few artfully scattered freckles. He's at least a head taller than she is, his long shiny red hair cascading almost to his waist. And the ears are pointy.

"You've changed," is all she comes up with, remembering the old hurt. He'd strung her on a leash for months, keeping her panting and guessing.

He grins. "So you need shelter for tonight, eh? Not safe for glowy girls out there."

"Are you going to let me stay?" He slides a cool finger down her still-hot arms.

"Maybe. If you'll do me a favor in return. I need a girlfriend."

What the hell does he mean by that? He's never wanted commitment. "I'm not in the market for a boyfriend."

"Just for tonight." Maedhros gestures with his torch. I don't want to go to the party alone. Help me out, will you? Then I'll help you."

She really needs that help. A party sounds innocent enough. Except she can't assume that. Elves have the weirdest ideas. The media says. She's never met any elves socially, because they stick together and wouldn't be seen dead at Macy's perfume counter.

"What does a girlfriend have to do?" she asks. Elves might not look like chans or sheldons, but she suspects they have a big dose of inner chan. And that's always been Mark's kind of guy.

"Nothing special," he says.

He seems fascinated with the way she moves her hands, the way light trails after them. She gets that, she often plays with herself in her dark bedroom.

"I loan you a dress, we eat, we dance, we celebrate. A party."

"Just don't touch my hair," she says.

"Ah yes, the hair?," he says and yanks off her cap before she can stop it. The luminescent strands, thick as spaghetti, tumble out, agitated and afraid. Stanmay can never hide her feelings.

Maedhros smiles tightly. "I'd forgotten about that." He lifts up his hand to touch the writhing locks, but she jerks her head away.

"Don't touch it!" she says. Her hands' luminescence strays into orange. Maedhros steps away a pace and holds out his hand.

"You're an even better substitute than I thought. Don't look so suspicious. It'll be fun. And we'll find a gown to complement your wonderful coloring. Come!"

She takes the hand, although she's having serious second thoughts. Maedhros' glee fills her with misgiving. But how bad can it be? It has to be better than the litany of rob, rape and beat she's escaping from. Maedhros will dump her when he no longer needs her, but she's used to that.

And, gown. Free dinner.

Pulled ahead by Maedhros' hand, she follows winding paths, lit by scattered torches, through a dark, sweet-smelling garden. She wishes she could see it by daylight. It's sure to be prettier than the rubbled lots around her aunt's apartment.

"Stop!" she says.

"What?"

"I want to take off my shoes. Maybe I'll be able to see where I walk."

"Why not?" The torch glints off Maedhros pointy white teeth.

She unlaces her sneakers and takes off her socks. Her toes look pale and greenish against the path. The grassy or herby stuff sends up sweet scents with every footstep. Her feet's glow is just enough to show her stones or holes in the path.

Maedhros grabs her hand again. How big is the enclave? More than a block, that's for sure. The city administration is in such ruins that the appropriation of whole streets might go uncontested. She tries to orient herself against the silhouettes of buildings surrounding her in the distance, but without lights, Manhattan is invisible at night. Maybe they've taken over Prospect Park. She's fairly sure her mother took her to the big aquarium once to see the veilfish. Her mother had a weird, mean streak in her sometimes.

In the middle of the great garden stands a large glass hothouse. It looks old, not like the elves built it. Elves aren't the building kind.

"The party will be in the pavilion," Maedhros says. "I'm taking you to my sister's quarters and she'll set you up with a dress."

Maedhros leads her to a small side-room. It's lined by mirrors reflecting the candle pinpoints scattered about the room. A tall narrow woman, her skin a deep mahogany against the red of her hair, Maedhros' color, sits cross-legged in the middle and gazes rapt at her own multiplied face. An adopted sister, Stanmay guesses.

"Luthien, this is Stanmay," Maedhros says. "She's consented to be my consort for the party. Will you help her dress and beautify herself?"

The woman lifts pale yellow eyes. Stanmay feels a sharp stab of connection as their eyes meet. "I will, brother. She glows."

"Use it," Maedhros says, and departs with a theatrical flurry of curtains and robe.

Luthien plucks the sneakers from Stanmay's hand and tosses them in a corner. Her socks follow. "Take your clothes off, I need to measure you."

It isn't cold, but Stanmay shivers. She doesn't want the elf woman to see her imperfect human body. But she has no choice. Outside, the night still rages and she'd be no safer than before.

She slowly peels off her black slacks and jacket and the white polyester blouse, dull neat workwear. Luthien throws something large and baggy yet lightweight over Stanmay's head before she can feel too much shame about her belly or her thighs. The garment smells of sweat and perfume. It's somehow comforting that elves haven't conquered body odor yet.

"Can I see in the mirror?" she says.

Luthien pulls a cloth off a large standing mirror. It isn't

very light in the tent, but Stanmay sees a pretty girl in a pale dress, a cross between Arwen and Medusa. Too bad she can't turn men to stone. That would have been such a useful power.

A gong sounds.

"Party time! The feast of Beltane!" Luthien says and grabs Stanmay's hand with her cold knobby fingers.

"The what?" Stanmay asks, but Luthien drags her along at such a clip that any answer gets lost in the swirl of tent cloth, snatches of conversation and the growing buzz of people talking.

Outside it's still night, although the dressing up seems to have taken hours and hours. Stanmay feels tired and disoriented. As if she's not in New York anymore, although the silhouettes surrounding the park are the same old buildings as always.

In the middle of the former great lawn, now just churned slush, another large tent has been set up. Where have they found such a thing, now that almost nothing new gets made in North America? Maybe elven seamstresses hand-stitched hundreds of bed sheets together. She sniggers quietly at the thought, but Luthien turns around as if stung.

"You're not on something already, are you?" she says. "We like our guests to be in pristine condition."

"Of course not," Stanmay says. "I just come off work. And anyway, I never use." Girls who lose control don't end up well.

"Good. Now, when we enter, walk up to the head of the table, slowly, bow to our King and Queen. Then wait until Maedhros takes you to your seat."

A swift flash of panic stings Stanmay's throat. "Where will you be?" Not that she likes or trusts Luthien, but at this point she's the most familiar face around.

Luthien doesn't answer. She opens the tent flap. A rush of air blows into Stanmay's face, scented with rich food, perfume and many people. She's ravenous. She tells herself she's safe tonight and her free dinner's waiting.

She steps through into the candlelit space. Across the table a huge fire bellows, an empty spit turning over it. The flower-crowned people at the far end of the beautifully dressed tables must be the king and queen. Stanmay picks her way to the throne, stepping over bits of tent cloth, pegs, dogs, children and random bits of junk. The contrast between what lays on the floor and what appears above table level is disconcerting.

"Stanmay! Here!" Maedhros walks towards her. He offers her his arm, like a gentleman in an old movie. It feels good to walk around the table beside him, people staring and whispering and wondering who she is.

She's Maedhros guest, in a special dress, and she's getting to eat special, free, food. Her heart lifts. As he holds out her chair for her, again making her flashback to old movies, she sits down carefully, so she won't damage the fragile old fabric.

Maedhros sits down next to her. Over a hundred elves must be sitting around the table. A joint of some kind of meat lands on her plate, and a stream of dark red liquid gurgles into her wine glass.

When she picks it up, it isn't heavy enough. Really, plastic? She'd have thought elves would have real glass glasses, real wooden tables, linen table cloths. She fingers the cloth below her plate, surreptitiously so her hosts won't notice she's checking out their wealth. Cheap synthetics.

"Stanmay, to Beltane! To your good health and my good fortune!" Maedhros lifts his wineglass to hers. He smiles down at her. His eyeteeth have been filed or genetically modified to be very sharp and pointy.

She suppresses a shiver. What on earth made him think it's a good look? In retrospect, the old Mark almost seems like a nice guy, just insecure and immature. Maedhros has evolved himself into something much more menacing.

She drinks. The first sip tingles pleasantly against her tongue, and she drinks down deep. Warmth spreads through her body, relaxation through her limbs. Whew. Powerful stuff. She likes it. She wants to start eating, but manages to wait until everyone else starts.

The food tastes unexpectedly good, despite its drab exterior. It makes her think all the restaurant food she's eaten before—not a whole lot—has been treated with food dye to make it look more attractive. Like food looked Before, when it was flown in from all over the world. Now New York, the elves included, has to rely on what can be grown in its own climate.

Maedhros pours more wine. She drinks.

The elves are beautiful people, in beautiful if ragged clothes, and they make great conversation. Maedhros kisses her fingertips. She giggles and feels it go straight to her groin. Uh-oh. She's going to do exactly what she's vowed not to do, and she doesn't even care.

But food, even for the lofty elves, is too important to get distracted away from it. So only after they'd fed each other dessert, Maedhros stands up and pulls her to her feet.

"Wanna go somewhere private?"

"Yeah," she breathes.

She keeps tripping over her dress, tearing it, but she doesn't care anymore.

Maedhros leads her through a maze of cloth tunnels to a secluded bedroom area. The folds of cloth make it into a cozy bower. The bed is large, the linens smell fresh. Although they seem to have walked quite a ways, she can still hear the susurrus of the banquet.

Maedhros pulls her to him and kisses her. "You taste amazing."

He touches her hair, which normally she'd have swatted off, but now she lets him. It's fine. He's fine. She's going to have fun. She feels lazy and replete, ready to be filled up and taken, to be ridden. She giggles again. Ridden like a horse. No, horses don't ride. Riders ride. No, yeah, she's the horse.

A slight push from Maedhros fingertip sends her sprawling onto the bed. Her head swims, but she's determined not to pass out before she's had the good stuff. Her clumsy fingers help or hinder Maedhros getting her dress off, and she's glad Luthien had her ditch the work-wear suitable bra and panties. What a turnoff those would have been.

She watches his face as he thrusts into her with delicious certainty. Life is hard. A girl has the right to enjoy herself once in a while, throw caution into the wind. And she's known Mark like forever, it isn't like a one-night-stand.

The dim, tent-like space is becoming lighter, or maybe her eyes have adjusted to the darkness. Maedhros lifts his head from her breasts and grins at her. His filed teeth ruin the effect and she closes her eyes.

But then she realizes why she can see his feral grin and she looks down at herself. Yep. She's starting to glow harder. Usually guys either freak out or are way too much into it, but of course Maedhros already knew. He continues single-mindedly with what he's doing.

He's doing it well. Better than he ever has before. She throws her head back and screams.

Maedhros follows her lead and she expects him to sink down onto her or next to her, but instead a breeze of cool air caresses her sweaty skin. Whatever. She stretches the full length of her body and lets out a long sigh.

Something's wrong with the silence.

She opens her eyes, propping herself up on her elbows. The bedroom tent is brightly lit by fluctuating oranges and pinks. She pays that no attention, that's just what she does when she comes. But the darkness at the foot of the bed is now lit as well, if not as bright as her own illumination.

And it moves.

Stanmay wipes a writhing hair out of her eyes and sits up straighter.

The silence breaks open in a round of applause. The faint moving shapes and tiny lights resolve into dozens of people holding up candles. What the hell?

They've been watching?

"Bravo. Maedhros, what a wonderful Beltane sacrifice! The goddess will be honored by such passion, such a unique glow!" a male voice calls out. The King, she thinks.

Her color changes from a rosy glow to a white hot brilliance. They were watching?

She jumps up and spreads her arms. "What the hell do you think you're doing, assholes?" she yells.

They laugh.

Maedhros grabs her arms and holds them behind her back. "The sacrifice, sire," he says to someone in the crowd.

The king lifts a huge-ass sword, the torchlight glinting off the blade. Suddenly the tent is bristling with steel, as if all the elves wants a part in her kill. Not swords, but kitchen knives. So that's what the empty spit was for. For her.

She explodes.

#

Stanmay's eyes feel gummy and weird. She's pretty sure she has a hangover, but she still needs to find out if she's late for work. Why can't she remember what day it is?

Her face seems to be covered with some kind of springy stuff. She needs her eyes to make sense of it. With her one free hand she rubs and plucks at the resistant stuff until it parts. Like a gum bubble that's burst in her face. She smiles. Those were the days, when getting gum out of your hair was the worst you could think of.

At last she can touch her face. She rubs at her eyes until the crunchy sleep stuff goes away and she can blink. She seems to be outside somewhere. It's darkish, with a pale glow on the horizon. She twists her head. Eastern. Almost morning. Why is she here?

It smells funny. Burnt, like a pork chop left on the barbecue too long.

She peels off the rest of the gummy shroud and scrambles up. A torn dress pools around her ankles. Now she remembers. The dress Luthien picked out for her. The banquet, Maedhros.

She's done something. Something wonderful and terrible at the same time. She got mad and then she turned into the sun.

As the real sun rises, she picks out more and more details around her. Everything is charred black. Irregular lumps of stuff, tree stumps, heaps of ash that get lifted by the dawn breeze, swirling into the air like black snow.

She wraps her arms around her shivering self. That charred bump over there is a person. A former person that she burned to death.

Her teeth clatter. She killed these people. Everyone. She remembers their swords and knives, and yes, they'd tried to kill her in their lame-ass Beltane sacrifice. Spit her, put her over the fire and broil her like a chicken. That doesn't mean she should have killed them.

But then again, what alternative did she have?

The sun rising over the ruined skyscrapers makes her

feel small and cold. She can't think of anything to do. She can't undo this. What she did last night is something she'll have to live with.

She shivers in the light of the new day. Her life will never be the same because she's saved herself. She's no longer prey. Granddaddy added something useful to her mix after all, and she doesn't know how she feels about that.

But she'll never have to be afraid again. Except of her herself.

Bo Balder

Studies in Shadow and Light

Su J. Sokol

"That hurt!" I say, pulling at my restraints.

Mister Jones laughs from behind the broad control panel. My mind reaches out towards his before I remember myself. I'm not at home and I've promised to follow their rules.

"Why did you hurt me?" I ask out loud instead. "And why did you laugh?"

You people I hear in subvocalization before I shut down that part of my perception.

"It was only a small jolt. To remind you not to lie to me," he answers.

I watch Mister Jones carefully—there's not much else to look at in this tiny, stark room. Though I was brought here by campus security, Mister Jones isn't in uniform. Like most of the university's security team, he presents male with short hair and a serious, almost angry expression. He appears to be in his forties, but I find age harder to judge here. What strikes me most is how expressive Mister Jones' face is. The people of the United America, though obsessed with feeling and thought privacy, don't hide their emotions very well.

Mister Jones doesn't explain his laughter. After a moment, I say, "I didn't lie. I know you didn't like my answer but-"

Pain shoots through me for a second time. I take a slow, deep breath and will myself to be calm. To wait before reacting, like a mature adult should.

"Your first semester at the university and you've already forgotten your agreement," Mister Jones scolds. "No mind reading. No psychic invasion."

Su J. Sokol

I want to argue. You don't have to be a mind-reader to know when you've pissed someone off. But I keep my mouth shut, scared of giving him an excuse to jolt me again. As my home parent Soraya is fond of saying, I may be foolish, but I'm not stupid."

"Let's try again," Mister Jones says, speaking slowly, as though to a little kid.

It's true that at seventeen I'm legally a minor here, but back home I'm considered adult. Trying to steady myself, I sink into the memory of my adulthood ceremony—my parents encircling me, close friends and other family members standing around them, then larger and larger circles of people radiating out, all of them projecting affirmations of trust. The memory's reassuring, but it doesn't wipe out the growing fear that my parents were right. I should never have left Nouvelle S'Entraide to study abroad.

"State your full legal name," Mister Jones demands.

"Sasha Imani Lavoie," I answer, though he already knows this. My name's on my Nouvelle S'Entraide identity chip and my student ID. When I first arrived in the United America, I couldn't believe how many security verifications I had to go through. Mica told me it would have been worse if their father, who works for the government, hadn't "pulled some strings."

"Mother's name," Mister Jones continues.

I pause as he fiddles with some controls. "Pardon me," I say. "I don't want to get this wrong. You know our family structures are different than yours ..."

His lips twist with distaste. "Just answer the question."

"My womb mother is Emma Sapir Lavoie. My home mother is Soraya Tony Imani."

He puts his index finger on the control he'd used to shock me. I hold my breath.

"Name of father," he barks.

"My ... my gene father is Malek O'Mar and—" I look to see if his finger has moved. "And Malek's ... husband's name is Robin." Mister Jones strokes the controller in a gentle circular motion, almost a caress. My stomach churns. "Pedro Maria Robin Volantes," I amend. "We just call them Robin."

"You're female, right?"

I stare at him, shocked. His finger presses and I cry out. When the pain subsides, I'm covered in a cold sweat.

"Is this what you call being cooperative?" he asks in that slow voice.

I take a ragged breath. "I'm sorry. Where I come from ... I mean in my comm, my community ... It's only that it's very rude to ... Please," I stammer, as he reaches for the control again. "I'll answer your question. My sex ... is female. But my gender is fluid, which means—"

"Shut up," he roars, standing and leaning over the table between us.

No jolt this time, but my body jerks anyway. Fear is making it hard for me to maintain an effective mind block, so his surface thoughts are leaking right through. It's like having speakers inserted into my ears with the volume turned up to the max while an overlay of ANGER/LUST/CONFUSION/DISGUST/FRUSTRATION vibrate in the background.

"Please," I say, ashamed of the tremor in my voice. "Let me contact one of my parents. Under your laws, a minor has the right to have a parent present when questioned by authorities."

"Typical 'pather. Lawless as savages, but when it suits you, you'll cite rules and regulations like a backstreet lawyer."

Despite my fear, I still want to argue. 'Pathistes are against rulers, not rules. Five minutes at one of our coordinating councils would cure anyone of that confusion. It's one of the things I looked forward to escaping—all those meetings where people endlessly debate everything. That last argument with my parents is still fresh in my mind.

"I know you find the meetings tedious, Sasha, but it takes hard work to create systems that prize freedom above coercion," Emma had said in her cold, intellectual way.

"Then why are you trying to coerce me into staying home!" I shot back.

"We're not trying to coerce you, Sash," Malek replied while Soraya and Robin projected calm, loving emos. "We're just concerned. It wasn't that many generations ago that the UA exiled all their mind-readers and empaths." My response was smug. "But now they're inviting some of us back."

"Wait here," Mister Jones says now. "My supervisor has taken a special interest in you." He smiles then. The smile looks so wrong, I shudder.

As soon as Mister Jones is out of sight, I breathe easier. After a moment, I examine my surroundings more closely. Everything in the small room is hard and sterile, white or metallic. There's no wood or cloth, or even bamboo. It makes me wonder if the rumor that the UA has used up all of its own natural resources is true, if that's the real reason behind their renewed interest in our small comm. We are, after all, just north of Nueva York and Vert Mont—two of their strategically important states. To me, though, their choice of materials just feels like a way to leech any possible warmth out of the room. It goes with the lonely brightness of the single light stick burning above me, casting everything else in deep shadow.

I strain my ears for the approach of this supervisor, nervous about their interest in me. Before deciding to come to the UA, I'd read every article I could find on the current social and political situation, but there are limits to what you can learn by reading about a place.

Among my four parents, only Robin, a musician, has travelled much. Emma, Malek and Soraya are all scientists, and even though they're super smart, they're kind of provincial. I told them that when the search for knowledge leads you from home, it's cowardly not to go. Malek had looked down, trying to hide his smile, while Soraya tilted her head, waiting. Emma pressed her lips together in disapproval. At that moment, I wasn't quite ready to admit just how much my long-distance romance with Mica had influenced my final decision.

I hear a small click as the supervisor opens the door. My head jerks up. A long, tall shadow falls across the room and I swallow hard.

~oOo~

"You can call me Mister Smith. How do you do?"

Mister Smith's smile seems genuine, so I relax a little. Still, I don't answer, not trusting my responses after my time with Mister Jones.

After a moment, Mister Smith goes on. "As I'm sure you're aware, we're here to talk about certain unfortunate incidents at the university and, well, your role in all that. If you cooperate fully and we find you weren't an instigator, everything will be fine."

I still don't reply. He hadn't actually asked me a question.

"Come now. How can I make you more comfortable?"

"Could you take these off?" I say, indicating the restraints.

"I wish I could, Sasha, but you've put me in a bit of a bind," he says, as though we were in this together. "My superiors claim you're a violent terrorist."

"*Your* superiors," I say. "But I thought ..."

Mister Smith gives me a warning look.

"I'm not sure what you want from me," I reply carefully.

"Just tell the truth. Did you plan the whole thing—the cyber-attack on the university computer system, the student mob actions?"

"No!"

The jolt of pain takes me by surprise. I gasp.

"I'm going to give you another chance. Were you the instigator of these actions?"

I hesitate, then answer honestly. "No."

Even though I'm prepared this time, I cry out when the jolt goes through me.

"Please. Let me contact my parents. Your rules say I have the right."

"If that's what you want. It would be interesting to meet your mother. Emma Lavoie is one of the greatest minds in cyber engineering living today—a topic of avid interest to my government."

"She ... she couldn't talk to your government about that."

"Oh, I think she might be persuaded. If we brought her into one of these rooms."

The beginnings of a different kind of dread creep into my bones.

"Or perhaps we should contact your other mother, Soraya. She might be interested in our procedures for curing empathy. We put two empaths in close physical contact, then subject them to excruciating pain. Eventually the stress causes the empath's block to break down so that the subjects are experiencing both their pain and the other one's pain. After that, well, their connection just burns out.

"Amazing how the body knows what's good—and not good—for it, and takes adaptive measures. Of course, there's often collateral brain damage. That wouldn't be very good for Soraya's work in psychology, would it? Perhaps we should send for your fathers instead. I understand they're peculiarly fond of each other."

"How ... why you know these personal things about my family?"

"We do our research and we choose very carefully whom to invite into our country. So what will it be, Sasha? Shall I contact one or more of your parents?"

I shake my head quickly. How could I have thought Mister Smith would have any more fellow feeling for me than Mister Jones?

"I'm going to have to ask you to speak out loud, Sasha. That's what we do here. None of that subvocalization or thinking hard at each other. Just plain, English words, alright?"

"Yes. Alright."

"Shall I contact your parents? Or do you give up your right to have them present?"

"No. Yes! I mean, please don't contact them. I don't want them to come."

"In that case, I need your thumbprint and signature here." He presses my thumb against a palm-sized screen. I sign beneath it. "Very good. I don't like causing unnecessary pain. That's from the bad old days, before we took a more enlightened path and simply kicked all of you out of our country. Maybe cultural exchange isn't such a good idea. What do you think?"

He's looks like he's measuring me—or trying to guess what I will do. Maybe it's some kind of a test, but how to pass it? I don't understand these people! But I'm beginning to understand what they're capable of.

"Okay," I say slowly, as I think it through.

"Okay, what?"

"I'll leave. Leave your country. Blame it all on me. I don't care. I just want to go home."

"It's not that simple, I'm afraid. We need a written confession, including an admission that you tried to incite a student rebellion in order to expand Mpathisme into the United America."

I hesitate. The idea of agreeing to such a lie makes me sick, but what choice do I have? Back home, folks will understand. And here, they'll just believe what their government and media tell them anyway.

"Alright, I agree."

"And you'll also have to provide, in writing, a detailed technical account of how you managed to hack into our system without a Unified National Identity chip. And that'll need to be pretty convincing, considering you had to bypass a biometric authentication."

A sudden image intrudes into my mind. Mica's pale wrist as it passed over the digital field, the look of pleased surprise on their face when entry into the database was granted—the same sweet face I'd kissed so thoroughly the night I'd arrived here, after two years of an intense virtual friendship.

"My father's wrong. Information wants to be free," Mica had whispered to me, breath warm and lips soft on my ear. How much of what Mica had done was motivated by a desire to impress me? I block these thoughts with the strongest block I can weave. I will not tell them about Mica, no matter what they do to me.

"Yes, I can do that," I tell Mister Smith.

"And lastly, you can never return. Nor communicate with any of our citizens. We'll bring you directly to the airport from here."

I open my mouth to argue, but something stops me. "Fine," I say. Suddenly, I want to cry.

"I sense a hesitation, Sasha. Is there something—or someone—you'll miss?"

"No," I say firmly. "After all that's happened, I can't wait to get home."

"Except?"

"It's just that I'm afraid my parents will be ashamed of me."

"So it's not because you're protecting someone? Perhaps a boy you're romantically involved with?"

"No. Not at all." Could he know about Mica? Mica insisted we keep our relationship secret. I don't know why, exactly—people keep so many secrets here. Maybe we're violating one of their many sexuality or gender taboos. Both of us are pretty fluid; it's no telling how our relationship would read.

"Tell me who you're protecting, Sasha."

"No one!"

"I'm going to ask you again. And if I think you're lying, I'll have to hurt you."

"No one," I repeat. And then I hear myself scream.

~oOo~

Mister Smith is crouching beside me, holding a plastic cup of water to my lips. Oddly, he's perspiring, while I'm as cold as ice. I don't know how much time has passed.

"Until I know the truth, I must do this, Sasha. I don't enjoy hurting you."

"Then why are you? Torture doesn't help anything. It just makes people say what they think you want to hear."

He smiles. It's a sad smile. "And what is it you think I want to hear?"

"I don't know!" I wail.

He stands and walks slowly to the panel. "Then I suggest you figure it out."

The next time I come back to myself, my throat is sore, and tears and snot cover my face. I continue to cry, all my self-control focused on not saying anything about Mica.

"Stop crying," Mister Smith says, the hints of pity I thought I saw on his face gone, replaced by age and exhaustion and what seems like a grim sense of purpose.

"I ... I can't," I sob. With my arms in restraints, I can't even wipe my own face.

Mister Smith grabs my chin and stuffs a gag into my throat before taping my mouth closed. I panic as I struggle to draw air into my lungs through my running nose. And then even the fear of suffocation is eclipsed as his finger goes to the button and pain engulfs me once more.

Unable to move, unable to even cry out, my mind finally rebels, breaking through its self-imposed block. *Stop! It hurts!* I scream without sound.

The pain abruptly ends.

A flood of images, fuzzy and rough, enter my mind. A young child—pale, with soft, longish hair—running, playing, a sweet smile on their face. Then that same child, nose bloodied, holding their ribs and limping. A tall man's arms, my arms, lift the child gently, comforting them while they cry. *I won't let you be hurt again. I'll protect you.* The child nods, all trust, and rests their head on my shoulder.

It's Mica! Mica as a small child. And-

The shock of realization hits me. My head shoots up. Mister Smith is Mica's parent.

I pull air hard through my nose and try to remain calm. Mister Smith is silent, watching me. After a moment, he appears to come to a decision. He walks towards me. My heartbeat accelerates. He bends over and ... removes my gag. I cough, choking on my own saliva. There's a bitter taste in my throat. Finally, I speak.

"You're-"

"Mica's father. Yes."

"But ... I mean, how could you ..." I swallow again and shudder.

"I needed to know—without any doubt—that you wouldn't give him away."

My mind feels slow. There's something still missing. I think back to my voiceless cry, how abruptly the pain ended.

"You ... You're an empath!"

"Why are you so surprised? Of course we weren't all found."

I think it through. "But empathic abilities are hereditary," I say. "So if you have them, then probably ..." As soon as the words are out of my mouth, I realize I've made a mistake. "Please, I'd never say anything. About either of you. If only you would trust me! My thoughts, my emotions, they're right there for you to read!"

Su J. Sokol

"I have superiors, you stupid child! Don't you understand anything? Whatever I did to you—they would do worse." Mister Smith turns away from me.

For a long time, I just breathe in and out through my mouth and nose, turning everything over in my mind— Mister Smith, Mica, empaths, our two peoples, so different yet not so different.

"I think I do understand," I finally say quietly.

He turns back around, thoughtful, and for a moment he resembles Mica—the pallor of their face, the delicacy of their cheek bones, the keen intelligence in their eyes.

Bending down once again, the man who calls himself Mister Smith slowly and methodically releases my restraints. I pull myself to my feet, unsteady, and turn towards the exit, too scared to hope. After a long moment, Mister Smith picks up a device and with a click, the door is unlocked.

I walk to the door. I want to run but my legs are shaking. What if he changes his mind? But there's something more important that I need to do. I turn to Mister Smith.

"Mica could come back with me, if they wanted to." My voice sounds sure, confident, despite the flutter in my stomach. "They'd be safe in Nouvelle S'Entraide."

I imagine I see the glistening of tears. But no, his eyes are dry when he searches my own, perhaps looking for forgiveness. I can't give him that forgiveness, but I meet his gaze without flinching and without hate.

He nods, once, seeming satisfied. "You're stronger than he is."

I don't answer. There are many ways of being strong.

"Alright, wait outside. Someone will come for you. And perhaps ... Perhaps someday soon Mica will also find himself studying abroad."

"You could come too." I don't want this, don't know why I've said it.

"I'm not interested," he answers, and I feel surprised when my relief is tinged with the smallest disappointment. "I'd find it intolerable, constantly bombarded by everyone's ... naked, unmediated thoughts and feelings. Most people are venal. Cruel, and short-sighted. It's why your country is a social experiment that's destined to failure."

"People are also full of goodness, when given the chance to show it."

"You're young. You haven't seen the evil I have."

"I've seen more than you think." I rub my wrists where they'd been shackled.

He gives me a small nod of acknowledgement before saying, "But far less than I have."

I reach for the door, ready to be rid of this place forever.

"May I ask you one more question?" Mister Smith asks.

"Alright," I say.

"How do you stand it? Looking into people's minds, into their hearts, day after day. All that ugliness. All that darkness."

"It's only shadow. There's light too. You just need to move aside and let it come through."

Mister Smith seems unconvinced. I try not to care. Instead, I push open the door, anxious to be out of that room, but after a few steps, I can't keep myself from looking over my shoulder to see if he will follow me out.

Su J. Sokol

Tarantula

Russell Hemmell

The red dust has a Mars-like quality, and so does the terrain—barren, desolate, crater ridden. But we're on planet Earth, and this is a perfect place for an ambush. We'll storm an enemy stronghold this morning—a new target area in the same endless war.

My units are deployed, W-RPGs ready to blast. They won't see us coming. My left eye switches into X-ray mode, while the receptors stream the live-vision feed to the medium-altitude drones.

"There's nobody here, Sergeant. Maybe your intel was flawed."

"Shut up."

In the field they call me Tarantula. Probably for the color of my eyes and hair, more black than black—or maybe for the deadliness of my bites. Both things, as it often happens, not far away from the truth. I've been called like that for so long that I've almost forgotten my given name is Susan. I'm a tarantula all right, night habits and nasty reflexes included.

I curb the impulse to slap the imbecile across his juvenile bovine face, and I move forward, my sensors zeroing on the target area: scattered houses on a battered ground just a few hundred yards in front of us. They're empty, meaning it's underground we have to focus on: that's where the enemy hides. But not for long—the deep-penetration missiles will make them surface as fast as vermin threatened with fire. The fact I've been in their place many times gives me a strategic advantage, one I'm not going to waste.

My insect drones swarm down in attack formation, while I do hand signs to the ground unit, the Swamp

Ferrets—Assume position. On my mark. The lieutenant the Central Command sent today, to observe and report, looks uneasy, sticking out as a sore thumb.

I ignore him. If he gets hurt in the action, it's his goddamn problem.

I give the signal, and in a moment the eerily quiet, derelict area becomes pure hell, with blast sites, sky-high columns of dust and debris, and deafening noise. The enemy emerges from the holes on the ground only to fall under my snipers' bullets.

"Load. Aim. Shoot. Reload."

The drones engage the few that run away, while, as calm as a Buddhist deity, I walk along the war site scanning the terrain.

The whole action has lasted one minute: thirty seconds, and now, when the dust settles down, there are smoke and ruins where bricks and mud used to be. Mauled corpses litter the area.

The men look at me, and I nod. We stop to observe, wounded enemy forces in the distance, slowly retreating, and a trail of blood on the ground. Then we collect what they have left behind.

The young lieutenant approaches, his eyes still fearful for what he has just witnessed, but with an angry line now firm on his mouth.

"What are you doing? Some managed to escape."

I glance at him. I have an enemy to destroy and a war to fight, and I have neither the time nor the patience to educate somebody that will probably be dead in a month's time, or earlier if he keeps behaving this stupidly. Otherwise, he should already know we never kill them all in these raids. Some of them must remain alive, and get away, and regroup with the others still hidden—so that I can happily exterminate the whole bunch. But I don't give a flying shite. I shrug and look away.

"I asked you a question, soldier," he snaps, grabbing my arm, "and –"

He has no opportunity to complete the sentence—a blink of my eyes, and he's on the ground, his face into a mire of mud and enemy blood. My hand forces his head deep in, allowing him to breathe only after several seconds of agony.

"I'm not a soldier, I'm an assassin—that's why I'm here doing what you people can't talk about. Clear off, or fuck off."

~oOo~

I slip off the dark-blue combat fatigue, examining my right shoulder. All skin and the first flesh layer are gone—one of the enemy's grenades has taken them out and now lucid metal shines out in all its terrifying splendor. Most of my skeleton is made of haserig, an alloy of titanium, graphene and lithium—and the result is astonishing performance. Especially in the legs—my legs, where micromachines have replaced every human cell—can reach the speed of a motocross engine when I run.

The best thing? If I lose them, they can be replaced—as simple as that. They're expensive, sure, but no expenses spared for elite warriors that can get the job done. There are other fancy gizmos I pack inside my body ready to be used when the action asks for them– wings, spikes, exoskeleton and marine fins. The pinnacle of war technology to engineer a perfect killing device.

Make no mistake—I am not the only one to be that special: hundreds have been bio-modified thanks to the Cyborg Research and Development Program—and more will be in the future. We can rightly claim to be a new race of humans. And if deploying us save lives—of our soldiers, not the enemy, of course—then it's right, and just, and something the world has to be eternally grateful for. Our president is, and the worshipping crowd follows.

~oOo~

There's a time to kill and there's a time for pleasure.

We're out for the night, my unit and I—visiting the only village in the area big enough to host a brothel. We go there regularly since we've been deployed in the region, and not just to get properly laid. The main town is near, and even though the village itself has always pledged neutrality, my

213

gut feelings say it's a hotbed of rebellion and a major organization center. Never have been able to prove it—so far. But if the ones that got away during our last strike have found sanctuary here, I'll have the proof I'm seeking. I'll know soon enough.

"You look far away—what are you thinking about?"

Topaz. Soft skin, perfumed, natural-grown flesh, eyes that bewitch.

She caresses my shoulders, her hands gentle, a concerned expression on her face. I got the habit to go and see her every time I finish off a target; over the months she has learnt to recognize me, no matter if sometimes I wear a mask on my face or I don't undress.

I take Topaz's hand—who knows what her true name is?—and put it between my legs.

"Just do what you do best."

~oOo~

There's an ugly side in every Tarantula-like operative they create: we belong to our makers, because they're the only ones there for us. This is what my parents—desperate, misinformed, and out of options—signed for when they left the care of their only child, horribly maimed by a terrorist attack, to the institution that promised to make her live and bought her, flesh and remaining bones included.

Nobody else was going to invest a few million dollars in a martyred and soon-to-be-dead 5-year-old body. They agreed to never see that entity again, comforted by the awareness that something of their little one would still breathe somewhere, somehow. –They didn't stop to wonder how, or to worry about the fact that the makers were entitled to claim lawful ownership of whatever could possibly survive– I was no longer a daughter, just a barely recognizable human.

Right or not, the result was the same: Tarantula now has no more rights than a dog, or any of the pets people love filling their houses with. They treat the pets well, generally, but it's out of a good will that can't be enforced in any court. At least, I've never heard of Rottweiler-led lawsuits.

For cyborgs, it's much of the same story. Like the dogs, we're trained and conditioned and programmed since day one to blind obedience and butchering tasks—in a life that has no space for anything else, nor the appetite.

~oOo~

The sun is not high in the sky yet, but the swarms of tiny drones are already buzzing in formation, prying the area for possible targets: the chase has started. As I've correctly guessed, the village's not as innocent as it looks like. I'm ready to bet all actions have been directed from there.

Well, not for long: one week, and there will be nothing left to direct and to shelter—or to breathe. Tarantula and the unit she leads will make sure of it.

Before I leave for the kill, I go to see Topaz for a last time—in case I don't come back. That possibility always exists, even for almost-perfect machines. This time, I don't even take out the upper part of my exoskeleton. With the full-face helmet, the graphene wings and a scary-looking dorsal spike I'm the closest living thing to an alien monster. But as soon as she sees my naked belly, she smiles.

"I'm happy you're back—so soon."

"How do you know it's me—am I the only woman who seeks your services?"

"No. It's for your scars," she says, touching my stomach. "What are they?"

"Battle wounds badly healed."

"Strange they keep changing every time, though. Three days ago, you didn't have this," her tapered fingers go through the long, red mark that diagonally crosses my belly from the navel to the hip.

"You talk too much, Topaz."

I keep my helmet on and lie down on the bed, eyes closed, legs spread, nails jabbed in the mattress.

~oOo~

I haven't lied to her. These are real wounds, but from a

different war, one I've lost in advance. And this evening, when on my way back to base-camp I kill the occasional enemy that crosses my path, I idly think she's going to mention it again—because those wounds will keep changing.

I enter my cubicle, I take off my uniform, layer by layer, and then I start with my body, skin and flesh, until the cold glimmer of haserig appears when the bones are more evident—the only nudity that makes any sense to my eyes. I unsheathe my favorite weapon, a silver stiletto always tucked in my glove, and I perform the Ritual.

Every time I kill one of them—or a thousand—I cut myself, one more slash on the flesh like the kiss of a razor blade, sweet and non-invasive. It looks beautiful, with the thin red line that appears on the white, tender flesh of my stomach—the only part of me that is still 100 percent human, and as painful. Over the years, those white scars have become an eerie cobweb, like a long-forgotten alphabet or the ensign of an alien code. To me, it has a geographic value, too: this is hell alive on the body, with its timeline, and images, and locations—each one worse than the others.

~oOo~

Blast, shock and awe, mayhem and panicked clamors—hissing into a spiral of chaos. A dawn of blood has taken the place of our twilight of ambush and waiting—and now, strapped as I am on the wings of a two-meter combat drone, I swoop down on my prey with my wide-open arms, distributing grenades and shuriken like a harbinger of doom, an angry demon from the depths of Hell. I see them crushing and burning like moths against the scorching lights—and I realize the myth of a soulless machine is just that, a legend. I do care about the lives I'm taking but still relish watching them on the ground– so peaceful and gracious, their lithe bodies finally scarred and in little disjointed pieces like mine.

~oOo~

"A great raid, Sergeant."

"I know."

Party time for the Swamp Ferrets, including the idiotic lieutenant, who's going to celebrate the victory in an action he has only watched from a safe distance. But he thinks he's entitled to revel and thrive, and to bathe in a glory he has no idea of the cost—or the price.

I suppose I don't care—I have my men for companionship and Topaz for pleasure.

Yes, all the units go to the brothel tonight, and we're lucky it's still standing. Located as it was just outside the blast zone, conveniently on the main road to cater for the travelers need, it could've been an unintended casualty. For once, we've been damn lucky—otherwise, I'd be busy to make myself happy alone tonight.

My feet lead me toward her place, bright eyes and smiling like a young damsel in her day of engagement.

~oOo~

"It was you, wasn't it?" Topaz asks, as I sit down on the mattress and remove my helmet.

"They said it was a woman. They said she could fly and run as fast as a hound, and it was impossible to shoot her down." She hits me across the face. "Answer me."

I don't even think of denying it.

"Why?"

"It's war, Topaz. There's no why."

"There's always a reason, as much as there's always responsibility."

I shook my head. "Responsibility—yes. Reasons—it's not up to me to find them. I have no need to know anything, apart from my targets."

"And people fall like radiation-burnt leaves. You see –" her eyes shine in anger, "I don't care if they're my brothers—the ones you slaughter on the killing fields— they've chosen war and have to accept what comes along. But you also murder the ones that had no choice but suffer and die—elders, children, disabled. That's not war."

"Call it genocide then." I read contempt in her stare, and disappointment. "Words don't really matter to me."

217

Russell Hemmell

"To me neither." Her hand waves at me like if she's slapping an annoying bug away. "You're not welcome here, Tarantula."

She has found out my name, and it's sweet to hear it on her lips, even if soaked in poison.

I put back my helmet and left the premises, back to the battlefield. I've my orders, and there's more carnage to take care of.

And I do it, day after day after day. Weeks that become months.

Topaz's words stay with me like a hungry leech that saps my strength and bleeds me dry—driving me to an exhaustion I don't take the time to contemplate.

~oOo~

Time passed by.

I've moved—a thousand kilometers from my previous area of assignment. A different operation theatre, for a different fashion of killing.

"How much?" The soldier asks, his rude hand stroking my hair.

"A lot."

They don't call me Tarantula any longer.

Here, in the village's brothel where I'm deployed—it's not a misnomer—I'm known as Red Sue, my hair color conveying an implicit promise of lust. Red Sue is the one that does anything you ask, provided you pay the full price: one I never disclose.

It's something that makes me more alone I've ever been, and yet it's comforting in an odd way. I took Topaz's unspoken suggestion on board and now I only kill the ones who have chosen to fight. The bio-engineered STD I now carry in my body fluids, is so pernicious that it suffices of one time to catch it and kills in a few weeks—whenever the infected has not already died in the battlefield.

Indirect contamination hasn't worked so far, but even in this way is rather effective. And palatable to the political overlords in their high palaces—now questioned over the Tarantula-style killer machines more than ever. No more collateral damage, no more hapless civilians. If nobody is innocent in this universe of blood, some are guiltier than

218

others, and they're the ones I reap.

"Here," he says, putting his money on the table. "Undress."

Something has remained the same, though: I still inflict wounds on myself—every time I sleep with one of those I condemn to a certain agony.

"What's that?" His fingers brush the skin of my belly, where fresh, crisscrossed cuts look ready to bleed again. "Charming. A client particularly kinky?"

"War scars," I say, while he fumbles with his belt.

He leaves not long after, with a sated smile on his face, without realizing that his nights of pleasure—and his nights tout-court—are numbered.

My hand reaches for the blade, and its soothing glimmer.

~oOo~

"They said the foreign whore is the best in town. They said her red hair matches the fire in her loins, and she knows the kinkiest tricks. They said she's a dangerous one to bed, but one you won't forget."

Her voice is calm, with a distinctive high pitch—one she used to have when she was in good mood. She comes inside my alcove—her elegant dress and well-manicured hands telling me she's no longer Topaz, nor a pleasure lady. She has a man that cares for her and her children. She deals in opioids now, furnishing the brothels of the region, including mine, and her name is a more urban Zarah.

She removes her scarf and unties her blouse.

"I don't want you on my stomach," I say. No expression could be more literal.

I see a light flickering in her eyes—surprise, understanding, or just an insulting pity. Golden tiles pile up on the table.

"Whatever this buys me."

She doesn't add, that doesn't kill me—but she doesn't have to. Many words have been exchanged between us, and they're going to satisfy our needs for conversation. We don't talk further that day.

Nor all the others after. She comes over now and then,

for long nights far too expensive only to rest on a stomach of badly healed cuts and a cobweb of white scars, and a hand that caresses her with too much tenderness to be effective. Not a lot for what she pays—and far less of what I'd love to give her.

But, sometimes, less is more than enough.

Long After

Bruce Taylor

You're sitting there at the bar, you know the kind, you see them no matter where you go, what space port, what planet, seems like—every place has gotta have a bar where you can get something good to drink that won't kill you. So, you're sitting there at that bar, nice one really, large, with a shiny, sky-blue quartzatine counter and a bunch of bottles and cans, and flasks of all sorts of brews from everywhere, on the shelves across the service aisle. You look at the shelves. The bottles. The flasks. You laugh to yourself. How many brews are there anyway? Some kinda familiar, others—incomprehensible.

You look at the one with the blue label at eye level right across from you—and some weird writing—you look at it, let your bion-implant eyes bring it into sharp focus, and the meaningless swirls and dots that announce the brew rearrange themselves in your vision-field, to read, "Ukkuy Ipsit," and <u>those</u> letters rearrange themselves to read in the best translation possible: "Big Breast Beer."

You think for a moment how that would translate into Old Earth English and then you muse that it might be: Great Bust Beer. You see the other labels; a red label, written in some swirling cursive writing translates out as "Hard Organ" and yet another one with a small label (and you have to focus your bion-eyes almost to stage one limitations) simply translates as "Wet-wet."

You ponder. You don't have a clue what that would be in Old Earth English. You look to another brown bottle and without reading the label, you point it out to the Fishnoid bartender (your name for it) standing nearby. *Guess that's fitting,* you think, *that a barkeep might have a not too distant relative from the sea, maybe a cousin or so still swimming about.* But the closest sea to NuNuyork on this planet, Nu-rth 16, is a ways away. Even so, the Fishnoid moves easily about almost as if the air is water and with its modified flipper digits, gets you a bottle from a low bank of fridges below the shelving and looks at you with pale green eyes and dull expression like it's been swimming upstream for a long time and is really tired. *Looks funny to see something like that in a white bartender's apron*, you think. *As if trying to make something weird look normal.*

It pops the top off the brew, pours it and nudges the full glass to you. You laugh, and think to yourself, Hey, some things never change._Still the best way to get a drink is out of a cold bottle and into a chilled glass.

You look around. Your bion-enhanced nose takes in the odor of the brew: *Fermented Kuzzle and Rotwhet; OE analog: like wheat and mint.* You've already figured out the not unpleasant smell of the bar, Cyclapurl—not too much of a stretch to say it's like cinnamon.

Yeah, not a bad place to wait for your friend Mikolo. Nice tables, maybe nine or ten, same quartzatine tops, open chairs of various shapes to conform or withstand all sorts of weights, sizes and butts. Mix and match. Bright interior from south-facing windows to your left, where the shelves of beer end. You turn back to your beer and a flickering white light through the high open door on your right catches your eye. Oh, yeah, you never get tired of watching the Proton-Class Heavy Lift Ships blast off, pounding out flame and fury with boiling, crackling racket as they thunder skyward and even though the launch port is seven kilometers away, the place still shakes. You kinda like that.

And then in through the doorway comes Mikolo. He's got that perennial look of having overslept, being late, no time to comb that fuzzy mass of blond hair. He's got another girlfriend hanging on his arm; an Etheral. Like most Etherals, long, copper-colored hair, skin faintly tanned, gorgeous creature with, as your bion-eyes focus discreetly on her, yellow—no, kind of a copper-yellow color for eyes. She's got a tight smile; it's a cultural thing you guess, since open smiling that reveal the teeth are really raggedy and scary looking, like they have just only recently evolved from some weird alien predator. Then you think, *Well, maybe they have. Lord knows what we did to make worlds safe for us and kinda like Old Earth. Even this city sorta looks like something you might have found in OE Arizona.*

But the smiles are nice.

And when Mikolo sees you, he waves, and huffs on down alongside counter and tables, almost dragging his girlfriend behind him as she hangs on to his arm, trying to keep up, trying not to stumble. She's wearing this subdued red one-suit. *She looks really hot,* you think, *oh, my God, does she look hot.*

Mikolo thumps up to you and says, "Hey, you old planet banger, how are ya?"

You look at him and you always gotta smile. Likeable guy, two meters high almost exact, and those blazing blue eyes, almost the color of the quartzatine in the bar, just drinking you and everything else in. He's got on a white shirt, blue OE-Pacific brand slacks and gotta say, he looks good but you gotta wonder why he never gets rid of what has to be ancient acne scars. With BeautiSurg always available, no one has to look like they were just coming in from battle but who knows and he slaps you around the shoulders and says, "Drink!" and points to a bottle on the back wall, the label of which translates to "IkSy Ik TwaToe." The letters rearrange themselves in your vision-field to read, "Big Wet-Boom." You <u>know</u> you don't need any more translation than that. His Etheral girlfriend puts her hand up to her mouth and is obviously giggling. He points to her.

"Richard, meet Nyrsh'la," you hear but your bion-cochlear implants simultaneously hear and translate what he says as, "Ric-erd, g'na Nychs-ala."

You extend a hand and she clasps it; a vaguely subtle grabby texture to the skin. In your head, you hear yourself saying, "Nice to meet you," but it comes out of your mouth as the vocal-synthz kicks in, as "Ulp-za fwuss nak-ja."

The Fishnoid has pulled out the bottle from the fridge and waits patiently as pleasantries finish. but before getting a glass, pauses just a second to look at the label and in his own Pisces way, seems to give Mikolo a side-long glance as it pulls a glass from beneath the counter and pours the brew.

You reach for your OE Card from your back pocket, but Mikolo already has his out and, with great fanfare, slaps and slides the yellow card across the counter to Fishnoid.

"Naw," says Mikolo, "on me," as he saddles up on the stool at the bar. "Hey, been a while."

"Yeah," you say, "sure has. How ya—"

But Nyrsh'la tugs on his arm and he leans over and she says something to him and for the first time, you hear the tinkle of earrings, bright, little delicate blue and yellow sparkly crystal things, and Mikolo says, "OK."

You laugh. Another remnant. "OK." Understood all over OE and now no matter what the place or planet, everyone and/or thing that hops, slithers, oozes or walks that has a cerebral cortex understands "OK."

He laughs, looks longingly at her walking away to meet other Etherals and simply says, "Wow! How'd I get so lucky. Wow!"

"So, you two known each other for a while," you say. A guess, but you really kinda do know the answer.

Mikolo turns to you and with sunny grin says, "Oh, yeah. Two OE (he pronounces it "Ohyeee" when the preferred pronunciation is usually "Oh-eee") weeks."

"You're in love," you laugh.

"For now," he replies. He looks back to her again.

You can just guess what the two weeks have been like.

"So how long you here for?" He takes a slug of the drink, puffs out his cheeks. "Woof. That's potent shit. But so good."

"Just a few days." You do the circle in the air with your right index finger which means this planet's days, not OE days.

"Oh," says Mikolo, "a month or so, OE."

"Yeah." You stop for a second. "God, it's hard to forget all the OE stuff, ain't it?" you continue. "It's like it's burned into our DNA."

Mikolo gulps another mouthful, closes his eyes, swallows and says, "Well, it is." Then he shakes his head. "Make some wild local beers here. Amazing."

You hear something that sounds like laughter or a close approximation. You glance over to the table and Nyrsh'la is sitting with others, and it looks like a fellow Etheran finds her interesting and they aren't just smiling, no, mouths open, laughing, and the teeth, well, to them, it's fine and lovely but you still wince and turn away.

Mikolo laughs. "You get used to it. They think our teeth are just as weird."

You nod, take another drink, savoring the flavor, the sweet bite. "Powerful stuff," you say, looking at the beer, then setting it down. "Doesn't take much." You pause. "Don't know why I keep thinking about-"

"S'cuse please," says Mikolo abruptly, "gotta find the critter's room." He hops up, walks past the table where the Etherals are talking and Nyrsh'la doesn't look up.

Boy, you think, studying your drink, *this is powerful crapola. Good, but*—and you kinda drift for a minute, looking down the bar to the high open doors, the street outside, the beings passing by. Then you look up at the deep blue-green sky with the huge moon, Tranquility, and Serena, farther away, hanging in the sky. Then, *Man,* you think, *man, in the short time we were out here, we sure turned everything we could into OE. As if OE hadn't changed. Turned out to be bad idea for lots of folks who just want to fucking forget the awful pain of what happened. What'd this place look like before we came?* you wonder. *All these folks better off?* You look to the Fishnoid. *Gave them adaptive mobility, ability to breathe air. Didn't we do a lot of good? We did—didn't we? Even gave them quartzatine which they just love.* You look down, closely examining the quartzatine of the bar, the subtle layers and hues of blue. *And this is the real stuff, not the imitation crap with microfractures. Lots of pride and money here.*

But--you gotta wonder. Even the street outside looks like an image of OE—um—you think—um—was it—um—Phoenix? You take another drink. Want to forget. Just want to—forget—great, great grandparents—want to forget just fucking want to forget—Mikolo returns.

"Whoo," he laughs and plops down beside you and puts elbows on the counter and rubs his hands together briskly. "Whoo. Powerful drink. Hope it don't fuck my kidneys."

"Nah," you say, "no matter where you go, it's pretty much Human Safe." you shrug, "well, Human Safe generally speaking." You wave your hand to all the drinks and then the interior. "I mean, you really do gotta know the HS ratings or maybe you could get into trouble. I guess."

You shrug. "Hell. I dunno. We all have embedded biozyme chips so if we get something nasty somewhere, it gets analyzed immediately, synthesized and antidote given, so who the hell gets sick anymore from anything, no matter where you are?"

Mikolo looks at you for a minute, then nods.

"Yeah. Guess that's right."

You take another drink. And you realize *Hey, this really is pretty damn good stuff.* You motion to the Fishnoid to bring you another and it moves as if it's right at home in an environment so far removed from its element. It brings the beer over, slaps it down, scoops up a glass, plops it down. You point to Mikolo's rapidly draining glass.

"Sure," Mikolo says.

"I buy," you say.

"No complaints," says Mikolo. He gets the same one as before. He grins.

"Gotta get ready."

Then you say, "So what's with you these days?"

"I'm liking it well enough here," he says. "Gets a bit toasty at times."

You laugh. "Not nearly as toasty as it got on OE before."

You stop. <u>Why do I keep going there?</u> You do *not* want to go there. You're too busy pretending.

Mikolo looks into his glass, his expression suddenly serious.

"Couldn't be helped," he sighs. "But enough got away in time and with the continual development and refinement of the new TransMatter Technology, new worlds to explore."

You laugh. "Wreck."

"Wreck," says Mikolo giving a laugh that actually sounds kinda grim. Out of black humor, you and he toast. "But anyway, more pleasant, got a good job with TransMatterTech," he says, trying to be up-beat. "Yeah, it's great to explore new applications of the stuff." He grins, takes a drink. "Get an obscene amount of money for having fun."

"Too bad you can't take that techno-stuff and reverse engineer."

Mikolo nods vigorously, his tousle of yellow hair almost as if dancing about his head. "Hey, some guys looking at that. Go back in time, go back to the 1980s of OE and show everyone what was gonna happen to the climate if we didn't do something—especially after they dismantled the EPA and prohibited mention of climate change. Yeah, yeah—the CO_2 went crazy—temps hitting 74C—that's what, 165F? in Chicago, in 2048 then the sudden massive methane release in the Arctic in what—2068 and *poof*—Venus redux."

Guess he meant to laugh, you think, but not much comes of it.

Mikolo just sits there next to you at the quartzatine bar, left hand on the surface, slowly moving his index finger in small circles across the quartzatine, right hand clasping the beer bottle, kinda coming across like a beer that's just gone flat, suddenly losing all its fizz. At length, he shakes his head.

"Sorry," he says, "sorry. Doesn't do anything to remember this shit, does it?" He laughs. "Guess I didn't have enough to drink yet." He sighs, says "Sorry," again.

You take another drink as does Mikolo. You both order more and you drink, trying to get silly again, pointing out the labels on the beer, guessing the OE meaning, guffawing—but—but in the end, by the time the evening was well on, after the second sun had set, and Nyrsh'la and her friends had gone to who knows where, you and Mikolo sit, drinking and doing what *so* many do when they drink these days—trying to—just—just trying to forget.

Bruce Taylor

Sandarakinophobia

Shelby Workman

Schools of fish follow you in billowing clouds as you make your way to work. Your footsteps are loud in the corridor, echoing off the walls that curve inward like ribs, the vertebrae of the ridged ceiling, as though you are exploring the vast, sunken carcass of some ancient leviathan, the metal and glass of this facility built over its fossils.

As you walk, you crack your jaw to ease the corks of pressure in your ears. The white-noise rumble of water outside hums in your bones. Your exhausted eyes burn; another sleepless night, leaving you aching for stimulants.

The fish in the windows are beautiful, bodies rippling like ribbons, scales flashing rainbows. Beyond them, coral reefs stretch on and on in riots of color. But it's an illusion; if you were to turn off the hologram you would see only a graveyard, miles of coral bleached bone-white and skeletal below the new farm-domes floating like jellyfish tethered to the rocks, the black-suited divers the only things swimming among them.

You move in long, quick strides, down the halls which will take you to the sprawling indoor farms, the rows and rows of vegetables blooming under LED lights and mists of nutrient spray, where you will spend the day measuring the hybrid potatoes' growth and splicing new strains in the lab before taking the sub-shuttle back to your coffin-narrow capsule apartment, where President Ivan Blackshear's latest speech on the tiny screen you can't switch off will bore into your brain until lights out.

You are fortunate, you know. You've heard of the

survivors on the surface world, the feral gangs scavenging in the radiation-soaked ruins, fighting for scraps under the eternal-winter sky. Guilt creeps up your spine when you think of it, so you try not to. You have your duties, and they can only feed so many. You repeat this to yourself often.

Everyone knows how it happened. No one knows how it happened. Vague details of Middle East wars that erupted into nuclear fire, efforts to cool the smog-cooked Earth by darkening the sky or seeding chemicals into the clouds that only made everything worse, until finally, in the year 2021, the human race abandoned the ruined land for a new civilization in the polluted, dying sea.

That was nearly twenty years ago.

Teachers and book-files speak of it as a time of hope, of people joining hands to create a shiny, sustainable future, as though the ruination of the planet had been some sort of opportunity. Growth from the ashes. But these underwater bases were military first, you are sure of it, before they became apartments and farms and laboratories. They must have been utterly unprepared for the rush of refugees. You don't like to wonder about the selection process, how it was decided who could stay.

Climate change. Far-away wars that erupted into nuclear fire. No one seems to know what the USA (as it was known then) was doing at the time, between the year of 2017 to the last days on the surface. Questions about this are rewarded with INFORMATION NOT FOUND results and zipper-lipped frowns on the oldest professors' faces. A gap in history that has nagged at you since you were a child, a rotten tooth no one would pull but that you couldn't stop tonguing. You quickly learned to stop asking. There is always someone listening.

President Blackshear's voice booms from speakers along the hallway, familiar and constant to you as the sound of water, as your own heartbeat in your ears. Promises to restore the coral, heal the land, the usual. Blackshear was the one who ordered the nation into the ocean, to the undersea farms and buildings, saving untold thousands of lives, but he only ever visits the colonies through screens, and no one knows where he broadcasts from. Sometimes you wonder if he is a hologram like the fish. He is running for re-election soon, his fifth term. You have never voted. You know of no one who has.

Blackshear is saying he will make the surface world habitable again through terraforming. You wonder what will happen to the people still up there, if they will be paved over, the new world built over their bones.

Then, in the corner of your eye, you see it: in the schools of fish, among the glittering scales of blue, gold, green, a flash of...

Orange.

A black curtain falls over your eyes. When the corridor blurs back into focus, you realize you are on the floor, shaking, sweating through your lab coat. The walls are too close. Your blood howls with the need to run.

You lift your head. The holo-fish are gone. PLEASE STAND BY blinks in the windows, only the safe black and white of orcas gliding past in them now. Sensors in the walls are reading your pulse, recognizing the panic attack. Recordings of whale song wash over you, melodic. Soothing. You start to breathe again.

Must have been a glitch, in the machine or of your tired brain. You can't have seen what you thought; the color orange is banned wherever possible. Carrots and round citrus fruits are spliced to be purple or yellow, solely for appearance. More than half the population in the colonies suffers from this same phobia. There have been studies.

Once, when you were young, your school teacher told the class to draw what monsters (her words) they could imagine lurking in the still-unexplored deep, the abyssal trenches and caverns in the seafloor where some life may yet thrive. You, and a few others, drew what such creatures looked like in the book-files: white murk-blind eyes, wiry fangs, organs and veins glowing through transparent skin. But most of the class drew creatures with saggy, human-like faces with orange skin, squinting rat-beady eyes and frowning lips. Some with the scaly bodies of dragons or sharks, some with pale, wig-straight hair, but all with the same face.

I see this in my nightmares, one little girl said, and the rest nodded uneasily. You kept quiet. The only reason you didn't pick up the orange crayons yourself was because you were too scared, you wouldn't have been able to draw for your hands shaking. You never knew why that one school had orange crayons to begin with. *(Unless someone was watching.)* You never admitted that they were your nightmares too.

You still have them. Bolting awake in icy sweat, that face branded on the insides of your eyelids. The face—like a human's, but how could any human be *orange?*—of some primal threat, maybe. Something that lurked outside the first campfires made by man, picking off Neanderthals in the dark, claws and fangs and blood-soured breath. But you don't think so. You think the answer is in those missing years in pre-ocean history, in what no one will say or remember.

There was life in the ocean once, richer and more beautiful than any hologram mimicry, now only coral bone-yards and darkness. Sometimes you turn the holograms off and stare into it until you can feel your mind fraying at the edges. What did this?

Underwater military bases. Scorched earth and iron-colored skies. Something, someone, erased from record but etched in terror into the cave walls of genetic memory. The missing space in history like the Deep where strange creatures prowl, eyeless and full of teeth. What swims down there, in all that blackness?

You carry out your duties. You create new plants to feed the people and you listen to Blackshear's speeches. You watch holo-fish drift across your ceiling at the end of each cycle and keep your thoughts from wandering to the dead world above. Except when you can't.

You are afraid to look into that dark, forgotten place, afraid of the teeth there. Afraid of the eyes that are always on you. You are afraid to know.

But still you lie awake, feverish with thinking, curiosity gnawing through you. Gnawing through the leash in your mind, eating your fear until only burning need remains. One day you'll be free.

And you can't sleep for the dread of that day.

About the Contributors

Sara Codair, the cover designer, is also a writer. They live with a cat, Goose, who "edits" their work by deleting entire pages. They teach and tutor at a community college, write when they should be sleeping, and read every speculative novel they can get their hands on. Sara's debut novel, *Power Surge*, will be published by NineStar Press on October 1, 2018. Find Sara online at https://saracodair.com/ or @shatteredsmooth.

Elizabeth Ann Scarborough is not a fairy godmother. She just writes about them and how they mete out social justice, kind of like warriors, only with more glitter. Scarborough is a Nebula award winner for *The Healer's War*, very loosely based on her experiences as a nurse in Vietnam during the war. She's the author of 40 books, 16 of which were co-written with Anne McCaffrey. Currently she's finishing the sixth novel in her SONGS FROM THE SEASHELL ARCHIVES series. She lives in Washington state with two black cats, Cisco and Pancho, sings shanties with the group Nelson's Blood, and designs and creates beadwork. She can be contacted through http://scarbor9.wixsite.com/beadtime-stories, and on FB at https://www.facebook.com/Elizabeth-Ann-Scarborough-162538643771710/?ref=aymt_homepage_panel

William Burns is a poet and a self-employed computer systems consultant who studied electrical engineering at the renowned University of Leeds. He is a frequent traveler and enjoys the company of others.

K.G. Anderson grew up in the Washington, D.C, area and worked as an East Coast newspaper reporter. Her short fiction— urban fantasy, space opera, alternate history, Weird West tales, near-future science fiction and horror— has appeared in anthologies including *Second Contacts, The Mammoth Book of Jack the Ripper Stories, Triangulation:*

Appetites, Welcome to Dystopia, Alternative Truths and *More Alternative Truths,* as well as online at Metaphorosis, Ares Magazine, Every Day Fiction and Far-Fetched Fables. K.G. attended the Viable Paradise and Taos Toolbox writing workshops. She herds cats and writes web content in Seattle.
More information at http//writerway.com/fiction

Laura Staley lives in Seattle with family, pets, books, computers and rain. Will read the ingredients off the back of a cereal box if nothing else is available.

Marcelle Thiébaux has published stories in The Delmarva Review, The Griffin, Literal Latté, Karamu (now Blue Stem), cream city review, The Penmen Review, Dogzplot, Grand Central Noir, Urban Fantasy KY, Keeping the Edge, dcomP magazinE, and Mondays are Murder. Her books on medieval themes include *The Writings of Medieval Women; Dhuoda, Handbook for her Warrior Son*; and *The Stag of Love: The Chase in Medieval Literature.* She has written about many women writers, e.g., Mary Wollstonecraft and Ellen Glasgow. She is the recipient of a Pen & Brush Club Award, and a Writer's Digest Award. She was nominated for a Pushcart Prize. She lives in New York

Samantha Weiss, a Rhode Island native, writes her funny and sometimes pointed fiction from her current home in Cambridge where she draws inspiration from the historic, and culturally stimulating surroundings.

Darren Todd, lives with his wife and occasionally dogsits for Kolu. He is a freelance editor for Evolved Publishing and studied Renaissance Literature at Arizona State University.

Paula Hammond has been in love with stories since she was old enough to read them for herself. When not hunkered over a keyboard, she can be found prowling London's crusty underbelly in search of random weirdness. She also finds time for Twitter: follow her at @writer_paula.

Chris Bullard lives in Collingswood, NJ. He received his B.A. in English from the University of Pennsylvania and his M.F.A. from Wilkes University. Finishing Line Press published his poetry chapbook, *Leviathan*, in 2016 and Kattywompus Press published *High Pulp*, a collection of his flash fiction, in 2017. His work has appeared in publications such as 32 Poems, Green Mountains Review, Rattle, Pleiades, River Styx and Nimrod.

J.G. Follansbee is the author of science fiction and speculative fiction novels set on an Earth and in a society transformed by climate change. A writer and former journalist who publishes independently, Follansbee explores themes of survival, justice, and tolerance with strong female protagonists and antagonists. Follansbee supports meaningful clean energy and transportation policies that combat the damaging effects of climate change. He lives in Seattle with his wife and an elderly chicken.

Kara Dalkey is the author of 15 published fantasy novels and over 20 published SF and fantasy short stories. She lives with her husband by the Puget Sound in Washington State where she is observing the world's events with growing disquiet, trying to age more-or-less gracefully, and playing way too much Hearthstone.

Frog and Esther Jones write speculative fiction novels and short stories from the depths of the rain forest on the Olympic Peninsula. When they are not writing they can be found camping, hosting gaming nights, or indulging in other general geekery.

Edd Vick likes books, Coke Zero, and quality entertainment. He loves his family, including the dog, the cat, and the variable number of chickens. He's lived more than half his life in Seattle, where he subsists on books, Coke Zero, and quality entertainment. It's a good life.

Yong Takahashi won the Chattahoochee Valley Writers National Short Story Contest and the Writer's Digest's Write It Your Way Contest. She was a finalist in The Restless Books Prize for New Immigrant Writing, and runner up in both the Gemini Magazine Short Story Contest and Georgia Writers Association Flash Fiction Contest. Some of her works appear in Cactus Heart, Crab Fat Magazine, Flash Fiction Magazine, Gemini Magazine, Hamilton Stone Review, Meat For Tea, River & South Review, and Twisted Vines.

To read some of Yong's stories, please visit: www.yctwriter.com.

Elana Gomel is an Associate Professor at the Department of English and American Studies at Tel-Aviv University. She is the author of six non-fiction books and numerous articles. As a fiction writer, she has published more than 40 fantasy and science fiction stories in The Singularity, New Realms, Mythic and many other magazines; and in several anthologies, including *People of the Book* and *Apex Book of World Science Fiction*. Her fantasy novel *A Tale of Three Cities* came out in 2013. Two more novels are scheduled to be published this year.

Ben Howels is a speculative fiction and thriller writer hailing from Devon, England. His short fiction has been published by Writers' Forum, Writing Magazine, Devolution Z Magazine, Phantaxis Magazine, The Arcanist, Earlyworks Press, Shotgun Honey, Red Sun Magazine, Lit Select, and Sirens Call Publications.
He recently completed his first novel (a dark supernatural thriller) and is currently seeking representation. He can usually be found writing on his laptop, training in the gym, or distracting himself on Twitter.Twitter handle: @BenHowels

Hannah Trusty works by day as a project manager while working towards dual degrees in journalism and English from the University of Kentucky. She has had numerous non-fiction articles printed, but this is her first fiction publication. When not writing or reading, Hannah spends her time drinking gin and tonics, eating Indian food, taking pictures of her cats, and playing roller derby.

Mike Adamson holds a PhD in archaeology from Flinders

University of South Australia. After early aspirations in art and writing, Mike returned to study and secured degrees in both marine biology and archaeology. Mike currently lectures in anthropology, is a passionate photographer, a master-level hobbyist and journalist for international magazines. Recent sales include to the anthologies *Mind Candy Vol I, Endless Apocalypse and Visions VII: Universe,* and the magazines Daily SF, Compelling Science Fiction and Nature Futures. Mike has placed some sixty stories to date.

John A. Pitts learned to love science fiction at the knee of his grandmother, listening to her read authors like Edgar Rice Burroughs and Robert E. Howard during his childhood in Kentucky. His favorite place in the whole wide world was the library where he could become so lost in story that he didn't want to ever leave.

He lives his life surrounded by books and story. A collector of myths and legends, John relishes the moment when an audience gasps or cries, laughs or winces at a particularly vivid tale. Selling his own tales still comes as a surprise to him.

The first three books in the Sarah Beauhall urban fantasy series are out from Tor Publishing (http://us.macmillan.com/TorForge.aspx)

Black Blade Blues, 2010, Honeyed Words, 2011, Forged in Fire, 2012.

His first short story collection, *Bravado's House of Blues,* came out Fall of 2013 from Fairwood Press. The fourth book in the Sarah Beauhall series, *Night Terrors,* has been published by Wordfire Press in April 2016.

John has a BA in English and a Masters of Library Science from University of Kentucky. He is a member of the Science Fiction and Fantasy Writers of America and the Dark Forces Defense League. He is said to have the hair of a Greek god.

Janka Hobbs lives in the Puget Sound lowlands, where she studies Aikido and Botany when she's not playing with words. Visit her blog at http://jankahobbs.com

Charles Joseph Albert is a writer of poetry and fiction living in San Jose, California, where he works as a metallurgist. His work (the poetry and fiction, not the metallurgy, though that would be pretty cool!) has appeared in First Lit Review, FreedomFiction, Dual Coast, The Wifiles, Asissi, the Ibis Head Review, the MOON, Chicago Literati, the Literary Hatchet, the Lowestoft Chronicle, Here Comes Everyone, and The Literary Nest.

Kevin David Anderson's debut novel, *Night of the Living Trekkies*, earned positive reviews in the L.A.Times, the Washington Post, Fangoria, and received a starred review in Publishers Weekly. His latest novel, *Night of the ZomBEEs*, revisits the zombie genre with a much more tongue-in-cheek "Shaun of the Dead" vibe, filled with geeky goodness and references from James Bond to Star Trek. Anderson's short stories have appeared in the pages of Dark Animus, Dark Wisdom, Darkness Rising, Dark Moon Digest, and many other publications with the word "dark" in the title. To learn more, go to www.KevinDavidAnderson.com.

Brenda Cooper is a writer, a futurist, and a technology professional. She often writes about technology and the environment. Her recent novels include *Wilders* (Pyr, 2017) *POST* (Espec Books, 2016) and *Spear of Light* (Pyr, 2016).

Brenda is the winner of the 2007 and 2016 Endeavor Awards for "a distinguished science fiction or fantasy book written by a Pacific Northwest author or authors." Her work has also been nominated for the Phillip K. Dick and Canopus awards.

Brenda lives in Woodinville, Washington with her family and four dogs. Sign up for her mailing list at her website: http://www.brenda-cooper.com.

Andrea Lopez is a Full Sail University Creative Writing Graduate. She consecutively wrote in diaries and journals throughout her life and fell in love with poetry at an early age. She enjoys film, music, art, and travel. Her short stories can be found in Down in the Dirt magazine and *Anthology Askew*. Her poetry can be found in Scarlet Leaf Review.

Bo Balder always wanted to be an sff writer. For that reason, she practiced a series of pointless professions like dishwasher, rowing coach, computer programmer, model and management consultant.

Bo is the first Dutch author to have been published in F&SF and Clarkesworld. Her short fiction has also appeared in Escape Pod, Nature and other places. Her sf novel *The Wan,* by Pink Narcissus Press, was published in 2016. She is a member of SFWA, Codex Writers and a graduate of Viable Paradise.

Su J. Sokol is a social rights activist and a writer of speculative, liminal, and interstitial fiction. A former legal services lawyer from New York City, she now makes Montréal her home. *Cycling to Asylum,* Su's debut novel, was long-listed for the Sunburst Award for Excellence in Canadian Literature of the Fantastic. Her short fiction has appeared in *The Future Fire, Spark: A Creative Anthology,* the TFF 10th Anniversary Anthology, Glittership: an LGBTQ Science Fiction and Fantasy Podcast, and the Glittership: Year One anthology. Her new novel, *Run J Run,* is scheduled to come out in 2019 with Renaissance Press. When she is not writing, battling slumlords, bringing evil bureaucracies to their knees, and smashing borders, Su curates and participates in readings and literary events in Canada and abroad.

Russell Hemmell is a statistician and social scientist from Scotland, passionate about astrophysics and speculative fiction. Recent/forthcoming publications in Aurealis, The Grievous Angel, Not One of Us, and others. Finalist in The Canopus 100 Year Starship Awards 2016-2017. Find her online at earthianhivemind.net and on Twitter @SPBianchini."

Bruce Taylor, known as Mr. Magic Realism, was born in 1947 in Seattle, Washington, where he currently lives. He was a student at the Clarion West Science Fiction/Fantasy writing pro- gram at the University of Washington, where he studied under such writers as Avram Davidson, Robert Silverberg,

Ursula K. LeGuin, and Frank Herbert. Bruce has been involved in the advancement of the genre of magic realism, founding the Magic Realism Writers International Network, and collaborating with Tamara Sellman on *MARGIN* (*http://www.magical- realism.com*www.magical-realism.com).

Shelby Workman lives in New Mexico with her family and the world's cutest dog. *Sandarakinophobia* is her first published work.

Manny Frishberg, the editor, was born just south of New York City and has made his home on the West Coast for over 40 years. He spent the first half of his life learning how to write and the second half learning what to write about, He is now spending the third half of his life making up stories, just like when he was eight years old. His stories have been appearing in anthologies and magazines since 2010.
When he is not doing that, he writes about things he hasn't made up for several magazines, and provides freelance editing and writing coach services. An independent editor, his anthology, *Horseshoes, Hand Grenades and Magic* was published by Knotted Road Press in 2016. He and his partner make their home near SeaTac Airport.